THE WORLD OF TARSUS

BOOK 1

THE HUNTRESS OF ARTISTAH

COPYRIGHT

All rights reserved. The Huntress of Artistah is in the public domain. All original additions are copyright © 2023 and may not be reproduced in any form without written permission from the publisher, except as permitted by U.S. copyright law.

ABOUT THE AUTHOR

Lonnie Wilcox is a US Navy Combat veteran. Born in Germany to American parents in 1961. Has lived in Germany, Turkey, and several States. Lonnie is currently living in an eighteen-wheeler and employed driving trucks east of Interstate 35. Lonnie is hoping that the sale of these books will give him the opportunity to settle down and do this full time. Lonnie is single and trucks and lives with his Chesapeake Bay Retriever "BUDDY"

Dedication

I wrote this book for a few reasons. First was to do something productive with what little off time I have, other than playing phone games. Second was to provide stories to my daughters, Granddaughters and Nieces, and great nieces. I wanted to give them a kick butt hero, that happens to be a female.

My influences have been Skyrim. I have been playing the Elder Scrolls series since Dagger Fall. Bethesda soft works once sent me a T shirt for Dagger fall that was one of my prize possessions. Dragon age is also another influence; we can also add world of Warcraft as well. As far as books are concerned, Ranger's apprentice The Royal Ranger and the Outcasts Series by John Flanagan. I have read all these books and loved every one of them. I credit John Flanagan for giving me the courage to follow in his footsteps. Of course, I must give credit to the Great J R Tolkien the elvish and other fantasy languages I use mostly come from him.

People.

Shanna, Amber, Chelsi, and Samantha. These are my four daughters. I hope they get a chance to read this book,

My grandchildren, My nieces, and great nieces. Special thanks to my friend and her daughter Nars and Ryzen for encouraging me to finish. Finally, my brother Kevin for listening and giving ideas, and just being a shoulder when I have no one.

Enjoy my labors.

Hug a veteran you might repay his sacrifice by saving his life. He could be having a difficult day!

Table of Contents

Chapter 1: The Huntress 1

Chapter 2: The Wolves of Mount Condie.. 7

Chapter 3: The Chase.. 15

Chapter 4: Secrets in the Dark... 19

Chapter 5: Tree Sprites Are Crazy Fun 25

Chapter 6: Let the Games Begin! 31

Chapter 7: A Night of Terror... 37

Chapter 8: Little Camp of Horrors 41

Chapter 9: The Aftermath 50

Chapter 10: Campaign of War 56

Chapter 11: Gathering an Army 60

Chapter 12: Nagging Questions... 64

Chapter 13: Defending Our Lands 72

Chapter 14: The Ride of a Lifetime... 82

Chapter 15: A Royal Visit.. 92

Chapter 16: Dragons for my friends 102

Chapter 17: The Reconnaissance Mission.. 110

Chapter 18: A Winged Attack 116

Chapter 19: Round One... 122

Chapter 20: The Royal Secret is Out.. 128

Chapter 21: The Council Decides 136

Chapter 22: The Colony Gets Started... 142

Chapter 23: Off to meet the High Elves 152

Chapter 24: Preparing for War 159

Chapter 25 Dangers of Being a Rider... 170

Chapter 26 The Shadow Lord 176
Chapter 27: Spelunking 184
Chapter 28: Another Royal 192

Chapter 1: The Huntress

Orchid studied the path; the deer she shot just moments ago could not have gotten far. Even though the dirt was hard, and tracks would not be obvious, she did see a very large drop of blood. Looking closer, she saw that there was a scrape his hooves made when he bolted. Orchid saw that the scrape visibly started where it was trying to gain traction, and then that hoof dragged back as it moved to become less visible. Because of this, Orchid could tell which direction it went. It could not have gotten far. The razor edges on the tip of the arrow would have severed anything it touched. The powerful handmade bow had a pull weight of around 70 pounds; it would penetrate a deer up to 218 meters.

Orchid was from Hielflander, standing 1.88 meters high with blonde hair and piercing electric blue eyes. She was from a crossbreed of people, half High elf, half Northmen. Hielflanders' average height was between 1.65 to 2.03 meters with women usually being taller than men. They are superior horse riders to every other race in Tarsus. They are also superb bow crafters and bow hunters. Both males and females learn to shoot at an incredibly early age, along with hunting, tracking, identifying herbs and herbalism, and healing using the gifts of nature. Once they make a kill, they use every part of the animal in one way or another.

For instance, antlers are ground for calcium to go into potions, poultices, salves, and necklaces. Bones are cooked for stocks and broth. Intestines are dried and used for sutures, sausage casings, lute strings, and even bow strings. However, Orchid's type of bow didn't use that type. She heard rustling in the bush and instinctively notched another arrow from her quiver. Stepping silently, she moved forward, searching, with her eyes and ears, shallowly breathing and controlling her heart rate. Each step was slow and methodical, only inches. She then saw her deer lying on its side, already dead. What had made that sound then?

She stopped in her tracks now, sniffing at the air, and was like a shadow. Another trait of the Hielflander was the ability to fade into shadow. She reached out with her feelings, searching for the presence of another life. She felt the plants, the insects, the trees, and the birds. These things in her mind showed up like a pulsing green mist; if danger lurked, it would come up as red. She reached out further and could now detect anything within a circle of 50 meters. There it was!

She homed in on the red mist in her mind, and immediately knew it was a Hielflander bear. Her heart started to race. She had to gain control and slow it back down again. She took out five more arrows, three of which she stuck in a close bunch in the ground in front of her. The other two she notched on her bow. The bear slowly came out of the trees heading to the deer carcass, unaware of her presence.

That was a good thing, she mused. *I really don't want to anger him ; I just don't want him eating my kill. I can't scare him. Hielflander bears are not afraid of anything. So, I will have to kill him. I guess if he knew I was here and was going to kill him, that would make him angry,* she thought. She had to suppress a laugh at her own joke. *Focus Orchid; this is very, very dangerous.*

The bear was now completely out in the open. Hielflander bears were normally big, but this one would be huge if he stood up. He would easily be over four meters tall and weigh 680 to 725 kg. She slowly drew back the bow. With several years of practice, her muscle memory was barely strained. The bow was steady in her hands as she stayed focused. He was almost at the carcass now, his head down, intent on just one thing, getting to that carcass and the choice parts of the deer to eat. Well, it was time to let him know it was not meant to be.

The bear was facing straight at her with a slight breeze coming toward her. She thought she could smell the sweat coming from it. She gave a sharp whistle, and it stopped in his tracks. Orchid stayed perfectly still. The bear could not hear or see her as it sniffed the air. Orchid had to concentrate more on her heart rate now to keep calm. She had one chance at a killing blow; there would be no second shot from this position. She would have to jump into a large tree and shoot from there. He was approximately 40 meters away now, sniffing and looking. Then the moment she was waiting for finally came.

Not being able to see or smell her, he started to stand on his hind legs to get a better look. He also roared a challenge to her. While standing up, he unprotected his throat. He roared again, but this time it ended shortly, as two arrows severed his vocal cords, while the third sliced through the jugular. Orchid already had the other arrows notched and let three zoom toward him. All hit body mass and ripped more holes into the bear. Within seconds he had lost so much blood and fell to the ground. Orchid notched another arrow for insurance.

She came into view and walked toward the massive beast. It watched her, unable to do anything, he was dying, and he knew it. He took a deep breath, shuddered, and went into a final hibernation. Orchid was sad, she did not want to kill it, but she needed this food for her village. She knelt to the now-dead bear and placed her hands on its head. She bowed her head and said a silent prayer to the goddess of the hunt.

Goddess Ursula, please carry the spirit of this bear to the forever forest, where he can dwell for eternity, never being hunted, hungry, or afraid again. As for his soul, let it now dwell in me; give me his strength, his cunning, and the power of ferocity of the bear. In turn, we will use this body to feed and supply our village, every part shall have a purpose and use, and from this death, life shall exist; for his sacrifice, we will pray and thank you for the fortune and blessing of a successful hunt. Thank you, Goddess Ursula! Orchids' people believed that everything in nature was interconnected. To kill an animal just for the sake of killing it was a crime. Everything was a delicate balance. If you held this belief with all your heart, then the goddess of the hunt would always see that you were successful. Hielflanders had many minor gods that looked at everyday things. The king of all the gods is "Aina Atar," elvish for (Holy Father) Orchid stood up. A tear ran down her face, and she wiped it with the back of her hand.

She let out two long whistles, and within minutes a tall horse came trotting through the bushes and trees. He sniffed the bear, then the deer, and then looked at Orchid as if to say, "Who do you think is going to drag this out of here and back to the village?"

Orchid giggled and said, "Godü, you know I had no choice. I will make it easy for you; I always do." Orchid had owned Godü since she was very small. All hunters were given horses to train with since they were old enough to ride.

They trained together in every aspect to grow a strong bond. Indeed, with the Hielflanders empathic abilities, those bonds were strong.

Orchid went to the saddlebags and pulled out two large tarps, a rope, and her knife set. She then went to work, cleaning and preparing the carcasses for transport. She made a makeshift hammock sled with the help of pulleys, a rope, and Godü. She got each of the animals wrapped and tied them on top of each other, sort of like a bunk bed. She then attached the long poles to the sides of the hammock sled and pulleys to reduce the weight. Orchid led the way, walking, holding on to Godü's bridle. They made it to the village about three hours after midday.

She brought the bodies straight away to the village butcher's house, where specifically trained villagers worked on the carcasses that are brought in. There was another building that tended to crops of all kinds brought in and another one still where farm animals are butchered.

At dusk, those that could not fend for themselves in the village; widows, the elderly with no family to tend to them, or orphans come to these buildings and are given food and anything else they needed. It is the family's responsibility to tend to their own families and to help neighbors when possible. Families that work in the village also have their needs met. The biggest trophy today would be the bear hide once it was tanned and softened. It would make for an amazingly warm blanket come winter. It would be offered to her first, of course, but if she declined it, it would find its way to a needy family. She had not made up her mind yet, but she could still use it. She had just moved out of her parent's house and moved in with another friend her age. Orchid had lived in her parents' home, but an accident on a lake took her parents from her. Her parent's house was a family structure with a large kitchen, dining area, and three bedrooms. She had a little brother, but a year ago, he died from an illness. Dayla, her friend, had been her friend back as long as she could remember. So, just starting out, they needed much.

She walked Godü to the stable behind her house, brushed him down, and put a blanket over him to stave off the night chill. She led him to his stall and fed him three apples and a generous portion of oats from his trough. She kissed him on the nose and went inside. Her friend, Dayla, greeted her as she came in.

"Any luck today, Orchid?" Dayla asked.

"Yes, I brought us some fresh venison and traded it for some vegetables. We have potatoes, onions, and some carrots I kept from Godü!" They both laughed. Godü loved carrots.

"Why don't you relax, Orchid?" Dayla said, "I'll make us some stew, and I also made a few loaves of fresh bread. You must be tired after dragging that deer."

"Well," said Orchid, "I killed a huge bear too!"

"A bear?!" Dayla exclaimed. "Are you okay?"

"Yeah," Orchid sighed wistfully, "he was so beautiful, the biggest bear I've ever seen. It was a shame to put him down, but it left me no choice. Hunting has been difficult recently, and the village needs the meat."

Dayla lowered her head and whispered the hunter's prayer. "His spirit will live on in us," Dayla said. "Ursula, be praised." The stew and bread revived Orchid's strength but also made her tired. She thanked Dayla and rose to go to her room.

"Orchid?" asked Dayla, "Would you like company tomorrow? Two bows are better than one!"

Orchid looked at her friend. "That would be great, Dayla," she said, "See you in the morning." She washed up, slipped into her night clothes, and then got into her feather and down bed. Before she knew it, she was fast asleep.

Chapter 2: The Wolves of Mount Condie

The early morning air was cool and refreshing; Dayla and Orchid were in the lean-to on the side of the log cabin where they lived. They were tending to their horses and packing for the day's hunt. They each carried water skins, rations consisting of dried meats and vegetables, and a pouch of spices. They each had a pot and a tarp, which could be turned into a single tent or connected to another tent tarp to make a tent for two. It also could be connected to others to make an exceptionally large structure and hold around ten people. They each carried two quivers of arrows, each quiver holding forty arrows (2 scores). They also wore short swords at their sides.

Dayla was remarkably similar in build to Orchid. However, Orchid had blond hair, while Dayla's was more of a reddish blond. They had been friends at a very young age; they always teamed up together at weapon practices. They were almost done packing now when they heard footsteps coming toward them.

"Wonder who that is?" asked Orchid. In a moment, a man appeared at the entrance of the lean-to. He was muscular and well-built; he had shoulder-length black hair and a black goatee.

"Excuse me, please. Good morning to you," he said.

"Good morning, Orlağul," the girls said in unison.

"Ladies, may I have a word with you?"

"Of course," they said again in unison.

"I wanted to catch you before you headed out this morning," Orlağul started. "I have a request; I need you to head east to Mikah's place. He has been losing sheep and goats and fears it may be a pack of wolves. He is afraid for his children and him not being able to protect them."

"Yes, of course, Orlağul," the girls answered.

"If it is wolves," Orlağul continued, "and you can spare it, can you leave some of the hides behind for Micah and his family to compensate him for his loss?"

"Yes, of course, we will," the girls answered.

"Thank you," said Orlağul. He turned and departed.

"Wow, wolves!" said Dayla. The price for wolf pelts in cities was very good and high this time of year, just before fall. In villages, everything went into a central hub, where everything was processed into usable or consumable goods. The depositor was allowed to keep what he or she wanted for personal use or to use as barter for something else.

For instance, if a farmer had goats, he would turn in collected milk, or sometimes as cheese. The farmer who turned it in sometimes kept some back to make a different kind of cheese, mostly for his family but word would get out, and eventually, people would come with other artesian-type things to trade. The farmer also kept most of the hides to use for trade. The village did not use a coin-based currency. How it is done by the villagers is, 'if I have it, and you need it, and it would not affect the well-being of me or my family, then you were welcome to it'. The things that mostly fell into that category were food, pelts, and hides that could be made into warm blankets.

Everyone in the village cared about and loved each other. There was no real leader or so, to speak of. There was an elder's council that got together twice a month to discuss things and to get into this group. You only needed to exceed 150 years old. In Hielflander, that was 3/4 of your life. Most people lived to 250. Some more, some less. Orchid and Dayla were both fifty and at that age, you leave your parent's house to start your responsibilities of tending to the village's needs. Orlağul was a messenger for the council. So, Mikah's message to the council must have triggered all this into motion.

Dayla was done packing her things up.

"Well, I hope there are a few of them; we could use those pelts," she stated.

"Well, for your sake, I hope there are plenty, too," said Orchid.

"What do you mean for my sake?" asked Dayla.

"Well," Orchid stated, "I have been thinking I'm going to keep the bear's hide. It will keep me plenty warm in the coming winter."

Dayla smiled. "Yes, I'm sure that will keep you very warm." Dayla and Orchid wore thin linen pants, a top, and a leather vest that functioned as armor. The pants, top, and vest had a small camouflage enchantment over them, giving them the ability to totally vanish into shadow. Hielflanders could also use their elf vision; one was a physical ability to see in the dark, like night vision, and the other was a mental ability that could see live things in a mist in their minds. They could also feel the emotions of creatures with that ability.

Dayla led her horse, Todah, out of the shelter, and Orchid did the same with Godü. They mounted and started heading east to Mount Condie. It would be mid-afternoon before they arrived. As they traveled, they interacted.

"Did you see how handsome Orlağul was this morning, Orchid?" Dayla asked.

"Haha, I knew it," said Orchid, "I knew you were thinking that. Did you read him?

"Read him?!" exclaimed Dayla. "No, I did not read him! That would be rude!"

"Well, I did," stated Orchid. "His heart was all a flutter. I'm surprised he didn't show how nervous he was on his face." Orchid teased, laughing. Dayla tried not to look amused and shocked at her friend, but Orchid's laugh was so contagious, and she busted out laughing with her friend.

"You know he is like the most eligible bachelor in Artistah," stated Dayla.

"Yes, but he is like 25 years older than you," Orchid said matter-of-factly.

"Oh, I don't care about that; he is a good man," Dayla admitted.

"Yes, I agree with you on that point," Orchid decided to change the subject. "I wonder if this wolf pack could be the reason for the lesser amount of game we are finding?"

Dayla thought for a moment before speaking. "It very well could be," she finally said.

Depending on how big the pack was, they could devastate a hunting ground. The children of Hielflander hunted small game in an area of approximately 150 acres for ten days, then moved to a different location and did not return for a year. The areas were marked with different colored banners hanging with the help of tall staffs bearing the village seal on them. Large game hunters did the same, except the area was 1500 acres. Also, once a quota was reached from kills in that area, they would also move locations. Anyone was allowed to hunt for food for their family; you just had to ask for an area to be assigned to you so as not to overhunt one specific area. It was all a balanced system for the sake of the wildlife.

Hielflanders, in general, were not greedy folk. They instead lived to help each other, and a successful village was everyone's focus. For the most part, everyone lived happy lives. If hunters, farmers, aviary farmers, beekeepers, and livestock farmers were successful, the village would thrive. If times got lean, they would all suffer together. For the most part, though, there was enough to go around. People from the village of Artistah were content with their fortune, friends, and lives.

Orchid was in a good mood, joking around with Dayla, when something on the path caught her eye. She stopped Godü and dismounted. She saw a faint set of tracks in the road, going across the road from east to west. She bent down and looked, studied, felt, and prodded.

"It's only horse tracks," said Dayla, looking down from her horse.

"No, I don't think so," replied Orchid. "The hooves are very narrow and not shod. Wait here; I want to follow them for a minute. Hold Godü, please. It will only be a minute."

Orchid started following the tracks; she saw that it was different tracks walking in a line. *What was this, and why were they trying to hide their numbers?* She pondered. The path was wide enough for three abreast mounted horses, but these stayed in one line. She looked more closely now and found three distinct prints belonging to three right hooves. She was sure now. One hoof was missing a diamond-shaped chunk from its outside front right hoof, probably stumbled on a stone. The second had uneven wear on its right hoof, and the last was in great shape, with no oddities. It was the size that stumped her; it was almost like large goats than horses. She returned to Godü and mounted.

"Well," Dayla asked, "Are you gonna tell me?"

"I don't have an answer," stated Orchid flatly. "I really don't know."

She explained what she saw to Dayla, but Dayla looked just as perplexed as she was. Within an hour, they made it to Mikah's farm. There were sheep in a walled-in area; at a guess, Orchid thought there were around 80. In another area, there were only maybe 50 goats. Mikah was mending part of a fallen wall, and when he saw the girls coming, he put his shirt back on and headed over to meet them.

"Greetings, girls, thank you for coming," said Mikah.

"Of course, we wanted to help," said the girls.

"Well, have you had a mid-day meal yet?" asked Mikah.

"No, we haven't thought about it, really," Dayla answered. Actually, they did think about it and secretly hoped it would play out exactly how it did.

"Boy!" Mikah yelled. "Come get these kind girl's horses and take them to the barn. Water them and brush them down."

"Okay, Dah," replied the boy. He walked over as the girls dismounted and handed their reins to him. He looked to be about twenty-five or twenty-six years old, well-muscled from working a farm. He led the horses away to the stables to get started. Mikah, on the other hand, was around 125 years old, and he was tall for a man, probably 1.88 meters. He had jet-black hair that he wore down to the middle of his back, but it was tied back with some thong. He held the door open for the girls and came in after them.

The farmhouse was very nicely built; it was warm and cozy. At the moment, it also smelled like good food was cooking. Orchid could see two females working in the kitchen. One looked to be about the same age as the boy who took their horses, and the other looked to be about Mikah's age. The older woman still looked very beautiful; she had long blond hair down to the top of her hips. Her beautiful straight, silky hair was in a ponytail to keep it from making her head sweat in the hot kitchen. The younger girl looked almost identical to the boy outside and the older lady. They both had full-figured bodies but were not overweight.

"Hi girls," the older lady called from the kitchen.

"Good day," the girls called back in unison once again.

"Anything we can do to help?" asked Dayla.

"No, girls, we were just finishing up. Very good timing," she teased. "There is a washing basin just there; feel free to wash the dust from the road. Mikah, wash your hands, please. I'm sure they are filthy," she said in a stern voice. Orchid and Dayla grinned at each other.

"Just sit there, girls," said Mikah showing them where to sit when they were done washing up as he headed for his turn at the wash basin. The table was made of a thick maple slab. Along each side was a bench, and on each end sat a wooden chair. It wasn't made to look pretty, just practical. The house itself was like most homes in Artistah, nothing flamboyant, just practical and very functional.

The two preparers brought in a platter of grilled mutton and some grilled goat. There were also roasted potatoes, mushrooms, corn on the cob, two round loaves of bread, and butter. They all sat down, and the older lady said the prayer of thanks to the goddess of the crops and domestic animals. Orchid bit into the corn, then put butter, salt, and pepper on it, and took a second bite. While she was chewing, she cut herself some bread. Opening it up, she put in a healthy helping of the mutton, added some mushrooms, and took a big bite of that. The food was amazingly delicious, and she was truly enjoying it.

She looked up at Dayla and saw she had her mouth so full that caused her to have a hard time chewing.

"By the way," said Mikah, "this is my wife, Lilly, and my daughter, Harmony." As he said the last name, the door came open, and in walked the boy who headed straight to the wash basin.

"That is my son and Harmony's twin brother, Echo."

"We are pleased to meet you guys," Orchid said between chewing.

"Thank you also for the food," said Dayla.

"Yes, thank you," echoed Orchid through a mouthful. She swallowed hard and took a strong swig of her water.

"Mikah, what can you tell me about the wolves?" inquired Orchid. "What are you missing? Did you see them? Are there tracks?"

Mikah looked down at his food. "Well, that's the problem. I haven't seen them, and there isn't any blood, fur, or bones, nothing. Just vanished," Mikah finished. The two girls gave each other confused glances.

"It has to be wolves," Mikah continued, "There are no other predators in this area." After a few moments of silence, he spoke more quietly.

"There is something else…." Mikah got up and walked away. "I found this, and I don't know what it means," he said as he walked back into the dining room, carrying something in his hand. He handed it to Orchid, who was still chowing down on the food.

"Oh," she paused and took the item from Mikah. "What do we have here?" It was an arrow, but like nothing she had ever seen before. The shaft was straight but shorter than the arrows she used. The tip was also very different and unique! It had six blades made of very thin metal. The blades were very sharp.

"Yes, I see your point Mikah, no pun intended," Orchid said. They all smiled uneasily. "This brings up more questions than answers. Hmm. I'm not familiar with this workmanship or craftsmanship. This is not a Hielflander arrow. I need to keep this if that is okay?" Orchid asked.

"Of course," said Mikah.

"Dayla and I will go see what we can see, scout the entire area, then bring this arrow to the council to see what they think of it. Echo? Can you get our horses, please?"

"Of course," said Echo, taking one more rushed mouthful of food. Orchid saw he had barely got to eat anything. "After you eat, of course," she rushed to say.

"Thank you," the boy replied gratefully.

They were not in that big of a hurry. *Besides,* Orchid thought, *I still want more food too!* Dayla was holding the arrow, giving it a thorough inspection. *That fletching is very odd,* she thought. Where Hielflanders used duck or goose feathers because they were waterproof and held up fairly well, these were from a falcon. They were short but slightly rotated, causing it to spin in flight, giving it speed and better distance. The shaft was from a pine; it was straight, fairly strong, and practical. No other detail jumped out to her.

"Well," she stated after some thought, "I can pretty much say this arrow isn't of any make that I'm familiar with." She showed the fletching to Mikah and Orchid. "See how this twists slightly? This will cause it to spin, meaning it will be faster and have greater distance. I don't think it would be harder hitting because of its length," she added, "but I'm not sure."

Around 20 minutes later, the girls were back on the road discussing different scenarios when they saw movement in the woods to the left about 170 meters.

"LOOK!!" hissed Orchid. Dayla looked sharply in the direction Orchid was pointing, and she saw them. They were running north, heading the same way as them. Their backs were facing them. *Did they see us and run away?* She reached into her saddlebag and pulled out her spyglass. What were they? She twisted the crystal around in the wooden tube, bringing it more into focus. She had never seen these creatures in person, but she knew of them only from drawings and legends. It was Satyrs.

Chapter 3: The Chase

"Should we give chase?" questioned Dayla.

Orchid thought for a second, then said, "Let's act like we didn't see them. Let them get a head start, and then we will track them to their camp," she finally said.

"That's a good idea," said Dayla, "if we give chase now, and they see us, they could decide to engage, and they outnumber us three to one." Dayla thought that it might be dangerous, but in the long run, she and Orchid had speed on their side. Their mounts were very long-legged, and therefore, very fast, and she also thought that their bows were superior at a ranged battle, although she wasn't positive. She thought Orchids' plan was a good one. Dayla dismounted, went to the front of her horse, Todah, and had him lift his right hoof. She bent over it and inspected it like something was wrong. Orchid dismounted also and walked over to Dayla and acted interested in what she was doing.

"Good thinking Dayla," said Orchid, "this will give them a chance to get further away. So, Satyrs? Can you believe it? What are they doing here, stealing?" Orchid sounded confused, surprised, and bewildered at the thought of Satyrs.

"Of course, I've never seen them in my life," exclaimed Dayla.

"No one has!" Orchid put in.

"What do you think this means?" asked Dayla.

Orchid looked anxious, replying, "Nothing good. I don't think this bodes well at all."

Chamura yelled to his men in the trees. *I don't think we have been spotted yet.* His small hunting/foraging party had been sent out earlier this morning, but the game was getting harder to find. So, they had decided to risk a quick jump onto this farmer's herd again but saw the two girls, so they fled back into the bushes and trees. They had strict orders to keep out of sight. Chamura was an ambitious man. His sights were set on rising to the position of division captain, and he knew that if they were spotted, he would be dealt with severely. His ambitions would be thwarted. The patrol leader now stopped, turned to see that they were out of sight, and told his men to stand down and take a breather.

"I'm going back to see what they are up to," he informed, "be ready just in case."

Each Satyr had a bow, one score of arrows, and two curved swords. The swords hung one on each side in a kind of harness that hung over their backs and fastened across their midsection. This had a locking rest for their bows, arrows, sword, and pouches that held water skins and food rations. Chamura started back the way they came. He was cautious and eventually got back to the edge of the woods. He peered out and saw the girls were right where they had left them. He breathed a sigh of relief. *Good, okay, let us get out of here.* Chamura walked back to the rest of the patrol.

"Okay, they didn't see us," he said to all of them, "let's get back to camp." They got into a single file line again and started back to base camp.

Orchid asked if he was gone.

"Yes," replied Dayla. "He was pretty worked up. I felt like he was scared, nervous, and even a little confused. We need to follow them, but it's almost dusk. Let's sit for some time and eat some of these leftovers Lily was nice enough to give us. Then in the cover of darkness, we will follow." Dayla finished.

"Sounds like a plan," Orchid agreed. They pulled the horses off to a thicket of trees.

"Let's start a small fire, too. That way, if they are still spying, they will think we are stopping for the night," Dayla suggested.

"Okay," agreed Orchid. They started to eat and rest. About two hours later, both girls knew they needed to get going, so they got up and packed their things.

"Well, this will be fun," they both laughed and started in the direction they last saw the Satyrs. They made their way over to the woods, and Orchid concentrated ahead of them using her vision. She didn't feel like there was anything amiss, so they trudged on. The Satyr's tracks were easy enough to follow because of their number. All walking or trying to walk in each other's footsteps, made the tracks deeper into the soft forest floor. Together with their night vision, they were not having any difficulty. They would take turns looking ahead and around so as not to be followed. The other would be following the tracks.

They were making good time. One kilometer turned into two, two turned into three, three into six, and before you knew it, they had gone 30 kilometers. They came to a very thick forest on the east side of the path they were following. They decided to move into the thickness and pitch their tents. They would connect the two halves to make one tent for both of them. There would be no fire, and the horses were trained for minimal movement. They gathered pine needles, leaves, and spongy moss to use as a floor in the tent to keep them dryer. They also put branches and leaves on the sides of the tent to give it more camouflage. The tents were a dull, drab green color anyway, but the branches would provide more breakup of the one color. The girls were experts in concealment, and the horses had trained with the girls as soon as they were old enough to ride.

The tent was not cramped, but neither was it roomy. Orchid put down their blankets and bedrolls. While she tended to the tent, Dayla tended to the horses' needs, brushing, feeding, and watering them from a collapsible hide bucket. There was a stream not far away, and Dayla had refilled their water skins as well as watered the horses. The spongy moss made it quite comfortable. The horses would wake them if something came snooping around, and after such a long day, they fell asleep.

It was just after sunrise when the girls got up. They immediately started breaking camp and getting the horses fed and packed. The girls ate the last of the leftovers, washed it down with cold water, and gave a contented sigh. *It would be rationing the rest of the journey,* they both thought. The weather was overcast, and it seemed like there was a chance of rain. The girls picked up where they had left off and started at a good pace after the tracks. They had been following the tracks for about 4 hours when Orchid held up her hand and sniffed the air.

"Wood smoke," she whispered. Dayla sniffed as well, "Yes, cooking fires." Orchid concentrated on the direction it was coming from. "It is a few hundred fires and people, an army?" she questioned in her mind. The girls quickly strung their bows, and they carried them unstrung so as not to weaken the wood or the string. They dismounted, walked the horses back into the thicket, and ordered them down and still. The girls now got both quivers of arrows and started out in the direction of the fire smell.

They both moved in unison, careful steps, balancing on the balls of their feet, in total silence. They went about 2 km when they felt like a lot of activity was ahead. They got off the main trail and moved quietly into the trees. Now, they went into shadow mode. They climbed a small hill and peered at the other side. They both took loud intakes of air and were startled. What they saw were 100s of Satyrs, tents, fires, and banners. This was a war party.

Chapter 4: Secrets in the Dark

The girls looked over the entire camp well as much as they could see from the hilltop. It was now around midday; it would be getting dark in about 6 hours. The plan was for Dayla to ride out, for there was a town a few hours from here. She was going to send word about the camp so a proper army could be arranged to defend towns and villages to counterstrike. Orchid was going to slip into the camp at nightfall. She wanted to eavesdrop on a few conversations to see what she could learn. There was a pit in her stomach, she had known peace and contentment all her life, and now it looked like she would soon taste war.

After a rest and some sleep, she woke at dusk. Dayla had left just after midday and was not back yet. She had taken the arrow they got from Mikah's house to show the unbelievers, and there would be those. I mean hundreds of legendary creatures no one had seen in centuries camped in our country. What did they want? *Well, hopefully, in a short while, I'll find out.* She decided to wait just a little after they finished eating, so full bellies would make them sleepy. The sentries had changed just after a meal. They would be fighting sleep. She slowly got up and covered herself with her camouflage cloak, the one with the enchantment on it. It also had a hood that hid her facial features. She was warm, excited, and all set to go.

She started down the hill, using her skill to stay hidden. The less movement, the less chance of them seeing her. She was almost at the first set of tents. She only had to stop once heading down the hill to keep a sentry from seeing her. Now, she was at the first way-point of protection she had spotted from the hill. She quietly snuck around the tents, keeping in the shadows as much as possible with something at her back. She was about to go around another tent when she spotted a sentry, then she slowly laid down and waited for him to pass. She was about to keep going when she heard voices from the tent she was lying next to.

"Kavak, why are we still here? Why haven't we started our raid?"

"Because little brother Mazak and Zajak, who joined with four hundred Satyrs each, have yet to get here. We are safe. No use putting our boys in danger till we have our full force of 2000."

"Kavak! There is barely enough food here for us without having to feed eight hundred more."

"Well, maybe they will bring their own food!" said Kavak.

"That would be nice," said the little brother. "Why were they against netting up the river for eels and fish?" he asked.

"Because Matoc," answered Kavak, "that stream heads to a town two hours from here. If the fishing went bad at a time of year it shouldn't, the townsfolk might come to investigate, and our surprise would no longer be."

"That makes sense," agreed Kavak's little brother, Matoc. "When do you think the two bands will get here? I heard Chamura complaining to one of his men that it could still be two weeks or so."

"Chamura was tired of trying to hunt here," Kavak informed him. "They say he was almost seen by two riders a few days ago but got away. They came back empty-handed, though, so now they have all the dirty chores. Hahaha!!" They both had a good laugh.

Orchid heard all she needed to hear. She slowly stood up and-

"THERE YOU ARE, YOU LITTLE THIEF!" Her heart went to her throat as she drew the short blade from her side and readied herself, but she didn't see anyone.

"Thief? Who are you calling a thief?" said another voice. She took a deep breath and started to calm her heart rate.

"I saw you back there; you took a handful of apples," said the first voice.

"They are there for us to eat, aren't they?" stated the second voice. "Yeah, but why are you being selfish and taking like six of them? Others are eating them too!"

"I'm not selfish," said the second voice, "I'm lazy, and once I get to my tent, I don't want to walk back out here."

"Well, at least you're an honest thief," the first guy laughed. Orchid had used the distraction to get out, and by the time the commotion settled down, she was halfway up the hill. She had also swiped a few of the apples herself as she snuck by. She was almost at the spot where she had started when she felt Dayla's presence.

"Hey girl, find anything out?" Dayla called from the shadows.

"Yup, I did," said Orchid proudly. She quickly filled Dayla in on all the information she had found out. "Here," she handed Dayla two apples, "compliments of our guests! One for you and one for Todah. How about you?" Orchid asked Dayla.

"Well, I got to Condie Village, where I met up with a member of the village council. He dispatched four riders to alert nearby villages and towns and one to ride to the Capital, Ursula." Ursula was deep in the forest. It was named after the Goddess Ursula and was one of the oldest settlements in memory. It was possibly 3,000 to 4,000 years old, but no one knew for sure.

"Wow," said Orchid, "but I guess we need to let everyone know. So, what do we do now?" asked Dayla.

"Well, legend has it that the last known whereabouts of Satyrs were in the Dragonspine Mountains. It's about a week's ride north. I suggest we head in that direction and see what mischief we can get into. Hopefully, in slowing the other two groups of Satyrs down," said Orchid. "We know where they are heading, and we know it's a large war party; it can't be that hard to locate them. Once we find them, we will keep track of them while the other sends updates to the villages so they can get word to the main body of defenders, wherever that will be," finished Orchid.

Dayla thought for a moment, then said, "Sounds like a great plan, so let's get started; that way, we can put some miles behind us before midday." They packed all their things while meticulously hiding signs they had been there. They headed north, and it was uneventful after a good hard ride that became slow, and they started looking for a suitable campsite. They found a flat grassy spot with tall trees to filter smoke, and it was next to a wide stream.

They went to work pitching the tent and starting a fire. Dayla attached a line to an arrow and shot two nice-sized salmon within minutes. She got them cleaned and prepared them for cooking. After dinner, they discussed the plans for the next day. They went to bed heavily fed and exhausted from the long day.

Dayla awoke; something was not right. She laid still, reaching out with her ability, seeking and searching for what woke her. She felt Orchid was awake, too, and doing the same thing, then she grabbed her hand and held it tightly. The air felt very thick and heavy. Slightly cool. Someone was out there. She searched harder, and there it was! She concentrated on the spot and realized there were half a dozen entities she could feel. However, she wasn't feeling any form of hostility. Meanwhile, Orchid had the exact same experience. Then something entered her mind; it was a voice.

"We mean you no harm; please come out of your tent. We just need to talk, do not be alarmed."

Orchid quietly rolled over and looked at Dayla. She looked like she had heard it too! The girls adjusted their clothes and pulled the flap to the tent open. There was a thick mist, but it seemed unnatural. As they left the tent, the mist started to disappear. It was then that they saw them.

There were six of them, each standing roughly a meter in height. They were dressed in green garb that seemed to flicker in and out of clearness and camouflage. The mist completely surrounded the area, and no one could see what was going on. Orchid had never in her life seen such a creature. One of the females stepped forward and spoke.

"Hello, greetings. I am Maple Blossom. I am a tree sprite. Some call us tree elves, while others call us tree fairies. We have been watching you, Orchid, and Dayla of Hielflander. We have sensed you have good souls and pure spirits. We have decided to give you information on your new enemy and now ours."

"They are waiting for another two parties, we know," Dayla interjected.

"Yes," stated Maple, "their army now chops sprout trees. Instead of using dead wood, they have many fires, which means more than just dead wood. We want to ally with you, and when the time comes, we will bring forth our forces to unite with yours. We may be small, but we have powerful mages, and we are great archers. We can take the form of a tree, bush, or other plant life."

Great for spying, thought Orchid.

"What is your plan, Orchid?" asked Maple.

"We are on our way to harass the two armies that are not here yet, to try to slow them down."

"This sounds reckless," Maple protested. Suspense hung in the air until her next words. "We are in!"

Orchid and Dayla sighed in relief.

"It sounds fun!" she stated matter-of-factly, and a very child-like giggle came from her. She let it evolve into a full laugh, and it took her over. Everyone joined in. First, Maple's eyes watered, and the smile lines on her face came out in full force. Then her whole body started shaking. She took deep breaths and gained control.

"I am sorry, girls," she apologized. "Tree sprites live to laugh!"

Chapter 5: Tree Sprites Are Crazy Fun

The other five sprites came forward and introduced themselves.

"Hi, I am Giggles," said one of the other females. Everyone started to laugh.

Giggles said, "I mean GiGi flower, but everyone calls me Giggles."

"I'm Ashen Oak," said the first male.

"And I'm Oaken Ash; we are twin brothers," said another male.

"I'm Hickory Root," said the last male.

"And I'm Dragonfly Willow," said the last female. Dragonfly was very distinctive in looks. She was very beautiful, but it was the way she carried herself that said something was amiss here.

Orchid bowed to Dragonfly, "Pleased to meet you, Princess."

Dragonfly started laughing aloud, "Well, that didn't take long! I forget you can sense things."

"Yes, your highness, but your secret is safe with us. We understand why you are doing it," Dayla said.

"Maple is my most trusted friend," stated Dragonfly. "She is also in command of 1,000 troops. You will find her highly organized, knowledgeable, and well; I was going to say serious, but that only happens when she is on task. The rest of the time, she is... well, she is... a sprite!" Everyone was laughing! "The rest of the sprites are commanders of our troops," Dragonfly finished.

"This is starting to turn out into a big fun adventure," said Dayla.

"Well, I'm not sure, but I don't think the Satyrs have fun in mind," said Orchid.

"Agreed," said Dragonfly and Maple Blossom in unison.

"Let's talk about what we can do to slow down the other two groups," said Orchid. It seemed she had been picked as the default leader, which was fine with her. She had many leadership qualities. She had been told that at an incredibly young age and had accepted it as a trait she would never be able to let go of, so she embraced it.

"Well," Dragonfly interrupted, "I think we could send word through the trees, and we could hear back by this evening. We could get the exact location of where they are. Then we call on an eagle to fly two or three of our numbers to get exact numbers and tactics; for security, they are deploying. With that information, we can produce a more perfect strategy."

"That sounds like a great plan, Dragonfly," said Orchid.

"Yes," agreed Dayla.

"Since we are staying here, let's set up camp and have breakfast," Dragonfly commanded. "Twins, see what foods you can gather. Gigi, Maple, please set up camp." Dragonfly was direct and strong with her orders. The years of giving such orders were evident. Orchid felt somewhat relieved, as she now had someone to share the responsibility of leadership with. She smiled warmly and invitingly to Dragonfly. Dragonfly understood all too well the underlying meaning of Orchid's smile. She knew that however capable Orchid was, it was good to have someone with like-mind to throw ideas at. This pleased Dragonfly; she was going to love collaborating with this girl. The twins had found a large pumpkin, various other root vegetables, and a few trout from the stream nearby.

After breakfast, Dragonfly took Orchid's arm and led her toward the forest. They softly talked as they walked away from everyone. Dayla smiled to herself as she watched them walk away. *Finally*, she thought. Someone else sees what she had always seen in Orchid. Dayla was a very capable young woman, but even she knew Orchid was so much more. Orchid was a strong leader but humble. She was capable of entertaining a princess or sharing sup with a homeless person. She was an extraordinary woman, and Dayla was enormously proud of her.

Dragonfly asked Orchid to stand still and observe. Dragonfly then sat down on the ground cross-legged next to an old oak tree. She motioned Orchid to do the same. Dragonfly reached out and took both of Orchid's hands in hers.

"Close your eyes, Orchid, and do not open them till I tell you to, okay?"

"Yes, Ma'am," replied Orchid. Dragonfly began to chant, the words were not familiar to Orchid, but she listened anyway. After what seemed like minutes, Orchid felt little tingles flow through her fingers. Then she felt queasy, but it went away quickly. Then it was as if the weather or atmosphere had changed, and then it was quiet. Dragonfly had stopped chanting.

"Okay, you may open your eyes now, and do not be alarmed. I will explain it as soon as you open. Okay, on the count of 3, 1......2.......3!" Orchid opened her eyes, and it took a few seconds since things were dark. However, she did hear a slight buzz. She read the emotions. There was a lot going on, but it actually was pretty slow emotionally. Then she caught Dragonfly's feeling that she was extremely excited and happy.

"We are not where we were, are we?" asked Orchid.

"Well, we are closer than you think," replied Dragonfly. "We are inside the oak tree!"

"WHAT?!" Orchid exclaimed. "But how can that be?" Dragonfly was impressed. There was no disbelief in her voice, just curiosity.

"Well, we are exceedingly small right now. We are the size of a grain of sand, in fact."

"Wow, wow, wow! What is next?" asked Orchid very excitedly.

"Well, I want you to use your ability to connect with the root system of this old oak. Use it to amplify your ability; seek out anything that seems unnatural to you."

"Yes, ma'am," Orchid said, unable to contain her excitement. Dragonfly heard Orchid take in a few deep breaths to calm herself, and she could almost feel the calm come over Orchid. *My my*, she thought, *this girl is incredibly good.* She took to being inside a tree like a sprite; it never fazed her. Meanwhile, Orchid reached with her thoughts. She felt like she had traveled away, extremely far away. She knew, though, that it was just her mind traveling, not her body. Then she felt heat, pain, and sorrow. She followed the emotion and came to a place where she could go no further.

'Who are you?' a young voice spoke in her thoughts.

'I'm Orchid,' she thought strongly in her mind. *'What's happening?'*

'There are monsters killing my family and burning them alive...' it replied in the darkness.

'Your family?' asked Orchid.

'Yes, the other trees in the Grove...' it sniffed sadly.

'I am so sorry,' said Orchid. The emotions were overwhelming her. She needed to go back.

'Little one, Dragonfly and I are coming as soon as we can,' she comforted with all the confidence she could muster up.

'Thank you, but it won't bring my family back.'

Orchid went back to Dragonfly, coming out of the trance, and found she was next to the Dragonfly again.

"Well, what did you find?" asked Dragonfly.

"I ran into a young tree... She said her family was all burned alive by monsters. She said the Grove is gone," she relayed somberly.

"The Grove? That is possibly Pine Grove," thought Dragonfly out loud. "While you were gone, I sent a message through the roots, so we will have answers soon," stated Dragonfly. "Well, it's time to return."

"Will I ever get to come back?" asked Orchid.

"Of course," said Dragonfly, "of course!" The two went back to the camp, where there was a fire going with food being prepared.

"How long have we been gone?" asked Orchid, remembering that they had just eaten before they left, and now there was another meal prepared.

"Several hours," said Dragonfly, "we meditated for an hour before we were small enough to go in. Then you were gone for three hours or so when you went down the roots."

"Wow," said Orchid, "I must remember that next time." Dragonfly smiled to herself; she had a student if she wanted, she thought.

"Can you teach me the chant?" asked Orchid.

Dragonfly's smile broadened. "Yes, but it takes practice," she said. Getting closer, they started smelling a stew.

"Mmm, that smells delicious," Orchid called out. She was in a great mood and in high spirits. "What am I smelling?" she asked Dayla.

"Rabbit stew with mushrooms, onions, potatoes, and parsnips, with some wine!" Dayla replied.

"Oh, wow," said Orchid. "When will it be ready?" she asked.

"Oh, about 40 minutes to make the rabbit tender," Dayla answered.

"Oh, okay," said Orchid, "need my help with anything?"

"No, it is in the pot cooking. Where did you go?" questioned Dayla.

Orchid explained everything to Dayla, who seemed totally interested. "Dragonfly said she would teach me the chant, and just you wait because I am sure your time will come. We can use this skill once things settle back to normal," explained Orchid.

"Will it?" asked Dayla. "Will it all go back to the way it was?" She was worried that life, as they knew it, was never going to be the same.

"I'm not sure, Dayla," said Orchid. "I just am not sure." They ate, chatting amongst themselves around the fire. Maple came over to where Dragonfly and the two girls were sitting and discussing various things.

"Yes, Maple?" asked Dragonfly.

"My lady, I mean.. Ma'am, we have heard back from some of the forests, ma'am... I'm afraid Pine Grove is lost," Maple informed sadly.

"Yes, we had heard that too."

"You did? How?" asked Maple.

"I took Orchid here with me this morning," Dragonfly said, pointing to her, "she used her abilities inside the tree, directly into the root system. It took her a while to navigate, but she figured it out in no time. She heard from a young tree spirit that her family had been killed by monsters and burned alive."

"Yes, well, that is not all. The two groups have now teamed up together and are unruly. The trees report that there is no discipline, constant fights, and even instances of killing each other. There does not seem to be any leader that can control them," finished Maple.

"Well," started Orchid, "that would make sense... They have been stuck in the Dragonspine Mountains for centuries. Now they have freedom and adventure; they don't know what to do with all that energy. I think we may have an opportunity to do more damage than we first thought." Dragonfly was content in letting Orchid have the floor; she was really enjoying watching Orchid in a leadership role. Dragonfly especially loved watching Orchid work things out in her head and talk them out aloud. The others were just engaging with her. Orchid was a true leader, and everyone seemed to greatly respect her. "If we make some mischievous attacks, we can really work up a bad attitude in their camp! We will place allies on various points to employ hit-and-run tactics. The aim will be to frustrate them, get in their heads, demoralize them, and break their spirits before they even get started. If we can beat them before they meet up with the first party, then we should have the advantage. After all, I believe we are learning more about them than they know about us," concluded Orchid.

Dragonfly felt like she did not need to say anything, but she wanted to show support for her new friend. She said, "Very good, Orchid. I agree with you on all points. In the morning, we will put your plan into action. Does anyone have questions?" Everyone was quiet, so they all retired to their tents that had been set up by the men before the meeting. Orchid and Dayla went back to their tent for the first time since they awoke. It had been a long day. Some important things happened, though. First, they didn't have to go at this alone. Second, they had backup. Third, the sprites were fun indeed!!

Chapter 6: Let the Games Begin!

The next morning Orchid woke up to more than normal noises outside her tent. She was about to get up when she decided to sleep a little longer. She, for some reason, was still incredibly exhausted and sore. She also was not as hungry as she usually was when she woke up, so she reasoned within herself that it wasn't dawn yet. So, she repositioned her pillow and fell back to sleep.

Dayla was already on her second plate of tasty, flat, sweet pan-fried cakes with honey, eggs, and fruit. She wondered what was taking Orchid so long. She thought she heard her moving about, but still no sight of her.

Dragonfly came over to her. "Good morning, Dayla," she said.

"Good morning," Dayla responded.

"Where is Orchid this morning?" she inquired.

"Well, I guess she is having a hard time getting up," stated Dayla, "which isn't like her at all. Not in all the time I've known her. She is always the first one up, the first one dressed, and the first to breakfast."

"Well, maybe we should check on her?" suggested Dragonfly. They both got up and headed to the girl's tent. Dayla came in first, then Dragonfly. Dragonfly crawled over to Orchid and tried to shake her awake. Orchid didn't budge.

Dayla placed her hand on her friend, closed her eyes, and went trance-like. "She is exhausted!!" she exclaimed, "She is also very sore in all her joints like she has been running all night."

"It's from the spell I put on her yesterday," stated Dragonfly sadly, "shrinking down to that size has its consequences. Let her sleep, and I'll make an energy tea for her that will revive her as good as new." Dragonfly crawled out of the tent and called out to Maple, who came running toward her.

"Ma'am, are you alright?"

"Yes, Maple, but our new friend is not. I need ingredients for my energy tea potion; Orchid is having a reaction to the shrinking spell I put on her yesterday."

"Yes, Ma'am, right away! We will find what we need."

"Hurry, please, Maple. I don't know how this will affect someone who is not a sprite," Dragonfly pleaded.

"Don't worry, princess; we will get her back to health. She has an extraordinarily strong will!" With that, she took off, calling Gigi for backup help. Off to the forest, they ran, searching for certain plants, barks, and fruits. Well, late fall berries, anyway. The fruits that worked the best were not in season. Also, one root vegetable is called a wild raddot, which is basically a red carrot that tastes like a radish. It held powerful properties, such as strength and energy restoration.

Dragonfly got a special stone bowl and a cylindrical crystal geode with a rounded bottom. She started putting things inside the bowl. She poured water into a large crystal geode that was open at the top and had a small hole at the bottom. She ran the water through three times. She added some moss from a nearby birch tree and also added some pine nuts. The girls came back and ran directly to Dragonfly, who was finishing up what she had started.

"Here is everything you need, princess," Maple said, setting everything down. "Are you ready for the Budhulug?"

Dragonfly replied quickly, "Yes, bring Daerwen here. Dayla can observe." Dayla knew the words were elvish but didn't know the meaning. She also didn't say anything. Dayla loved to watch and learn new things. At this very moment, she was extremely interested in activities going on in the camp.

Dragonfly was making a magical tea. The girls, Gigi and Maple, were making a large circle out of stones. Oaken Ash was bringing an exceptionally large box, or was that Ashen Oak? She could not tell the difference between them just yet. The box was placed before Dragonfly. Everyone sat in a semicircle, with Dragonfly on the open side. Dayla was motioned to sit on the left side of Dragonfly. Everyone got quiet. Dragonfly looked at the box and started talking in a quiet, elvish tone. A small cauldron was placed in the middle of the stone circle, but there was no wood under to produce fire to heat the ingredients in the cauldron. Ashen Oak slowly opened a door at the top of the large box. Dayla heard a loud buzzing sound come from the box, and all at once, a very large dragonfly took flight from the box.

It flew straight up, like an arrow speeding around the group. The princess called out to it, "DAERWEN, come here, girl." The dragonfly Daerwen looked right at the princess, and then flew to her. Daerwen was around a meter long with a 2-meter-and-a-half wing span. She had two levels of frontal wings, an upper level in the shape of an 'x.' She was amazingly fast, and instead of an insect head, she had the head of a dragon. The princess talked to it in elvish, and Daerwen went to the cauldron and circled it thrice. Then it breathed a purple flame on the tea, which immediately started to boil. Then the sprites started feeding it grapes. Daerwen calmed down and then returned to the box.

Dragonfly approached the cauldron with a long root in her hand, and she was mumbling elvish. She held the root out in her hand, on the edge of the cauldron, and circled it thrice. Then she put the root inside and circled it again counterclockwise this time. At this time, Maple came forward with a wooden ladle to pour some of the hot liquid into an earthen mug. Upon reaching to where Orchid was in a rush, she had just woken up. So, they gave her the tea straight away.

Maple explained to Orchid what had happened to her and also explained the reason Dragonfly wasn't there. She, too, was recovering her strength. The magic spell drained her energy and zapped her strength. Making the tea left her without strength, but she also drank some of it and would soon be fine. Dayla came in to be with her best friend. Maple told Orchid that the first time is the roughest but the more she did it, the easier recovery would be. She also told her that they were going to stay in camp one more day. Maple held Orchid's hand and was talking to her as if Orchid was a sister. Orchid was very relaxed and very much enjoying Maple's company.

"Orchid?" Maple asked, "I think I have a plan for tomorrow."

"Really?" asked Orchid. "Please share it with me."

"Okay," said Maple. "Well, not too far from here, there is a forest that grows a special tree called an elven ear tree. The leaves look like elven ears. There is a lichen that grows on it, and it glows in the dark, making a light like a firefly."

"Wow!" interrupted Orchid.

"Well, I thought we could collect a large amount of it and make a large human figure with the lichen on like an oak. A figure with red glowing eyes and a huge battle ax. The lichen and a geode on the eyes can be commanded to glow and go dark. Dragonfly's wand can make that work. We wait till the Satyrs are down for the night when it is dark. We get the sprites to build the figure, and in the early morning, way before dawn, we cast a spell to make it flicker. Oaken Ash and his brother have low voices. We can have them speaking through a hollow tree, telling the Satyrs to leave his forest.

"Although you didn't get to see it, the princess has a very rare pet named Daerwen, a rare species of dragonfly. This one is a little over a meter, but it also has a dragon's head and a scorpions tail, it can breathe flame. Daerwen is also magical. I think we should let Daerwen start burning down tents with his purple flame while the Satyrs are distracted by the glowing figure; it will cause total chaos." Orchid couldn't hold it back as she burst into laughter. Maple was taken aback, her feelings clearly hurt, and she let go of Orchid's hands.

Orchid immediately grabbed her hand back and apologized. "It is not your plan I'm laughing about Maple," explained Orchid, wiping a tear from her eye, "just for a second in my mind, I pictured the Satyr's faces: purple flames on one side and a 5-meter-tall warrior on the other!" Orchid said, still laughing and trying to breathe. This caused Dayla and Maple to start laughing. When she gained her composure, she hugged Maple.

"That's an amazing idea," she told her. "It also sounds so fun." She paused, then said, "I have a question, though. Won't that put Daerwen in harm's way? The Satyrs are all archers!"

"Well," started Maple, "first, Daerwen has extremely hard scales. I'm not saying you can't kill him with an arrow, but it would be very difficult. Second, Daerwen is incredibly fast, and in the dark, you will be very hard-pressed to even see him. Let's face it; most will be fighting fires or peeing themselves from the horror we create in the forest. The fire will seem like it is a spell from our warrior friend. Then you and Dayla will be picking off a few to slam the point home." Orchid smiled at that.

"And protecting Daerwen," added Dayla. "What if they regroup and charge the forest?"

"Well," Maple answered, "the warrior will be as if he disappeared; we will simply extinguish the light, and it will look like an oak tree with moss. Besides, I think they will be trying to save the camp. If they don't give up, we can repeat it the following night and up the terror by animating the oak!" finished Maple.

"Wait, what?" asked Orchid and Dayla in unison.

"We are tree sprites," stated Maple. It takes a lot of magic, but we can make the tree move and even attack with its massive branches.

"Oh, my!" said Orchid, giggling. This will be the best time ever!"

Chapter 7: A Night of Terror

Maple left the girls; they had planned to stay one more night so Orchid and Dragonfly could regain their strength. They were to leave early in the morning at first light. Maple headed to Dragonfly's tent. "Princess?" Maple called out. "I'm here, Maple," answered Dragonfly. "We have decided to stay one more day so Orchid and you can regain your strength," said Maple. She then explained the plan she had discussed with Orchid and Dayla. Dragonfly started giggling; even though she was exhausted, she couldn't wait till they got started.

Early the next morning, there was a hustle and bustle around the camp; Dayla woke up and looked toward the direction where Orchid would be. Light from the campfire and her vision abilities enabled her to see that she wasn't there. Orchids' stuff was already gone, and there was no sign of her. *'Well, back to being second again,'* she thought. She got up and dressed and started packing her things. She was excited about what the day would bring. As she exited the tent, she saw Orchid eating a plate of breakfast, "Leave some for me!" she yelled playfully at Orchid.

Orchid giggled and yelled back, "Too late! I ate most of it already." Dayla walked to the fire and saw that there was plenty of food left. She threw her pack pillow at Orchid; Orchid ducked and then put her last spoonful in her mouth from her plate. She set the plate down and quickly got up and ran toward Dayla. Dayla planted her feet and took a defensive pose. Orchid stopped just short and threw a front kick, but Dayla was very ready for that move; it was Orchid's favorite, and they had trained many years together. They both kicked and punched, counter-kicked and counter-punched; they knew each other so well that it was like fighting a copy of themselves. Dayla finally stepped back, "Okay! Stop, Orchid! I want to eat before we must leave." "Maybe you shouldn't have slept so long," countered Orchid, laughing. "Try the wild potatoes and green onions fried in butter; there are fresh eggs there too." Dayla's stomach grumbled, "I guess I'm hungrier than I thought." She headed to the fire after she got her eating plate and fork from her pack. Orchid picked up her dirty plate and headed for the stream to wash it, and then headed back to the camp after she was done. She finished packing her stuff, and then packed it all on Godü. She un-sheathed her short sword and took out her sharpening stone, and sat cross-legged next to her best friend, Dayla. Dayla was eating her breakfast, and Dragonfly and Maple were sitting next to her.

"So, are we ready to do this?" Orchid asked. "Yes, we will be leaving in about 10 minutes. It will be fun," Dragonfly said.

The Party moved north. It was now almost dusk on the first day. Messengers in the form of hawks came in throughout the day, altering the party's path in the right direction. It seemed like they would be near the Satyrs camp the early evening of the next day. Suddenly, Orchid held up her hand; she had been riding lead and now called for silence. She quietly and slowly got off her horse and grabbed her bow, which had already been strung. She slipped the quiver over her shoulder and took a step toward the wooded area on the right. She smiled as she felt the ground give way a few steps behind her; without looking, she knew that Dayla had mimicked her and was 3 meters behind her.

They walked into the woods with slow, methodical steps, Dayla stepping in the exact spots her friend was stepping in front of her. She did this to minimize the chance of stepping on a branch or even a trap, but she also knew that Orchid was looking and skillfully watching her own movements. Orchid stopped, and she drew back her bow. Dayla looked and saw a small deer. All of a sudden, an arrow flew past the deer. Orchid immediately swung to the right and shot an arrow in the opposite direction of the other arrow. There was a scream and the sound of metal leaving leather. Orchid was reloading when she heard an arrow fly past her and a second scream, then a third as her second arrow left her bow, and a fourth as Dayla hit her second and final target. In less than 10 seconds, 4 Satyrs were down. The girls slowly stepped toward the fallen Satyrs. As they were moving, Dragonfly and the rest of the wood sprites came running behind them with various weapons drawn. "Form a semicircle, and do not let your guard down. Move cautiously toward them."

As they got closer, Orchid could see an arrow protruding from the first Satyr; it was a kill shot to the heart. The second Satyr had a curved sword drawn but also had an arrow protruding from the same exact spot as the first, the third Satyr, which was the second one Orchid shot, met a similar fate. The fourth was writhing in pain. The arrow had traveled through the upper thighs of the left front leg and the right rear leg. He was trying to get up but could not put weight on either leg. He was reaching for a dagger when a small dart came from the area the sprites were; it hit him in the left shoulder. He went stiff immediately.

He screamed but could not move; in a common tongue, he yelled, "Why I can't move?"

"The dart you were just hit with was laced with a toxin. It paralyzes your muscles, provides pain relief, keeps you from escaping, and will slowly kill you if you don't get the antidote within about an hour," said Dragonfly smugly. "What want?" asked the Satyr. "Oh, we want much," continued Dragonfly. "Let's start with where are you from and... where are you going?" Meanwhile, Maple started tending to his wounds. "We wouldn't want you to bleed out before we get information from you," stated Maple. Orchid wasn't sure, but she thought she saw a mischievous look in Maple's eyes. *These sprites*, she thought, *you never know when they are joking or serious*.

"We from Satyr Canyon, in the mountains, we hungry we look for food." "Don't you know these woods and forest north of here are haunted?" asked Dragonfly. "Spirit Warriors steal souls and take them to dwell in the fiery pits below the ground. More importantly, these are our forests; they belong to the tree folk," Dragonfly finished. "We no care; these will be our lands soon," stated the Satyr. "Well, not for you," Dragonfly put in. "You have 40 minutes to live." "I tell you the answer: why you don't give a potion fix to Blutok?" *Potion fix?* Thought Dragonfly. "Oh, you meant antidote! Well, I don't think you are telling me everything," said Dragonfly. "Don't go away," she added. She walked back to where Dayla and Orchid stood around 40 meters away, examining the bow and arrows the Satyrs carried. She started talking to them in hushed tones.

"Okay, first, that toxin won't kill him, but it works in stages. Next, in about ten minutes, he will go blind, and then about 10 minutes after that, he will have really bad cramps, sweats, and muscle pain. 40 mins of that, and it starts to return to normal," explained Dragonfly. "I want to set the guys up to his right once he goes blind. I want them to use the spirit warrior voice. I want us to scream in terror and run loudly back to the horses. I'll hit him with another dart, the herbs on that one will speed the other toxin through his body and give him the energy to get out of here. He will go back and set the stage for tomorrow with the other Satyrs." They all smiled. Orchid smiled, then said, "I love being with you sprites."

Chapter 8: Little Camp of Horrors

True to Dragonfly's words, Blutok started screaming, "ME NO SEE, ME DYING, YOU LIE TO BLUTOK!" Blutok was in total panic, "ARGRRR, WHAT GOES ON HERE?" A booming voice full of growls was screaming at them from the right side of Blutok. "I HAVE COME FOR YOUR SOULS." The girls and the sprites started screaming and running away from the forest. Dragonfly shot one more dart from her blowgun, it hit Blutok, but he didn't feel it. He was screaming and crying. The sprites and the girls jumped on their mounts and left, but they didn't go far. They stopped and just started laughing. Gigi fell from her pony, which made everyone laugh harder.

"Gigi, when you're quite finished, slowly ride back, hide your mount, take a form, and make sure Blutic or Toc, whatever his name is, gets to his feet and starts going north, then catch back up with us," ordered Dragonfly. "Maple, you doubled up on the healing salve, right?" "Yes, Ma'am," answered Maple, "He will be sore but should be able to walk once that toxin wears off," finished Maple. "I stitched the tears. It was an amazing shot. No vital bone or muscle was hit; it was a perfect immobilizing shot." Dayla smiled but flushed with embarrassment. She hated attention. She was so content in letting her best friend take all the limelight.

Gigi returned a bit later with confirmation for her friends. "Blutok had indeed recovered enough to hobble away, cursing the tall elves and swearing revenge on all of us each time he fell, which was half a dozen times or more," she had said, laughing. "He kept looking around for the Warrior; he was so scared. He also checked the bodies of his comrades, and can you believe he took everything of value?" Gigi added. "Well, it isn't doing them any good. I guess it's practical, just a little immoral unless he will give it to their families, which I can hardly imagine," said Dayla.

Orchid had been quiet; she was thinking about what Dayla had just said. *Had those Satyrs had families? Did she just cause a family now to go hungry with no father to provide?* Dayla looked at her friend. She was emotion-reading Orchid and felt sorrow and guilt. She loved Orchid and wanted to address this situation but knew this wasn't the time. The rest of the journey through the day went pretty uneventful. That night in the security of the tent, Dayla approached the subject with Orchid. They lay under their sleeping rolls. "Orchid?" Dayla asked. "Yes? Dayla, I know what you are going to say, and the answer isn't an easy one. We hunt," Orchid responded. "We rarely think about what we kill because we believe that the goddess provided for us. After our kill, we give thanks, and we put the idea of the killed animals' families in her hands. There is a closure there. Here it is different; there is no closure. I must look at it in a different way, like if a bear or badger was to attack me in the woods and I kill it because he gave me no choice. In a sense, that is what is happening, the Satyrs are here in our lands, and they are up to no good. They leave us no choice. Dayla, like Dragonfly earlier, knew that sometimes her friend needed to talk things through, out loud, to make better sense of it."

"You are right," Dayla put in.

"We didn't go taking over their lands. They are so bold. Did you hear Blutok say 'these will be our lands soon', Dayla? How are you doing? You killed today, too. You seem to be doing better than me." "No, it's different," stated Dayla, "my first shot was defending you; he pulled his sword. For the second one, I only wounded so we could get information. At least, that's the way I thought about it later. You are right, though. I defended you, and we are defending our people and friends," finished Dayla. Orchid rolled over to Dayla and gave her friend a big hug. "You are the best friend a girl could have," said Orchid. "I believe the same about you, Orchid," said Dayla. "Well, let's get some sleep; we have a big day ahead of us tomorrow." Dayla fell right to sleep, while it took around 40 minutes for Orchid to catch some sleep.

The next morning came; Dayla and Orchid sat by the fire eating breakfast; their horses were packed and ready. Oaken Ash came running into the camp. "Two riders are approaching," he called out to Dragonfly. Orchid and Dayla leaped up and ran to their horses and retrieved their bows and quivers, each nocking an arrow. The two riders stopped at the fringes of the camp. "We are looking for a lady named Orchid," the first rider said. "I am Aarik, a knight in the royal guard of Northland!"

Orchid studied him; he sat on an excessively big Warhorse that was tall and strong; both horses wore armor. Aarik was wearing fine, strong chainmail; there was a longsword in a scabbard along the left side of his horse and a shield with an emblem of a crossed ax and sword, and a silver Crown. His hair was shoulder length and the reddest she had ever seen. He had no facial hair, and she couldn't see his eye color, but reasoned with hair like that, the eye color must only be green. Her final conclusion was that he was very handsome. The second rider was very dark-skinned. He was wearing all black leather; there were three short javelins in a leather carrying harness strapped to his huge battle horse. He had a shield, and the emblem on the shield was a dragon head. The dragon was wearing a gold crown.

"This here is Drakk; he is from the island called Drakconia. He is a dragon rider in his country's royal guard. His lands are north of mine, across the sea. Our countries have been allies for a thousand years, as with yours, my lady. We mean you no harm," stated Aarik. Orchid realized she still had an arrow half drawn in her bow. "Oh, sorry," she said, disarming the arrow, a little embarrassed. *She was flustered, and Dayla was enjoying this, serves her right*, she thought, remembering days ago at Orchid's teasing about Orlagül.

"You may dismount, sires," said Orchid, totally recovering, to Dayla's dismay, and enter the camp. "I am Orchid." "Lady Orchid," said Aarik, "a pleasure to meet you. One of your countrymen brought a message to Borderlund, a city on the borders of our two countries. He stated that Satyrs were invading you. Is this so?"

"Yes, Sir Aarik," said Orchid. "And also, I am without title. It's just Orchid."

"Well, with such a beautiful name, you don't need a title," said Aarik, dismounting his horse. "I agree," Drakk chimed in, wearing a big smile showing off beautiful white teeth as he dismounted. For the second time in just as many minutes, Orchid was flustered.

What is wrong with me? She thought. "Hello, gentlemen, I am Princess Dragonfly of the Tree Realm," both Aarik and Drakk went to one knee and bowed their heads.

"That's not necessary; we are comrades, are we not? Please rise! Let us sit by the fire and discuss the past few days." It was Orchid's turn to watch royalty employ her skills as a diplomat and use charm and practice at dealing with ranked individuals. Royal guards are considered high-ranking officials. It wasn't long before everyone was comfortable with each other. Orchid tried to stay quiet; she wasn't confident that her nervousness wouldn't be noticed after being so strong the past couple of days. She wasn't sure, but she really liked Aarik, and that made her really uncomfortable. Every time he looked at her, she could not breathe.

"Well, we need to get going," stated Dragonfly. "We have a lot of work to do before the, um, festivities." Everyone started laughing. Gigi, take Daerwen, run on ahead, be careful, take form, and watch them; if they start to move, send him back with a message scroll!"

"Yes, ma'am," Gigi replied and took off to the back of the supply cart to retrieve Daerwen. Everyone heard the buzzing start. Aarik reached for his long sword, but Orchid was standing next to him and put her hand on his and softly told him it was alright. Daerwen leaped into the air and flew by everyone, not unlike a dog curious to meet everyone.

"My Lord! A Budhulug," exclaimed Drakk, totally excited; he heard Dragonfly say something to it in elvish. Daerwen immediately flew to Drakk and just hovered so Drakk could touch and pet it. It purred like a kitten. Everyone smiled because this intimidating-looking warrior was transformed into a kid just laughing and smiling. Dragonfly called him back, and Daerwen obeyed. Then flew to Gigi and started messing with her hair.

"My lady Dragonfly, do you know how rare those are?" asked Drakk in awe. "Unfortunately," said Dragonfly, "sadly, I do! They are such amazing creatures. They are kin to our dragons, a subspecies of Dragon," stated Drakk. "So, what are my orders, Lady Dragonfly? Otherwise, I will be here all day while this one talks about dragons," asked Aarik. "The leader of this attack is Orchid; she will direct you and Drakk." "I am sorry, ma'am," interjected Drakk as a royal guard. "I am not allowed to take part unless it is repaying a favor. I can only observe."

"Well, that's de-sapping a tree," exclaimed Dragonfly. "Maybe we can come to an arrangement," stated Drakk.

"What kind of an arrangement?" Questioned Dragonfly?

"Well, my lady, I am a royal guard. I ride a Dragon into battle. My weapon is the javelin, of which I carry three. Once thrown, I have no attack. I could go closer to use my sword, but that puts my dragon in terrible danger, and the dragons are sacred to us. If I could make an arrangement with Miss Orchid to train us to use a bow from a dragon, this would be an acceptable trade," finished Drakk.

"You want me to travel to Drakconia," asked Orchid. "Please, the legends we hear of your people's use of the bow and arrow, not to mention the crafting of such, would mean so much to her Highness. We would also need supplies of bows and arrows we would generously trade with your villages," finished Drakk again.

"Let's talk more on the way," stated Orchid. The party mounted and slowly headed toward the Satyr's camp. The new plan was now put into place. Orchid, Dayla, and Drakk were deep in conversation, hashing out all the plans to train the Royal Guard of Drakconia. Aarik was riding on Orchid's right. He looked at Orchid and said, "I was hoping to spend time showing you around the Royal court in Northland. The flower gardens there in the spring are like no other."

Orchid turned her head around fast and looked him in the face, and emotion-checked him and felt truth and fondness for her. She was speechless.

"Well, maybe you can stay a few days in Landia, the Royal city before you head to Drakconia. I might even escort you there myself," finished Aarik.

"Escort me to Landia? Or Drakconia," asked Orchid teasingly.

"Both!" answered Aarik shyly. "That would be genuinely nice. I would like that," stated Orchid.

They kept riding in silence for a few meters. Orchid braved a glance at him and then giggled. "You can close your mouth now, Aarik," she said. Aarik did not know what to think. He liked this girl, something about her made him believe that he had just met the girl of his dreams, but how could that be? He had only just met her. The night was falling, and there would be no moon tonight; they could not have planned it better. Daerwen had not come to them, so they kept heading to the last known location.

Orchid was in the lead, well, kind of. Aarik was still on her right. They kept on for another hour and started hearing the camp.

"Okay, this is it."

They all dismounted. Orchid and Dayla walked to the thickest part of the forest and tied their ponies. Orchid whispered to everyone, "Okay, Dayla and I and the sprites will head on the east side of the camp. Dayla and I will provide cover while the sprites do their thing." "Aarik, you and Drakk know your parts, right?"

"Yes, miss Orchid," answered Aarik. "Very well," acknowledged Orchid.

Everyone except Aarik and Drakk started heading East, following Orchid. While they were walking, Orchid was thinking to herself, *Wow, he went right back to being professional and a royal guard taking orders from a girl with no battle experience.*

They found an advantageous place to set up Sir Moss, as they jokingly called him. They had 160 arrows between the two of them. Dayla and Orchid set themselves up with plenty of cover; they both wore their enchanted cloaks with hoods up to hide their faces. They melted into shadow. They both stayed quiet, and the night air was getting chilly. Then it happened that a huge fireball was launched from 20 meters or so back and to the left of them. It flew into the first row of tents, setting as many as a dozen on fire. Then a huge lighted warrior with red glowing eyes and a 3-meter red-glowing sword. Orchid thought to herself, *had I not known it wasn't real, I would have been scared to death too!*

"I HAVE COME FOR YOUR SOULS," the warrior bellowed. Another fireball, this time hitting the middle row of tents. All of a sudden, tents on the far side of the camp erupted in purple flame. The camp was in total chaos! Then Orchid saw 3 Satyrs heading right toward them with swords drawn. Orchid let loose the arrow she had already nocked. The right Satyr fell simultaneously with the one on the left. Orchid knew Dayla got the one on the left. Another fireball and more tents were set ablaze. The Satyr that was in the middle turned back in the direction he came; this was more than he could handle. A group of about six started shooting arrows at Sir Moss when another fireball fired straight at them. To them, it seemed like the fireball came from the left side of the giant warrior. It was too much for them to handle.

They, too, ran away from the warrior. "I NEED MORE SOULS TO TAKE TO THE FIERY PITS," bellowed Sir Moss.... There were Satyrs running every which way, screaming orders no one was listening to. "MAZAK, I HAVE BEEN SENT TO BRING YOU AND ZAJAK TO MY DEMON LORD, SHOW YOURSELVES, YOU COWARDS," bellowed Sir Moss, this time blue flame shot from his mouth. Orchid decided to take down a few more, 800 was a big number; if they hooked up with the approximate 1200 at the main camp, which could very well be unstoppable. She started with the ones that were trying to regroup and attack. Every time a Satyr went down from seemingly nowhere, it caused mass panic. Dayla was pretty much doing the same.

Aarik and Drakk were quietly hiding in the thicket. They both had shields and swords at the ready. Drakk gave out a long yawn, and it triggered an even bigger yawn from Aarik. All of a sudden, out of nowhere, a huge fireball landed on a row of tents, catching them ablaze. "Now, that's an attention-getter!" exclaimed Aarik. Soon more fireballs, then Aarik started seeing Satyrs falling and knew his new friends were applying their deadly skill. Two Satyrs started running toward them, separating from the main group. It was their job to take out the stragglers, literally thin the herd. They jumped out from hiding, Drakk launched his javelin and then picked up his sword, his javelin hit one right in the chest, and he went down. The second one already had his sword drawn, Aarik engaged him, but the Satyr was no match, and it ended as fast as it had begun.

Others saw something they could engage in and charged the two. "7 to 2!" yelled Drakk. "This should be interesting."

The two friends stood side to side; both planted their feet and stood steadfast. One Satyr fell, then two more. Aarik knew Orchid was watching over him; she was on a rock outcropping. He couldn't see her, but it was the perfect spot, and she oversaw most of the camp. That last shot had to be 400 yds. Damn, she is deadly. Aarik thought. One more fell, then they were among them. Drakk took out the first one and was engaged with a second when an arrow slammed into his shield. "Look out, Aarik, Archers!" yelled Drakk.

Drakk looked to the archers as he was fighting a somewhat skilled swordsman. There were six archers grouped together. Aarik dispatched his skilled opponent and started helping Drakk, they together finished him and knew the arrows were gonna fly, but then the six started dropping like flies. "Drakk!" the girls again, yelled Aarik excitedly, "they live up to the legends, don't they?"

"They sure do," agreed Drakk.

"HAHAHA, I'VE GOT WHAT I NEED. I WILL BE BACK FOR MORE SOULS TOMORROW! GRRRRAH, YOU SHOULD HAVE STAYED IN THE MOUNTAINS! HAHA, HERE IS A PARTING GIFT!" A fireball bigger than all the others was launched; it exploded in the middle of the camp catching dozens of more tents on fire. Also, more and more tents were burning purple. Drakk and Aarik started back into hiding, then headed back to the horses. About 40 minutes later, everyone was mounted and riding away. About 20 km (12 miles) away, they all stopped at an abandoned farmhouse; it was small but dry and cozy. Daerwen arrived a little later. He started a hot purple fire in the fireplace, then took up watch on the roof.

In the light of the flame, Dragonfly read the message scroll. "Gigi is staying behind to assess the situation in the morning. She will catch up with us," said Dragonfly. "How does she know where we are?" asked Drakk.

"She gets directions from nature, like trees and animals; we are tree folks," answered Dragonfly. "Like one of the four races of Nature Elves." Dayla asked, "Who are the other races?"

"Well," started Dragonfly, "there is us, obviously. We are called sprites, and then we have the Druids; they live west of here. They are the oldest known Nature Elves, and they are probably the most powerful among us with healing magic. Then there are the water sprites; they are like us, except they interact with water as we interact with trees. Last, we have the Shadow Elves; they pretty much stick to themselves in the darkest reaches of the forests, mountains, and plains." The heat of the fire was putting everyone to sleep.

"Girls? That was the most amazing thing I ever saw. You are truly the best I've ever seen," said Drakk. "And sprites, had I not known that was you, I truly would have died of fright. It was a sight to behold; eight against 800. Haha, sounds like the biggest lie ever told." They were all very tired, Dayla and Orchid set their bedroll opposite the fire; the sprites preferred to be as close to the fire as possible. Aarik and Drakk set up next to the girls, with Aariks bed roll almost touching Orchids. It didn't take long till all were asleep.

Chapter 9: The Aftermath

"Orchid! Awoke, She was bound somehow. Something was constricting her movements. There was pressure both over her shoulders and around her waist. She was lying on her left side; she worked her right arm free and pulled it out of her blanket. She reached for the bonds. It wasn't a rope; it was an arm, Dayla's arm. It was close and confined in the house. What was over her waist, though? She reached down to remove that too. It was another arm, a much bigger arm that belonged to Aarik!

Well, to tell you the truth, she had no idea how she felt. She left it a little while longer! Enjoying the closeness of him. She had never had a boyfriend before, so she never knew this feeling of being this close. Alas, though, it was time to get started with her day. She picked up Aariks hand and gently put it back alongside him. She left her bed roll where it was because she didn't want to wake anyone.

Orchid moved outside and took a look around. It was very chilly, and she wrapped herself a little tighter. She was thinking about going back inside when she heard a familiar buzz. Within seconds she saw Daerwen heading straight for her. Daerwen stopped right in front of her.

"Quenya Daerwen," said Orchid. Good morning was an elvish phrase she had picked up in the last few days.

Daerwen purred at her. She patted his head, and she said in a common tongue, "Wish you understood me." Daerwen purred louder than cooed; he then bumped her head with her. "Ouch, that hurt! Wait, are you trying to tell me something?" she looked at him and emotion-checked him. Immediately, visions came into her head. She saw hundreds of creatures like him. They all had homes with people, her people. "You were once part of my people's lives?" She got another vision. This was a creature like him, playing with a little girl. She was running and playing; the creature was flying, trying to catch her, and she was giggling and laughing.

They ran into the woods where a Hielflander bear was waiting and grabbed the little girl. The creature went in to protect it in the fight; it was attacking with its flame but only in quick short bursts so as not to hurt the little girl. The bear got mad and attacked the creature; he pushed the little girl, and she lost her balance just as the creature went in for an attack. The flame hit the bear full in the face, and just as the little girl ran into the scorpion's tail, the half-meter stinger pierced right through her, and she died instantly.

Orchid realized she was crying out loud, sobbing uncontrollably. Sometimes during emotion checks, emotional transference happens. Emotional Transference is where the emotions of the person you are reading is transferred to you. The heartfelt sorrow and pain was real and true. "There is more, please I must show you," she heard Daerwen in her mind.

She resumed a vision. This time it was hunters hunting down the Budhulug, killing them on site. Again, she heard the voice of Daerwen in her head. "They killed 90% of all Budhulugs. We were outlawed as companions to your kind." "Couldn't you talk with them like you are talking to me now?" Orchid asked.

"Now, I have picked up many languages over the years, Elvish, Common tongue, Dwarfish, and being around the sprites, I have learned Entish too. I don't dare go to one of your towns, but when I saw you and felt you have a good heart, I decided to give it a try." said Daerwen.

"I'm glad you did. Thank you for trusting in me," Orchid said out loud. She reached out and hugged Daerwen. He just purred!

"So, what are we going to do about this," asked Orchid. "Wait till we have finished this campaign, then we will talk. Drakk was right; we are cousins to the dragons. Maybe we can find peace on an island near them. Just a thought!"

"That's a good idea." Orchid heard the stirring of everyone waking up and going on with daily chores, starting breakfast, packing, feeding horses, washing up, and getting ready for the day.

"Can Dragonfly talk to you, Daerwen?" asked Orchid.

"Not as well as you," replied Daerwen. "She can use telepathy but cannot convey or receive images like I just showed you, our conversations are basic. I'm hoping I can use you to help her expand her vocabulary. She does not possess the emotional ability that you do; your ability to read emotions and actually feel them is a compartment in your brain. It is the same compartment that telepathy is located in. Telepathy is the name of a skill to talk with your mind like we are doing. I'm sure if you practice, you and Dayla could do this too! It could prove useful at times when you don't want others to hear you." Dragonfly approached, asking as she walked toward them, "Taking a liking to my beloved friend, are you Orchid?"

"He was teaching me of the history of his kind with my people centuries ago," stated Orchid. "I'm afraid we were the cause of the extermination of his kind." She continued, "Because of my emotion check ability, I can actually talk with Daerwen using something he called telepathy." Dragonfly looked at her, slightly stunned.

"Can you talk?" she managed to get out.

"Yes," answered Orchid.

"As you can, but in much more detail, he can project images in my head. He wants the three of us to work to help you see it too!"

"Please tell me he is happy with how he is treated here with me," mentioned Dragonfly.

Daerwen flew to her and purred; Orchid laughed and said, "I don't need to translate that. Well, what is next for us to do? So, has Gigi come back?"

"No, I was about to send Daerwen to check on her," stated Dragonfly. "He said he will go right now, my lady." Orchid translated Daerwen's response as he told her. With that, Daerwen took off.

Gigi was in the form of a tree branch, about 3 meters from the ground. She had a great view of the entire camp. Most of the fires had been put out, and there were various groups bunched up. Some had packed and were headed north. Others were burying the dead; there were close to 100 graves, while others were still packing and heading for the other camp south. There were approximately 500 still in the fight, so to speak. When added to the southern troops, there would be slightly more than 1700. This would be a very large and formidable force, thought Gigi. She couldn't head back to the others yet; she would be seen. She just relaxed and watched.

Aarik came out of the house, headed to the wash barrel, and washed his face in the freezing cold water. He kind of cried out or growled at the shock of the water hitting his face. So, he dried his face on a rag, straightened himself up and headed to the fire where breakfast was being prepared. There was hot water in a big cauldron, and smoked meats were frying.

"If you had waited, you could have washed in warm water," Maple said to him.

"Ahhh, this woke me up and was invigorating," stated Aarik. "Suit yourself," commented Maple.

"Boy, I slept hard," stated Aarik.

"Yes, you did," said Orchid mischievously. Aarik looked at her, puzzled. He heard the tone of her voice, and the tone said there was more to her statement.

"I would never have guessed a man of your age missing his stuffed bear," stated Orchid smugly.

Most people in the camp now listened but kept doing their tasks, pretending not to be listening. Aarik sensing something had happened, laughed a nervous laugh, "My lady?" he questioned. "I awoke this morning to your arm around me, snuggling me like I was your stuffed bear; I assumed that was the reason," Orchid continued, looking at him; she had to try really hard not to smile or laugh. His face was red, his mouth wide open; she emotion-checked him, making sure he wasn't getting mad.

All she found was complete confusion. "Um, my lady Orchid, I am so sorry; please forgive me. I meant nothing by it. I would never have done that had I been awake; the quarters were small and cramped." Orchid started walking toward him; she said out loud, "I guess no harm done." As she walked by him, she brushed up against him, and whispered to him where only he could hear, "I kinda liked it."

This girl! thought Aarik. *Wow, so amazing, so confident and bold, she is fearless.*

Dayla had been listening as she was picking up her things as well as Orchid's things. She was smiling; she knew her friend, and she also suspected that Orchid liked Aarik. Orchid came into the house and said, "Oh, thank you, Dayla."

"You didn't have to do that, well," answered Dayla. "You were busy teasing our new friend; flirting is probably more like it." She laughed.

"Well, you had an arm around me, too; it was almost like you were fighting over me," stated Orchid, also laughing.

"Well, that's nothing new," said Dayla. "We have been best friends for our entire lives, and we are very comfortable with each other. This wouldn't be the first time we snuggled up for warmth away from home." Orchid explained the situation. When she woke up, she thought she was bound; she told her she almost panicked but realized the binds were not tight. She told Dayla of finding first her hand over her shoulders, then Aarik's. "Then I found Aariks arm around my waist, but I didn't remove it right away; I kind of put it back around me for a few minutes." She and Dayla had a good laugh.

"So, you like him?" Dayla asked.

"Yes," answered Orchid.

"Well, then, you need to know a little more about him," Dragonfly said, coming in through the door.

"What do you mean?" asked Orchid.

"He isn't married, is he?" asked Orchid, "No, and I'm sure your emotion check would've figured that out," Dragonfly said.

"He hasn't told everything about himself, though."

"You see, he isn't just the captain of the guard. He is the first-born son of Queen Anora of Northland," Dragonfly added. Both girls stared at her.

Finally, Orchid spoke, "Royalty? Figures, I finally meet a guy I like, only to find he is out of my league." Orchid felt her heart sink, and sadness crept in. "Well, that's not entirely true," stated Dragonfly.

Chapter 10: Campaign of War

"How much do you know about your family line Orchid?" asked Dragonfly.

"Well, my dad was half High elf and half Northlander," answered Orchid.

"Okay, on your dad's side, keep going."

"My grandfather was A Northlander," Orchid continued. "What do you remember about him?" asked Dragonfly.

"Well, I didn't get to spend much time with him, but he was nice and always brought me gifts when he came to visit. He was loving, and my grandmother loved him so much," said Orchid.

"Yes, she did, she really, really did," said Dragonfly.

"Wait, you knew my grandmother?" asked Orchid.

"Yes, her name was Lady Lilly; she was a high elf," stated Dragonfly. "She was married to Olaf, your grandfather. He was the son of Queen Amakir, High elf Royalty who passed the crown to her Twin sister, Amastacia, so she could marry a Northlander Royal Guard, your great grandfather, Elkhazel."

"So, you see, technically, you are royal blood. Did you think your skills in leadership, your charisma, your dedication, and your abilities to fight and lead battle-hardened men was just chance?" asked Dragonfly. "No, my dear, you are royal."

Dayla was looking at her friend now; tears were running down her face. She was so proud of her.

"I guess I've always known," Dayla said.

Orchid laughed a nervous laugh out loud at her and said, "Glad you did because I sure didn't."

Dragonfly continued, "That's why I have let you lead these past days; I wanted to see if there was a sign that you carried that bloodline. I must say that I'm very impressed with everything I see with you."

"Does Aarik know?" asked Orchid.

"No, he is like your great grandparents, not really caring for titles or power. He is a good man," finished Dragonfly.

"My lady Orchid, can you please help me finish packing? I'm not your servant yet," giggled Dayla.

"However, this one," Dragonfly pointed at Dayla, "she should have been a sprite." They all laughed!

"My lady," Maple called from outside. "Daerwen has returned!" They all rushed outside. Daerwen flew to Orchid and hovered near her. Orchid concentrated on her emotion check so Daerwen could tap into that.

"Gigi is fine. I couldn't get close to her; there are still quite a few Satyrs in the area. There is a significant amount of them heading south. If I was to guess, I believe 500 would be the approximate number. Approximately 100 have died, and the remainder are headed back to the mountains," Orchid relayed the message to everyone.

Drakk came up to Orchid now and stood before her. "Miss Orchid," he started, "I request your leave. I need to head back to Drakconia and inform and update my queen. I would have them prepare to March troops to our aid."

Orchid thought for a second. "Yes, Drakk. That would be a great help, thank you," she stated.

"Captain Aarik? That wouldn't be a bad idea for you either. We will need all the help we can get," Orchid said to him. "I will also send word to my people along the route to have food and water along your route. It might not be much, but it will be something. It is the very least we can do for those defending our home."

"Yes, lady Orchid right away," Captain Aarik said. With that, he got his things together and packed his horse, and mounted.

"I shall return in 5 days with the heavy and light cavalry." With that, he took off in a gallop.

"As for us, Dayla, we need to shore up the security in the towns nearby and warn of danger. Next, we need to get word to our hunters and troops about where to meet."

"Okay, let's get going," stated Dayla. The two of them started packing the horses. Dragonfly came over to them, "We will wait for Gigi, then go back to Teldrassil and prepare for war. I will send Maple with you so she can send information and your progress through the trees. Will that be okay?"

"Yes, Ma'am," answered Orchid. "We will love to have her, and we will take good care of her."

"Good then," replied Dragonfly. "Let us begin the work of ridding ourselves of these invaders."

With that, the girls mounted up and headed for the nearest town. Maple rode on Todah behind Dayla because her pony wouldn't have been able to keep up with the other two girls' horses. They were quiet at the beginning of the trip. Each of them was thinking about the coming days. Maple was concerned for her people, Dragonfly, and also Gigi. Dayla was thinking about the last few days and all that had transpired. She was thinking about how this adventure broke up her boredom with life back home in Artistah.

Her thought was that she was going to miss this, and it would be difficult to go back to her old life. Orchid was deep in thought of the things that Dragonfly had told her of her lineage. *How could she be a royal? Did she really want that kind of life? Did she want to be in a castle ruling over people? Did she want a life in court?* These questions kept swirling around in her head. She did know that she did not want to be separated from her friend, Dayla. So, if she was forced to follow this path, she would make sure that Dayla had a part to play.

She also did not know what to think about the handsome Royal Guard Captain. She did like him, *if he could be a royal and still be a captain of the guard, there was hope for me to escape being cooped up in a castle all day,* she thought. The biggest concern, however, was for the safety of her people. Most of her people had known only peace in their long lifetimes. How were they going to be able to cope with the horrors of war? She was struggling with it even now. She was used to taking life; she was a hunter.

However, she told Dayla it was for food, and it was always put in Ursula's hands. This was different. In the coming days, would she have to deal with the loss of a friend? Dayla? Maple? Heaven forbid, Dragonfly? She had only known the sprites for a few days but had totally become attached to them. She loved them, the way they loved to laugh, the practical jokes on each other, their playfulness, etc. Yes, she loved the sprites; they were very special indeed! Part of being an empath and reading emotions as you grew attached to those people. How could she keep Dayla safe? She was trying to answer that in her head.

I can't; First reason is Dayla was just as good with a bow as herself. Second, she felt safest, with Dayla guarding her back. Third, it was not right to send others to their possible deaths and protect your friends. Last, Dayla would never forgive her if she did that, and she loved Dayla, and if this was going to be my last days on this earth, I want her beside me, she thought! Lastly, she was thinking about the last thing Dragonfly said to her as they were leaving. She had told her to keep the royalty thing a secret for now until the right time. She said that in the future, Hielflander was going to need true leadership and a born leader. At that point, it will be time to play her cards. She would have the backing of 3 different people; Northland, Drakconia, and the tree spirits of Teldrassil. Not to mention; her Bloodline.

Chapter 11: Gathering an Army

Drakk and Aarik were riding together, talking about the last few days.

"Your army will be unstoppable after Orchid trains your troops," stated Aarik.

"If my men can learn 30% of her greatness, we will indeed," remarked Drakk.

"The skill she has…I have never seen anything like it," said Drakk.

"Dayla was just as good," added Aarik.

"I agree," stated Drakk.

"Strategically speaking, we need to equalize the Satyr archers," he continued. "We won't have bows by the time of the engagement. Breathing flame and frost from the dragons will help a bit, but we want maximum damage before we use your Calvary and troops, Aarik."

"Well, I'm sure the troops that Orchid brings from her Home Country will be devastating. It's possible that we can put Orchids archers behind barriers on high ground, like the other night. That must have been terrifying for the Satyrs. Also, you can't count out the sprites." They both started laughing. "I cannot imagine what they have planned; it almost makes you feel sorry for the Satyrs, doesn't it?" They both started laughing uncontrollably.

"Aarik?" said Drakk seriously. "Are you going to tell Orchid who you are? I see the way you look at her. I believe you are becoming serious with her. She is a very skilled and worthy companion, and she is beyond beautiful, but she is NOT a royal. Your family will not approve!" Aarik gave a nervous laugh. "Yes, you are right about how I'm starting to feel about her. Yes, you are right about how my family will not approve, but tell me, Drakk, we have been friends for almost 50 years. You know me better than anyone; when has that ever stopped me from being who I am? I have no aspirations for the throne; I have no desire for a life of Court. I am a simple man with simple wants and desires that happen to have royal blood," finished Aarik.

Drakk looked at his friend. "You are much more than a simple man," he stated. "You are a man I would willingly give my life for. You are my friend, and although I am not part of your country. I would willingly call you Captain, and I would follow you into battle as my King. You have all the qualities I consider worthy of a King and leader. That being said," Drakk paused for dramatic effect, "Orchid is way out of your league!"

Those last words hit Aarik hard; he was about to say something when he saw that Drakk was unsuccessfully trying not to smile or laugh. Aarik let out a loud, roaring, full-belly laugh. Immediately, Drakk lost his composure and joined his close friend. They both laughed so hard that tears were streaming from both of their eyes. It was hard for them to catch their breath. They were still trying to gain their composure when they were approached by three riders on horseback.

"Sirs, we are from a village close to here, about 2 kilometers from this main road. We got word that you may need refreshment and food and water for your horses." Aarik looked at the riders. Two were male; the other, the one who spoke, was a female. She met Aarik's gaze. She had electric blue eyes like Orchid; she held herself upright and confidently on her horse. There was a Hielflander bow across her lap and a quiver of arrows strapped to her back. She had long, straight black hair, a short sword was strapped to her waist, and was within drawing distance.

She was wearing reddish-colored leather armor; stunning to look at, with her blue eyes and black hair. She lowered her eyes. "I am Serephine of Artistah. Orchid has sent word to tend to your needs. I am also to escort you, sir Aarik, and you as well, sir Drakk, to the edge of our borders to ensure your needs are met and that there is no delay in getting troops to defend our home. I am also to update you with information. We have gathered 80 archers in a field 5 kilometers south of Artistah; more are coming every day, sirs!"

"Ms. Serephine," Drakk addressed her, "thank you for your hospitality. We are ready to follow you; please lead." Serephine turned her horse around and headed down a side path. She was followed by the two men; both had brown hair and were carrying bows and short swords. They were dressed in well-made leather armor similar to Serephine's. Drakk couldn't keep his eyes off her. Aarik smiled to himself. He couldn't blame him. Had he not been smitten by Orchid, he would be interested in this girl very easily. They trotted the two kilometers to a sizable village. There, people were milling about where a large table had been set up near a cooking fire. The meat had been cooking, fresh bread and fruits, vegetables, and jugs of cold water drawn from a deep spring well.

Aarik and Drakk dismounted along with Serephine. They walked over to the table and were served healthy portions of perfectly cooked wild boar, hard-crusted pieces of bread, raddots, sweet potatoes, late fall wild blueberries, blackberries, and an assortment of squash cooked over the fire. Aarik and Drakk were famished and ate heartily. Serephine gave them their space as a sign of respect.

Other than the refilling of their water glasses and asking basic questions like, "Will there be anything else, sires?" the villagers kept their distance.

"I could get used to this," said Aarik.

"I would like it a little more if Serephine was over here," stated Drakk.

Aarik laughed as he put another mouth full of bread and meat in his mouth.

"You may get that chance," he said, swallowing his food. Serephine started walking over to them.

"Sires, would you like to trade your mounts for fresh ones?" she asked.

"No, I think they will still perform top-notch," answered Drakk. "We are not going to ride them that hard unless we get word that the situation is…more desperate. We are what? A day and a half from Aarik's border, Ms. Serephine?"

"Yes sir, it's about a day and a half at a good trot to Borderlund," she answered. "We still have a few good hours to ride tonight once your horses are rubbed down and resaddled."

"Thank you, Serephine," replied Drakk.

"May I ask you a question, Sir Drakk?"

"Of course," Drakk answered,

"Sir, I was told you are a dragon rider. Is this true?"

Drakk smiled. "Yes, it is true. If you escort us to Aarik's Capital Landia, you will be able to see my dragon Khelek-bril, which is elvish for Ice crystals; she is a frost dragon."

Serephine didn't know what to say.

"Well, I am tasked with being your liaison and messenger, so I guess it will be okay!"

"Well, it's settled then," stated Drakk!

"Just like that Drakk," asked Aarik?

"What do you mean, Aarik?" asked Drakk with a confused look on his face. He then looked at his friend and saw a smirk on his face and knew he was being teased.

"If it's too much trouble, Sir Drakk," Serephine began, only to be cut off by Drakk, "No, Ms. Serephine, Aarik forgot his place and who was in charge!" Aarik had to turn his head and work really hard on suppressing laughter.

He cleared his throat and said, "You are right, Sir Drakk. It was not my place." Drakk continued with the banter, "See that it doesn't happen again." Serephine was confused; she thought it was all serious.

Drakk continued, "As I was saying, we might even get Bril to give you a flight." Serephine took an intake of breath; she didn't know what to say; the emotion she was feeling was pure excitement and fear. She emotion-checked Drakk to see if he was being truthful. She found out he was, but also found another emotion she wasn't expecting; he was trying to impress her because he liked her. Well, this was not going to be the boring diplomatic mission she thought it was going to be.

Gigi had returned to the cabin. The sprites were almost prepared to leave. Dragonfly had debriefed Gigi. She caught up to the last few days of events that had happened here, and she was fed. They were now all mounting their ponies and heading to Teldrassil.

Chapter 12: Nagging Questions

Orchid, Maple, and Dayla rode through several towns talking to town council members, giving them strategies for the defense of their villages. Word had already spread through most of the towns and villages of the coming possible danger. It was also said that Orchid would be put in charge for the time being since there was no formal army to speak of other than town defense forces. She was known not only as one of the best hunters but most likely the best archer in Hielflander.

Her mother had won many archery competitions and was a Hielflander champion in a competition held every three years back when she was younger. On the other hand, Orchid won that event at age 13, beating out women twice and even three times her experience. She had been the only person to have ever been crowned the Grand Champion 5 times consecutively. Dayla became the Grand Champion the following three times, and then Orchid won again. Then another girl from their village Artistah, named Serephine, won the next two times. The three of them were best friends and trained together.

It was said that Artistah very rarely went entirely out of food with those three hunters circling around. Serephine was also highly trained with a sling with rounded stones and hunted smaller animals like ducks and rabbits. The stones did not damage the meat like an arrow. Orchid and Dayla used blunted arrows with rounded tips and only quarter to half pulls on the string. However, that was difficult to do when your muscle memory was used to draw back full strength. Of course, there were different tips that were used for different games. When hunting, each hunter carried a variety. Her skill, the confident manner in which she carried herself, and her natural charisma made it easy for others to follow and carry out her orders.

The same could also be said about Dayla. However, it was obvious that she was much more comfortable in Orchid's shadow. However, if she was carrying out a mission for Orchid, she did that with confidence and authority. They were now heading to the Capital of Hielflander, Ursula!

"Are you excited to be going to our capital Orchid?" asked Dayla. Orchid didn't answer. Dayla looked at her friend; she was deep in thought.

Dayla emotion-checked her; Orchid's emotions were all over the place. There was concern, anxiety, and although only a little, there was fear, but she didn't detect doubt. There was confidence and determination. Dayla stopped to wonder about the situation. Here was this girl, her best friend, in the last week she had learned about the existence of a creature thought to be a legend. She had led troops into battle; she had killed, strategized, found out her royal bloodline, and now was riding out to meet the high council and lead a nation's army into battle!

All this stress and weight must be taking a toll, but in reading Orchid's emotions, she did not find any negativity; she was accepting of the situation and striving to complete what was expected of her. Dayla decided not to repeat the question and let her friend be. She had so much on her plate.

Maple spoke up, "She is deep in thought, isn't she?"

Dayla answered, "I'm afraid for her. She has never had this much responsibility placed on her before."

Maple continued, "Well, she is doing a great job being her first time and all; I believe in her."

"I do, too," stated Dayla. Maple then said something that made Dayla think. "I'm worried about Dragonfly."

Dayla questioned her, "And why is that Maple?"

Maple answered, "Well, I'm next in line to take charge of the tree sprites if something happens to her. She is my older sister." "Wait, you are a royal too?" asked Dayla.

"Well, technically, yes, but I have always found it much more comfortable in her shadow," Maple finished.

"I exactly know what you mean," murmured Dayla, but loud enough for Maple to hear. "Who is your Queen?" asked Dayla. "The Nature elves are divided into groups, as my sister explained the other night. We are the tree sprites clan, Dragonfly is our highest leader, and her title is princess. Then, you have the Plant sprites, who are into plants and herbs; I think you know them as Druids. They are mysterious and stay in the shadows. Their Princess's name is Violet. Her title is equal to my sister's. They are taller than us and serious in nature. We trade with them often. Trading mushrooms and medicinal herbs for potions and healing balms. Then come the Water sprites. They are very much like us, up to lots of mischief. Playing in the water, emptying the fishing nets of those who fish like your people. They live both in fresh and salt water. Their Princess's name is Nen, that's the elvish word for water. Last is the Ruling elves that live in the impenetrable forest called Darkwood. That's where the Queen and King lives. They are a mixed race of Sprites and High elves. Yes, I know that's a silly combination, Sprites being as short as we are and High elves being very tall. Ruling elves' average height is 1.7 to 1.8 meters. They are the tallest of nature elves. They will leave the Darkwood Forest to go to Teldrassil; it is our sacred place. They will bring our smaller cousins, the Pixies and Brownies armies. We will show the Satyrs they messed with the wrong countries," Maple finished.

"If it's called the impenetrable forest, how do they get out?" laughed Dayla.

Maple laughed, "There are tunnels and paths only they know. Also, the trees and plants are enchanted. They hide and change their paths. You elves are something special, but...." Dayla's voice trailed off for a moment. "Something isn't right," she stated. "The Satyrs we have encountered have not been very intelligent; there is something driving them to do this. They don't possess the skill, confidence, or leadership ability to pull something like this off. Someone or something else is behind this, and it has me worried!" At that moment, Orchid stopped her horse and turned back to look at her.

"I have been thinking that exact same thing," Orchid said. "They can't get organized; there is fighting in the ranks. No single leader stands out or is taking charge. What if this is a rouse to pull our forces away from their main objective? Then, when we have assembled, the real enemy strikes! I don't like this at all!" Maple and Dayla were stunned.

They just sat there on their horses, staring at each other. Dayla spoke first. "How would they have known where we were going to assemble? We only made that decision yesterday," Orchid looked at her. "Well, they must have known we would find them sooner or later. I think that they were maybe being told to wait; the first part of the Satyr army was the bait of some sort. The other two clans were sent out late on purpose. Knowing that one of the groups would probably be spotted, our scouting would happen, and the camped army would be located. At that point, we would assemble our army in close proximity to theirs. We played right into their hands; we were perfectly manipulated. They also probably knew that we would call for aid to our allies to the north because we didn't have our own army."

Maple looked at them. "To what end?" she asked. "What is the final outcome they are hoping to achieve? Take our land? Remember, Blutoc said, *'These be our lands soon.'* Or was that what was promised to the Satyrs to get them to divert us, so some other objective could be obtained?"

"Maple, I need you to send word to Dragonfly to tell her we are heading north to Landia. We need to bring this knowledge to Drakk and Aarik. Drakk can scout faster on the back of a dragon, and Aarik needs to defend his lands, not come here. I believe Northland is the prime target. Think about it, Aarik moves his armies south to help us; this will weaken Northland's defense. Drakk moves a good portion of his army to help us; this weakens Drakconia. A large enough army can now sweep in and take both Northland and have access to taking Drakconia," stated Orchid. They all sat up on their horses and stared at each other again.

"Maple, can you send all that through the trees? I also need her to stage an army south blocking them from the retreat."

"I believe I can," stated Maple. She then jumped off the horse and ran to a large oak tree. She placed her hands on the tree and closed her eyes, and concentrated. She was perfectly still. Orchid and Dayla sat on their horses waiting.

"Dayla?" asked Orchid, "I need you to go to Ursula first. Warn the council, get our armies north between the encampment and Northland. Have them set up defenses, and be prepared with all the arrows and archers we can find. Do this, and move with as much secrecy as you can. Unfortunately, we must leave the southern villages to defend themselves at first. Once we have our defenses in place in the north, then we will send reinforcements to the southern Villages. After you explain all that to the council, come find me in Landia!"

Dayla thought for a moment, then spoke. "How about Triangulus? It's a well-fortified ancient fortress. It is easy to defend with all the archers we will have, and it's in the way to get to Northland from the east and south."

"Hmm," thought Orchid, "that just might work. Tell the council our plans." With that, Dayla whirled Todah to the west and took off at a blisteringly fast pace. Orchid looked at Maple; she was still in deep meditation. *She will be mentally exhausted when she is done*, thought Orchid. She got off Godu and took her bed roll to make a make-shift backrest with a few sticks and twine, all so that Maple could sleep and recover while they went north. Maple's pack was strapped onto Godu as well. Maple was in meditation for about an hour. Orchid saw her disengage from the Oak tree; she took a step backward and stumbled. She was exhausted. Her eyes were closed, and she fell but was caught, by Orchid. Orchid carried her to Godu and put her in the makeshift harness that she had made. She then mounted and took off toward Northland. Maple was secured in the back, so Orchid took off at a fast gallop.

Meanwhile, Aarik and the company were getting ready to stop and camp for the night. Aarik was having a conversation with yet another Hielflander girl named Lindale (pronounced LIN DAH LAY) (meaning music in elvish). She was about the same height as most females from Hielflander, about 6 feet. She wore the same reddish leather armor, yet she carried no bow but had a shield and longsword. She had reddish hair that went to the middle of her back, beautiful emerald eyes, and the lightest airiest voice.

They stopped their horses, brushed them down, and fed them. They gathered wood and stretched out their bed rolls. Serephine pulled out leftover boar meat and bread with some vegetables and shared them with the companions. Some water was put in a pot for herbal tea; one made to make you relax and sleep soundly. They were sitting on their bedrolls when Lindale got up, went to her saddlebags, and pulled out a lute. She sat back down on her bedroll and began to strum. The music was soft and light, but then she began to sing.

It was as if the angels were singing in the trees. Her voice was as beautiful and as light as the lute she played. The lyrics were in another language. Aarik asked Serephine what language it was and was told, ancient druid. "She is a bard," Aarik was told. "Her songs can be made into spells, and I asked her to put us to sleep. Lindale will take the first watch, she will wake me in 4 hours, and I will be on watch till we leave. So, sleep, regain your strength; we will talk in the morning."

With that, they drifted off to sleep, listening to the spell-enhanced lullabies sung by Lindale. Drakk had never heard anything like this; the music was enchanting, and the magic powerful; before he knew it, he was asleep. It felt like only seconds before they were woken up by Serephine. Aarik rose to find he was well-rested and full of energy, although hungry.

Cold meat and bread had been laid out for them to eat while packing everything up. Aarik took and ate a large portion knowing they probably wouldn't be stopping anytime soon. Drakk did the same and was also amazed at how well rested he felt. Serephine was about to speak when she felt something in her mind. She immediately emotion-checked, and at the same time, knocked an arrow into her bow. Lindale saw this and quickly had her sword at the ready. Aarik and Drakk followed suit but much slower than the girls. Serephine was concentrating on her emotion check.

"It's Orchid," she said, withdrawing her arrow and putting it back in her quiver. "She is coming at a gallop, she has a sense of urgency, and has someone with her, although this person is exhausted and sleeping. Orchid is also exhausted. Quick, restart the fire, get water on, and get food ready!" Everyone rushed to do what she asked. Within 5 minutes, Orchid came into the clearing. Aarik rushed to her to help her off Godu, Drakk was helping Lindale get Maple off, and he carried her to his bedroll that had not been packed up yet. Orchid collapsed into Aarik's arms. She tried to speak, but her mouth was dry. Aarik grabbed his water skin and handed it to her, and sat her down on Serephine's bedroll.

"What is it?" he asked her. Orchid explained the thought process that they had discovered and her suspicions of the main target. Drakk and Aarik looked at each other. All of this made perfect sense to them. Then, Drakk got up and ran to his horse.

"I will ride now to Northland and then to Drakconia; we will take to the skies and find this enemy!" exclaimed Drakk. With that, he put the horse in full gallop and rode north. Aarik started tending to Orchid, getting food and water for her. The girls were making tea and finishing the packing. Orchid looked at Aarik.

"I knew I had to get word to you; you need to prepare. Maple sent word through the trees to the sprites. I told her to tell Dragonfly to station her armies to the south to have the Satyrs surrounded. I wanted all archers from Hielflander to station north between the Satyrs and Northland. You have high peaks of the Travallah Mountains to the east of Triangulus with only one pass that you could move a large army through. To the west, The Dark Mountains, but they are impassable, razor-sharp cliffs and such. The only way to get north is around Triangulus unless you go south 270 kilometers, around the Dark Mountains, and then back north, exposed the whole time. No, I don't see them doing that. They will want to hit fast before anyone knows what is happening."

Aarik looked at her, his mouth was open, and he was in awe. "When did you become a war strategist?" he asked. "Your country has not known war in a millennium. What you explained to me just now, I would have expected from a well-seasoned campaigner. I have officers under me that couldn't have thought that out any better than you just did. Some would have never figured it out. What was it that made you question our original plan?"

Orchid blushed as she said, "Something just didn't feel right; I didn't know why. It didn't occur to me till Maple and Dayla started talking about it."

"Well, I agree with your conclusions," stated Aarik. "Stay here, recoup your strength, get some sleep, then come to Landia."

"NO!" said Orchid, a little more forceful than she meant to. "Sorry, Aarik, but I must go with you," she said. "Serephine will escort us too! Lindale, will you please look after my dear friend Maple? When she is well, both of you head for Landia, okay?"

"Yes, Ms. Orchid," Lindale answered.

"Aarik, the tea will revive me," Orchid started, "and give me energy. I must see the Queen and escort you through our lands. Our troops will be on high alert now to all strangers if Dayla has delivered my message."

"Ms. Orchid, I doubt my ma… I um ah, the Queen will see you."

"Prince Aarik, there is no time for this," said Orchid, sipping the cup of tea she was just offered. Everyone looked up. "Yes, I know who you are, and it doesn't make any difference to me. I recently found out I am not who I thought I was, either. We will talk about it on the way. Ni estel tye, (trust me Elvish)." She whispered to Aarik, who looked at her in amazement but gave her a nod of his head.

Over the past few days, she had picked up on the Elvish language; it was also a language that Aarik knew being a diplomat. She didn't want to embarrass Aarik, but the lack of sleep and the stress of the situation had pretty much done her in. This was not a time to be diplomatic.

Aarik finished packing his gear, Maple was moved to Lindale's bed roll, and Drakk's gear was packed up and put with his. Aarik and Orchid mounted and set off; they would gallop 5 miles, trot 5 miles, and then walk 5 leading the horses, so as not to wear them out. They should be there by early tomorrow morning. Lindale sat with Maple; she picked up her lute, and began to play a song, then infused a spell into the words life-giving energy and strength. Maple slept on.

Chapter 13: Defending Our Lands

Drakk had ridden through the night; he had a sense of urgency. He was thinking to himself as he rode. *Orchid*, he thought, *was an amazing girl. She had figured out this whole scenario and then came up with a plan to counter it. It was a good counter strategy too! Then Dayla and Serephine were amazing as well, and last night Lindale and the lute.*

He thought that he had to spend some more time with these girls, especially Serephine. When this was all over, he thought to himself. *I will definitely have to seek her out.* He was getting close to Borderland now, and he would be in Landia in about an hour. The big patches of forests were now scarce, in its place now were small woods and open meadows. He came upon a herd of elk that scattered as he drew near. His mount was starting to tire, so he slowed it a bit. He leaned down and stroked the horse's neck and whispered words of encouragement to her.

"That's my girl, I'm sorry I have to ride you so fast, but it is very important, or I wouldn't do it," he told the horse in a soothing manner. Meanwhile, he kept stroking her. Her ears kept twitching, and she seemed to take in the soothing words from her rider and sped up on her own. 30 minutes later, Drakk looked up and saw the city of Landia looming in the distance. Her tall archer towers on the wall, and the royal fluttering in the wind. There was also a flag of Northland, a green flag with a purple border, and a white stag in the center. Below that was the royal flag, a purple flag with a silver crown in the center. He drew near to the gates and slowed his horse down a little.

The guards on duty recognized and saluted him by putting their right arm across their body, with a fist over their heart. Drakk nodded to them as he rode under the portcullis and headed toward the stables. Once there, he dismounted. The stable hand ran to him, taking the reins. Drakk heard a gleeful screech coming from a very large stable in a separate building at the far end of the main stable. There were four such buildings meant to house the mounts of

Drakconia. Drakk reached into his money pouch, pulled out a gold coin and he flipped it to the stable hand.

"What's this, sir?" the stable hand asked. "Your mounts stay here free. It's paid for by the Castle, as per our treaty. Besides, this amount would house five horses for a month."

"That's for you," Drakk said as he was getting off the horse.

"Please feed this mount a few raddots and a few apples, I rode her extremely hard, and she deserves them. Also, an extra-long brushing and rubbing down, if you don't mind, if you do all that for me, well then that coin is yours and well deserved."

"I will, Sir, and thank you." Ari, the stable hand, took the horse into the middle of the stables and started to do as he was told. The horse was dead tired and appreciated the rubbing down and brushing; he was eagerly munching on raddots and apples out of a pail. When Ari was done, he led the horse into her stall. He had just cleaned this stall, and it had fresh hay, and he filled the bucket with water and the troth with grain and oats, with which he added another big scoop. He put the best blanket he had over her to ward off a chill after such a hard ride.

He liked Sir Drakk, and this money was desperately needed. His salary was 65 silvers a week, so this one gold coin was more than he made in a week, one gold coin being 100 silvers; there were also copper coins, and 100 coppers equaled one silver. Ari knew that the Drakconian people loved and took great care of their animals. Being around animals all the time, Ari respected Drakconians. It was said that the dragon riders could talk to their mounts in some way and that when they rode dragons, there were no reins; it was performed by using pressure from the knees and taps on the neck with hands. It was also thought that they talked and used telepathy as well, flying fast with the wind whipping by you; you wouldn't be able to hear very well.

Drakk ran to Bril, "Hey girl, we need to hurry home, we have important work to do." Bril shivered with anticipation and excitement. Drakk hugged Bril's neck and then mounted her. They trotted out into the fenced-in area where horses graze. With a few steps Bril took to the sky, the ground fell away, and they headed north. Drakk had to pull his cloak tightly around him as the weather was changing and fall was at its end. Winter was just around the corner. The flight home was uneventful. Drakk headed straight for the royal hall after he put Bril in her private stall and fed her the hind quarter of a goat. As he approached the entrance, a guard at the entrance announced Captain Drakk was arriving. All in the hall looked to the entrance as Drakk entered. He walked to within 20 ft of the queen, then went on one knee.

"Thank you, sir, Drakk Darkconius. What seems to be the urgency?" Queen Alora was about 5"10'. Her weight was proportioned to her height. She had long black hair that went past her shoulders and brown eyes. She had a lighter complexion than most Drakconians. She carried herself with confidence and assurance. She was very well educated, and unlike most royals, she was aware of those around her, down to the cooks and maids. Alora never talked down on them as she knew that every person in the castle had a role, and it ran much more smoothly when everyone was working together. That being said, however, she was a staunch judge when you shrieked your duties or broke the law, but she was fair in her judgments.

Drakk started, "My lady Alora, as instructed by you, I flew to Northland to meet up with Captain Aarik. However, just as I arrived, a messenger from Borderland arrived also. The messenger said that there was trouble south of Hielflander. So, I accompanied Aarik. We met up with a Hielflander girl named Orchid; she was in company with sprites, including Princess Dragonfly. They stated that the land was under attack from Satyrs." Drakk explained all the events leading up to this moment.

When he was done, Queen Alora looked straight at him. "You did well, Drakk. So, the Hielflanders are as good with the bow as the stories, is that right? Well, you did a good service bringing them here to train our riders. Do you think we are in danger?" Drakk thought for a short period, "Not at the moment, he responded, but we should do all we can to defend Hielflander and Northland to keep this enemy south and away from our borders, to keep it that way."

"Tell Lieutenant Donush to get 25 riders ready to ride; I want all Dragons fitted with armor for safety. I will put you in charge, Captain Drakk. Also, take three messenger dragon riders to bring word back to me," finished Alora.

"It will be done, my lady," Drakk stated. With that, he rushed off to the officer barracks. It was there he found Donush. Drakk told Donush what was going on and gave him his orders. Drakk told him to have everything ready by dawn and to wake him about an hour before. With that, he went to his quarters, ate a little, and then collapsed on his bed.

Dayla was nearing the capital; she was tired, wet, and cold. It had started to rain about an hour ago, and she had to slow down for safety. She didn't want Todah to slip and break a leg. As she came to the city gates, one of the few cities in Artistah that had them, she noticed what appeared to be several guards at the entrance with bows in hand. *Wow,* she thought to herself, *for a country with no standing army, they sure mobilized fast.* As she got close, the guards were positioning themselves to stop her. "Good afternoon Miss. May I have your name, please?" asked the guard.

"I am Dayla of Artistah!" she answered. "I bring word from Orchid." The guards instantly took a less defensive stance, "Ms. Dayla, the council members are waiting for you just down the road there, a very big and tall building. There is a wooden sign with a gavel on it. Ms. Dayla, we were told there would be two of you. Where is Captain Orchid?"

"She is probably in Landia by now," she said, as she prodded Todah to go faster. She found the building the guards had described. She dismounted, and a young stable girl took her horse. "I'll take him," she said. "I'll dry him and give him some grain."

"That will be great, thank you," Dayla said. *Now to get ME, dry and warm,* she thought. She walked up the stone stairs to the top, then opened the entry door. From there, she walked down the hall to the Council chambers. As she opened the door and went inside, all eyes turned to her.

"Good day, elders. I am Dayla of Artistah, and I bring a message from Captain Orchid," she stated. She used the title that the guards had given her. *Orchid would be amused,* she thought.

"And where is Orchid?" a pudgy little man asked.

Dayla looked at him; he had dark pants and a bright yellow shirt. He had an arrogance about him that Dayla immediately disliked.

"She is in Landia, securing an army with Northland and Drakconia."

"Well, why must we worry about the Northlanders and Drakconians? They are not of our concern," the man stated flatly. "I am sure we can settle our own affairs. We have not had dealings with them in years," he continued, looking around the room at the other elders faces but not finding a smile or nod supporting him to this point. "THAT shows just how little you know!" barked Dayla interrupting him and making him jump! "DID YOU…. not vote for Orchid to take this leading role in charge? Well, she is now Captain because of that vote, and I am her lieutenant. As is our law, she is now our top-ranking official till the danger is defeated or has come to an end. That puts me second in command!"

The man lowered his head, as his attempts to intimidate her failed. He could sense that several of the female elders were angry with him as well as some of the males. He didn't really care, though. He was one of the oldest of the council, not as if it meant anything; they all had the same authority. He just liked to think that it did.

"As I was saying," continued Dayla, "we have uncovered a bigger plot. There will be close to seventeen hundred Satyrs right about here." She pointed to a spot on the map hanging on the wall. "We have most of our forces here," she pointed to another spot near Artistah. "We are going to slowly withdraw them at night, little groups at a time over several days, and reposition them at Triangulas. The smaller villages will have to defend themselves till we can secure a defensive hold at Triangulas. Then we will send any extra forces south to help. Princess Dragonfly of the Tree Realm will also place some of her army south to cut off retreat to the south and to bolster our own forces and defend the villages." A lady from the back spoke up, "You have made a lot of allies since this started, strong allies, like Hielflander of old."

Dayla looked up to see the lady talking. She smiled when her eyes met the ladies. She was tall even for a Hielflander, with short curly blond hair, although now there were streaks of gray. It was Dayla's and Orchid's history teacher, Mrs. Silverman.

"Yes, Mrs. Silvermen, we are now allied with the dragon riders of Drakconia, The Northlanders, and the four divisions of elves from the Tree Realm, and they will hopefully bring the pixy and brownie armies. Here is why we think we will need all the help we can get."

Dayla then proceeded to explain the theory they had produced and also gave them the account of the battle that had already happened. She explained the reason that Orchid had galloped north. The majority of council members looked impressed.

"What will you do now, Lieutenant Dayla?" asked Mrs. Silvermen.

"I will rest tonight, then head to Landia in the morning to assist Orchid in any way I can," answered Dayla.

"Then rest well, Lieutenant, I think I speak for MOST (she Emphasized the word while she was looking at the pudgy man) of us here; we are proud of you and Orchid and are comfortable in knowing you will not let us down. There is no one I would trust with this more than you and your friends. As for a place to sleep, there are guest quarters to the left and down the hall, there is a caretaker there, and he will show you to your room. He has already been informed," stated Mrs. Silvermen.

With that said, Dayla turned and headed to the armory after asking directions, and after getting some battle armor for her and Orchid, she went to the stables and got her pack, then dropped everything at her quarters. She then headed to a clothing store and bartered for some furs she had for new clothes and undergarments. Then another trip back to the stables. She approached the stable little girl.

"Will there be something else?" the girl asked.

"What is your name?" Dayla asked curiously.

"Sorry mistress, I'm Tara, Tara Horsemen."

"Horsemen?" Dayla questioned.

"YES, she is my daughter Ms. Dayla," a voice from the entrance answered.

"Darian!" Dayla ran to the man and hugged him. "HAHA," Darian laughed, and his face was turning red.

"I thought I recognized Todah," he said. Darian was very tall for a male Hielflander. He stood 2.0 meters, whereas Orchid and Dayla were 1.88 meters. He was very muscular, especially for his age. He wore his dark hair shoulder length but tied back with a leather thong. He was an 8th generation

Stablemaster, and he personally trained all of the hunter's horses. Orchid, Dayla, and Serephine had trained with him a long time ago. When Godu, Todah, and Balah Serephine's mount were ready, he brought them down to Artistah. He stayed with the Orchids family till Orchid and Serephine were comfortable with riding and training the horses.

Darian was a genuinely nice man, and Dayla was truly fond of him and happy to see him.

"What brings you this way?" Darian asked.

"Orchid is putting together an army to fight off an invading army of Satyrs," Dayla answered.

"Satyrs?" questioned Darian.

"As usual, you are Orchid's second, is that right?" asked Darian.

"Yes, that is right, I am her lieutenant. I came to inform the council. I came back over here before I turned in to sleep to ask you for an extra horse. I need to empty the armory of arrows. I will have one ready for you. It will be in the stall next to Todah in the morning." She hugged Darian again, and then Tara ran up to her and hugged her too. Dayla had noticed Tara emotion checking her; Tara must have seen how fond she was of Darian, and so she hugged as well.

She headed back to her quarters and stripped herself of her wet clothes. She then washed from a bucket of hot water that was put in her room for her. The warm water brought some feeling back to her icy body. She then put on her new undergarments and washed her old clothes, and hung them by the wood stove that kept the room warm and cozy. She ate some apples, bread, and cheese, and then got under the covers and fell fast asleep. Very early the next morning, she got up and packed everything and loaded the armor, bows and arrows on the extra mount, and took off for Landia.

Meanwhile, Orchid, Serephine, and Aarik had gotten a late start, letting Orchid sleep, but they were now nearing Landia. As they neared the gates, the guards stood straight up and saluted their captain. Aarik and the girls trotted by; Aarik acknowledged the salute with a nod. They went straight to the castle and to the throne room. The three of them walked to where the queen was seated.

"Hello, Mother," Aarik said.

"Aarik, who are these people with you? Why are they here in this chamber?"

"They are my guests. May I introduce?"

"NO, YOU MAY NOT!" interrupted the queen.

"They have important information for you."

"I do not speak to Commoners without an appointment."

"I AM NOT A Commoner!" interjected Orchid boldly.

"I am the highest-ranking person in Hielflander currently, and I also am of noble birth. A noble birth between both our countries. I also carry a royal message from Princess Dragonfly." The Queen was taken aback.

Aarik stood staring at Orchid. Once again, his mouth was open.

"Your kingdom is in danger," Orchid uttered. "Captain Aarik, can you please explain everything to the queen?"

Aarik proceeded to explain all that had transpired in the last week. He explained the theory that they had of another enemy. The queen was still fuming about the way Orchid had interrupted her and her outburst, but her chastising of Orchid would have to wait.

"Well, what do you ask of the court?" asked the queen.

"Nothing, your majesty. We were merely informing you of the situation. Captain Drakk will arrive with some dragon riders. We will scout the area and come up with a plan. Meanwhile, I have asked Captain Aarik to muster one hundred calvary and two to three hundred pike and swordsmen. We will have close to a thousand Hielflander archers. We should be able to hold our own. We plan to defend the fort at Triangulas. This should hold any army from getting to your lands," stated Orchid.

"What is your rank, Orchid?" asked the Queen.

"I have been voted by our council to the rank of Captain of our armies," explained Orchid. "The council is not aware of my royal bloodline. I just found out about it myself from Princess Dragonfly. If I'm not mistaken, I am the only royal blood in Hielflander, so that would make me a Queen if I decide to pursue it, that is. As far as being a Captain, the rank alone would give me all authority over the land as long as the conflict had not ended." For the first time Orchid saw Serephine, there were tears running down her friend's face as she stared at her. Orchid smiled at her and then nodded at her friend. Serephine was beaming inside; her friend was a royal. Serephine thought for a second, she kind of thought that she somehow knew it.

Her thoughts were interrupted by a guard running in. "My Captain…... Captain Drakk has returned with about two dozen riders." They all headed outside. It was at this point they met up with Lindale, and Dayla was back as well. After a hug between Dayla and Orchid, Dayla explained what had happened with the council. Orchid smiled and said, "Thought as much." They all walked over to where the Dragons were landing. Aarik excused himself to ready his troops.

Orchid saw Maple and ran to her,

"Are you okay?" she said as she held the sprite tightly in her arms. "I'm so sorry I made you do that," Orchid said, choking back tears.

"Hey, hey, I'm okay, Orchid," said Maple.

"Just in case that happens again, though, some honey, fresh and still in the comb, does wonders to sprites in that condition. I carry some in a jar in my pack, just so you know."

Just then, Drakk Landed.

Bril was so beautiful. She was several shades of blue in color. She had a big square head; she stood about six meters high with a wingspan of fifteen meters. From the tip of the snout to the tip of the tail, she was 25 meters in length.

Orchid was in awe. Drakk dismounted by stepping down the wing; Bril lowered her head for a nuzzle. Her head was every bit as big as Drakk. Drakk hugged her and started to walk toward everyone when Bril playfully pushed him with her head.

"Ms. Orchid, what do you think?" He did not wait for an answer; the look on her face told everything. "I have a gift for you from my queen."

He then placed a whistle in his mouth and let out a sharp whistle; a dragon that had been circling slowly above started descending. As it got closer, Orchid could see the dragon was also blue, although much lighter than Bril. She also had streaks of silver/white and some highlights of red; she was much smaller than Bril, about half the size.

"A gift?" Orchid said in disbelief. "Well, how can you train us if you don't know how to ride a dragon?" stated Drakk.

"Captain Orchid, when she lands, you must walk to her, look her in the eye. Do not drop your gaze if she nuzzles you and rubs your neck. This means she accepts you, and you must ride her."

"WHAT!" asked Orchid. "I don't know how to fly."

"She will teach you," Drakk said. The dragon landed and walked toward them. "One other thing, Orchid," said Drakk, "she is the first female dragon born to the queen dragon, she is a royal, treat her with respect. Royals do not pick eternal riders very often but will let you ride her in times of need like this. To ride a dragon is sacred to us, but riding a royal is an honor I have never experienced. Let us see what you got," he finished saying.

"How will I know if she picks me to be her eternal rider?" Orchid asked. You will experience something we call wiruthwix if translated into the common tongue; it would mean "rebirth." Orchid took a deep breath and started to walk toward the beautiful creature.

Chapter 14: The Ride of a Lifetime

Dayla was trembling with fear and excitement at the same time. Serephine was standing next to Drakk. As Orchid drew near, Serephine grabbed Drakk's hand and held it. Drakk smiled,

"Hey, don't get too scared. If they go up, you are going up with me," he said to Serephine. She got so excited that she hopped from one leg to the other, like a young schoolgirl.

Dayla moved next to Serephine and took her left hand and held it. She, too, was excited about what was going to happen to her best friend. Orchid got close to the royal dragon and did as she was told. The dragon stared back; this went on for several minutes. The dragon took a few steps closer. Orchid froze but kept still; she could feel the intake of air as the dragon sniffed her. Her hair was caught in the vacuum and then released upon the exhale.

All of a sudden, a female voice entered her head, it was a young girl's voice, no… it was a young girl's thoughts!

"She…. SHE IS A ROYAL!!"

"Yes, I am," she said back to the dragon, using the same technique she used with Daerwen. The dragon took a step back.

"Can you talk to me?" she asked. "I knew you were royal. I can smell it in your blood." Orchid was shocked. "Yes, I am a royal," Orchid stated proudly, out loud. "I need a rider, and I find you worthy. I am First Sister, and what might your name be?"

"I am Captain Orchid of Artistah. Did you say your name was First Sister?" answered and asked Orchid.

"It is tradition for an eternal rider to name his or her dragon. Until that time, we go by sibling rank. In the position we were born. I am First Sister. I have three older brothers; the eldest is First Brother, and the next is, Haha, Second Brother, understand?" questioned First Sister.

"Yes, I understand," answered Orchid, First Sister lowered her head and nuzzled Orchid.

"ORCHID of Artistah, are you ready to fly?" Orchid took a deep breath and swallowed hard.

"I accept you as my rider," announced First Sister.

"I accept you as my Dragon," answered Orchid. She lowered her wing so Orchid could climb on. Orchid noticed that she was trembling all over; she was extremely excited to fly. She got comfortable, then looked out at the crowd, looking for Serephine and Dayla. She waved back as she saw them waving at her.

She practiced drawing her bow first on the right side and then on the left. She noticed she couldn't shoot under the dragon's neck from that side. She felt the dragon shiver, and big goosebumps started appearing on her neck and back.

"Are you okay?" she asked First Sister.

"I am excited. I feel like something special is about to happen," the dragon answered.

"Are you ready, my lady?" First Sister asked.

"Yes, let's do this," replied Orchid. First Sister took two running steps and extended her wings. She then jumped in the air, her wings flapped, and the ground slowly started moving, and away they went.

"Now, I will start flying; we are talking now, and that is fine, but under battle situations, sometimes there are too many mental distractions. So, if you want me to go in the left direction, just put pressure on my left with your leg, and also put pressure with your hand on my neck. How will you know I am not just trying to hold on," asked Orchid.

"The more we fly, the more comfortable we will be with each other," said First Sister. "If we experience Wiruthwix, there will be an awfully close bond; we will be able to know every thought of each other. With your natural ability to sense people's feelings, it might be a powerful Wiruthwix moment. It might be awfully hard for me to handle the emotion of feelings of your kind. In normal circumstances with Drakconians, that is not an issue. But before you make me feel that, first you must feel THIS," she playfully said as she went into a dive straight down at a sharp angle. Orchid's stomach went into her throat, and her breath was stolen away.

"BREATHE, little lady, enjoy it."

They got to within meters from the ground, banked right, and went back up. Orchid started to relax a little and started to just enjoy the ride. Something told her that it was not her that was doing it. The calming was coming from First Sister. Where she was cold a few minutes ago, she was now warm. Again, she felt like it, too, was from First Sister.

"So, you and Dayla are as close as sisters," and the thoughts of First Sister were coming into her head.

Then they both started laughing as Orchid had the thought that she had enough thoughts in her head on her own; now, it was going to be much more crowded.

We are doing it, they both thought.

Orchid thought of heading back down and to the left before the thought even fully formed; First Sister was performing the maneuver. They were now thinking in unison, and it was as if they were both one being. It was as if they were born to fly together. They thought that what they were feeling was way too fast, and learning usually took dozens of long flights together, and here they were as one already. Orchid accessed the new compartment of her brain. Well, their brain now. She learned that First Sister's breath was a twin breath of frost and shock. She also learned that Royal Dragons sometimes got a third element when they reached adulthood. The breath they now had would hit a target with frost then the electrical part used the water as a conductor and shocked the target.

Just then, a herd of elk flushed out. First Sister flew downward; the wind in Orchid's ears was deafening and the hunt exhilarating. First Sister and Orchid flew as one, picked up an elk, one in each claw. *This will be for a celebration,* they thought. They headed back to the castle of Landia. In the distance, they could see another dragon; in fact, there were two. One was Bril, the other was Carnaxx. Drakk was riding Bril, while Serephine was on Carnaxx. She knew this name because of First Sister's memories. There was another

Drakconian rider and Dayla. Orchid could feel First Sister look over Dayla and then use Orchid's emotion-check on her.

Both Orchid and First Sister felt the excitement coming from her, but it was quite different from before. The feeling was so much more powerful and raw; it was almost as if that emotion was coming from her and First Sister. Orchid could feel First Sister trying to control the feelings. She could hear her thinking that this would take some getting used to. Serephine had her arms around Drakk and her head laying between his shoulders. Orchid initiated the emotion check this time. She felt the excitement again, but there was a more powerful emotion, one of trust and understanding, and she could feel love kindling there.

She quickly checked Drakk and found contentment and also love kindling there as well. "Ooo," thought First Sister. "I like this," Orchid laughed aloud,

"OOPS, I forgot you can hear me too," laughed the dragon in Orchid's mind.

"How is this happening?" asked Orchid.

"I really don't know," the Dragon answered. "With Drakconian riders, it takes many hours of flying; it is normal to not even be able to communicate at first and even into the second week. Well, how can it be that we were communicating within minutes? Is that normal, too?" Orchid asked.

"I have never heard of such a thing, to tell you the truth," answered the dragon. "Could it be that only a few days ago, I talked with a smaller Dragon? I spoke with a Budhulug; he showed me pictures in my mind," stated Orchid.

"A BUDHULUG??? Those are almost extinct!" stated First Sister.

"I know we can talk about that later," said Orchid. "Remember, Orchid, you are my first-ever rider! I am as new at this as you are!" stated First Sister.

"I have never felt like this before!" stated Orchid. "I cannot remember a time in my life that I have ever been this happy."

"Oh, that is you being happy? I thought it was me," said the dragon. "It's getting hard to tell anymore." They both started laughing hard.

"Hey, concentrate on flying," Orchid told First Sister.

"I can fly with my eyes closed," said the dragon. "Watch," she said as she shut her eyes.

"Wow, that's pretty good," said Orchid after a few minutes. First Sister started laughing.

"What," asked Orchid. "Oh, nothing, said the Dragon." "Orchid shut your eyes," she told her. "Orchid shut her eyes. And now try to see without opening them."

Orchid tried to see, and then she could but through First Sister's eyes.

"Oh, my goodness!" exclaimed Orchid.

"Orchid? We are learning things at a hurried pace. I think that if we keep working on it, we can be the first-ever Royal Dragon and Royal Rider. I am sure in a few weeks; we will experience the "rebirth." Just do not get discouraged. My mother has never experienced it. She is now an ancient dragon, and she will never have another rider. It is funny, but the thought of flying alone does not even appeal to me anymore."

They saw the landing area and headed for it. They landed, and everyone started clapping.

"We need to come up with some kind of harness to keep scores of arrows where I can get to them."

"Hmm, we can talk to the smithy in Drakconia; he is familiar with such things," Orchid started to get down.

"Hey," said First Sister, "slide down my wing. Do not walk; it will be more fun for you."

"Haha," answered Orchid, "okay."

With that, she slid down her wing. She got to the bottom and then stood up. She took two steps then she felt nauseous and everything went black! As consciousness started coming back to her, she felt wet and sticky. She tried to move but could not. She was trapped.

Dayla jumped off her dragon and ran to Orchid, but the Drakconian guards stopped her.

"Let me go. I must help her!" yelled Dayla.

"She can't be helped by you, Dayla," Drakk said from behind her.

"She is bonding with First Sister; it is the Wiruthwix, the "rebirth." They are experiencing each other's birth. Orchid is now hatching from an egg, and First Sister is going through the birth canal. They have accessed each other's deepest memories. Memories that have long been forgotten. This is unheard of. This kind of bonding takes weeks and long hours of collaborating with the dragon and rider."

"Yes, Captain, it took me six weeks before it happened to me," said the guard standing in front of Dayla. Dayla felt a hand hold hers; she did not even look because she knew it was Serephine. They were both crying; the emotion to help was so strong. Dayla emotion-checked Orchid, she was confused and on the verge of panic. First Sister just moved her legs every now and then. The Drakconian Guards were all emotional, it was as if they were reliving their own experiences. Most had tears or pained faces.

Orchid pushed hard with her hands; she could not break free. So, she slammed her hand into it, and it cracked a little. Then she did it again; this time, she could see some light. She pushed with both her feet and hands. This time a large chunk busted over her head, and she pushed more. She could hear loud purring. So, she looked down at her hands and noticed they were sharp claws; this startled her.

I'm a dragon, she thought. A guard approached Drakk; he handed him a golden dagger and a golden chalice. Drakk then headed to Orchid; he took her by the arm and sliced it open. He let the blood drip into the chalice. Dayla gasped, and then Drakk headed to First Sister. He sliced open her wing and added her blood to Orchids in the chalice. An orange-colored dragon breathed on the blood in the chalice. Drakk mixed the blood together, then headed back to Orchid; he called to the girls, "Come here please, hold her down; this will hurt." Drakk poured the mixture of blood over Orchid's wounds, the blood bubbled and then was sucked into the wound.

Orchid screamed, but the wound disappeared, not even a scar. Drakk headed to the dragon and did the same. Orchid started acting as before, like what had just happened never took place. She took the claw and raked it down the enclosure. It fell open, and she rolled out. She was a sticky wet mess. Then the purring got closer, and a big tongue started cleaning her. At that moment, she felt herself again and immediately looked down at her hands. *Oh good,* she thought, *no claws.* She looked around and then ran to First Sister.

The dragon was just coming out of it as well. She opened her eyes in time to see Orchid throw her arms around her neck. The emotion in their hearts was so overwhelming that they both just stayed in Orchid's embrace. Their heartbeats started to go back to normal.

"Okay... maybe I should not have picked an empath," said First Sister. They both started laughing. "I guess you're stuck with me for eternity," said Orchid. "Yesssss, it would seem so. I think we are breaking all the rules. There has never been a Wiruthwix on the first day. Never! There has never been a Royal Rider and Royal Dragon together ever! Let us just hope we don't die on the first day too!"

The dragon pointed her head at the crowd. "They are waiting for us to give permission to them; they don't want to spoil the moment." Orchid waved to her girls, and the three of them ran as fast as they could and jumped on Orchid; they hugged and squeezed her.

"We did not know what was happening, and the guards wouldn't let us come to you," said Dayla. They were hugging in a group when a smaller person was trying to wiggle her way into the embrace." "Maple!" Orchid said, squeezing her. "Let me introduce you to my new Eternal Mount. Wait before I do…"

"Drakk, can you please call everyone?" Once everyone was situated, Orchid spoke. "For those of you that are confused by what just happened, let me speak for my dragon and I. Welcome to the club. We understand what we just accomplished has never been done. Maybe it is because I'm an empath, or maybe it was just destined to be. What I will say is that it has brought both of us so much joy. Because it happened so fast, we are having some trouble adjusting to certain things. For her, it is dealing with my ability to feel other beings' emotions. We now feel it together. It is now stronger and much more powerful than I have ever felt before. That being said, however, I would not change it for the world. Now, I have thought about this, and I will now announce it to all of you."

Orchid turned to First Sister, "I accept you as my Eternal Dragon."

"And I the dragon," First Sister said through Orchid. "Accept you, Orchid, as my Eternal rider."

"I, Orchid, now remove from you the name First Sister and give you a new name by which you shall be known. That name is Daylphine."

Everyone cheered. "Daylphine, may I introduce you to the first part of your name? The D A Y L is for Dayla," Dayla smiled and came up to Daylphine; she curtsied to her. Then asked if she could hug her, Daylphine nuzzled her so she could give her a hug. "The last part of your name from Serephine." Serephine copied what she saw Dayla do.

"Welcome to our sisterhood, oh, and our honorary member Maple of the Tree Realm." Maple stepped closer only to have Daylphine start to sniff her. "Yes, Daylphine, she is a royal too." Everyone looked at her, so Orchid explained, "Maple is the younger sister of Princess Dragonfly." Daylphine kept sniffing. "Orchid, I smell dragon on her, but unlike anything I have encountered before."

"Yes," answered Orchid aloud so everyone could understand. "Her sister has a companion named Daerwen, and he is the Budhulug I was telling you about. A faerie dragon, those are very rare," said Daylphine. "Yes, and it is because of my people long ago. That hunted them almost into non-existence."

"Well stated, Drakk. Maybe this is redemption. Long ago, your people gave up dragon companions, now the fastest Rebirth ever has just taken place. Hielflanders and dragons are now reunited. Men get the fires going and wood collected, and tonight we will feast. Donush, take charge. Do not start without us. We must present Orchid and Daylphine to the queen and now both their mothers."

Dayla handed Orchid some new leather armor and a new warm cloak, also an extra quiver of arrows. She hugged her friend tightly. She then looked at Daylphine, "Keep her safe." Daylphine nuzzled her. Dayla kissed her on her head, then turned around. Orchid looked up just in time to get swallowed up by Aariks' arms, and he kissed her full on the lips.

"Hurry back; we have, umm, strategies to talk about."

"Oh, is that what we are going to talk about?" said Daylphine through Orchid.

Aarik looked at her funny. "That was not me; that was her talking through me. We went through wiruthwix. Already?" asked Aarik. "I thought that took weeks, if at all. Apparently not," stated Orchid.

"Look, Drakk and I are heading to Drakconia. We must be introduced to the queen; it is a formality. Ask him to come; you two are an item, she needs to meet him too!" stated Daylphine.

"Aarik, go get a warm cloak; we are taking you with us. Up there, oh no, I'm not Drakconian," stated Aarik. "I just thought you wanted to be with me all close and cozy." Aarik looked at her with a puzzled look again.

Orchid just pointed at Daylphine. "This will get old fast. Going to get my cloak, dear," Aarik said as he headed to the castle. Drakk and Bril walked over to them. "Ready," he asked.

"We are waiting for Aarik," Drakk laughed as he said. "You're taking him with you," he laughed again, "I've been trying to get him up there for 50 years."

"Yes, but you don't look as pretty as I do."

"Daylphine, will you stop using my voice? Or at least use a different tone so people know it is you, not me!" Drakk started laughing.

"Nope, never had those kinds of issues. You two have built in a few hours a bond closer than riders who have ridden their whole life. It is uncanny. Your mother will be ecstatic," said Drakk. Orchid Got back on Daylphine and waited for Aarik. As he approached, Drakk yelled at him, "So, now you are going up there?"

Aarik laughed. "I trust her more than I trust you." Drakk laughed.

"She has been flying for maybe 2 hours, and I a lifetime," stated Drakk. "Yeah, but me holding on to her won't be as weird as me holding on to you." Everyone laughed.

Aarik started to climb Daylphine's wing; Orchid held her hand down to help him. The moment they touched, Aariks' hand started to freeze, then a huge shock, and he flew backward and landed on his back. Orchid slid down the wing and ran to him. "I am sorry, I don't know what happened. Are you alright?" she said in a panic. "Not the kind of flying I thought we were talking about," he said, dazed and shaking his head to clear up the cobwebs.

"What was that?"

"I don't know," said Orchid.

Drakk spoke up, "It looked like Daylphine's frost breath, but it came out of your fingertips. It felt like an ice horse kicked me." Aarik interjected. Everyone chuckled.

"Yeah, it's funny now, but... WOW. Sure, you don't want to ride with me?" asked Drakk, laughing. "Oh, I am determined now." Aarik picked himself up from the ground; Orchid climbed back up on her dragon. Aarik started climbing back up. Orchid held her hand down again, Aarik then reluctantly took it, and she pulled him up without a mishap. Aarik got comfortable behind her.

He put his arms around her, then whispered in her ear, "You didn't have to shock me into submission. Every time you look at me, you shock my heart."

"OOO," came Daylphine's voice in her head. *We love that man, yes, we do.* *Shut up and start flying so we can get back here to the feast,* thought Orchid. With that, they took off into the air. Aarik held onto Orchid a little tighter.

Chapter 15: A Royal Visit

Daylphine was kind of quiet.

"What's the matter?" Orchid asked her.

"I am hoping my mom, well, our mom now, will be happy for us. She has never had an Eternal rider. I hope this does not make her feel sad," finished Daylphine.

"I am sure she will be delighted for us. From the memories I have seen that you have, she seems to be a beautiful and loving mother," stated Orchid.

"Thank You, Orchid," said Daylphine.

"Aarik, what do you think of flying?" asked Orchid because Daylphine was bugging her to ask.

"I liked it a lot more than I thought I would," he said in her ear." The bass inflections in his voice made her ear buzz and gave her goosebumps. **Woah, what was that?** thought Daylphine. *I don't know,* thought Orchid.

"But it tickled, and at the same time, made me fuzzy all over." "I know," answered Daylphine. "I felt it too!" Aarik leaned over to her ear again, "I know you two are talking about me, so share this." With that, he kissed Orchid's neck a few times, then whispered in her ear, "I am falling hard for you. I think I must warn you." Orchid was left speechless. Even Daylphine was silent. Eventually, she answered him.

"I am falling for you too, Aarik, but this is not the time. I have just gone through something very traumatic and emotional; I am also bonding a new relationship with Daylphine, not to mention leading my country's defense. I will promise you, however, that once this is all over, I will commit to all the time I can to pursue a relationship with you."

"That is good enough for me," answered Aarik, "it's all I ask for."

Aarik questioned Orchid, "Are you sure your mother will approve?" Orchid immediately emotion-checked him, she found some anger there, but it was not aimed at her. It was anger for his mother. "She and I did not actually get off on the right foot," Orchid uttered. "In fact, I'm sure she is very angry at me."

To Orchid's surprise, Aarik started laughing and said, "She had no idea what to do, she is not used to being openly questioned and interrupted."

"I am sorry, Aarik. I am sorry I lost my patience. That was not very professional of a person of my new station," stated Orchid.

"It needed to be said," Aarik stated as a matter-of-factly. "None of the other court members would have been so bold! Therefore, she would have continued to belittle people. It is one of the main reasons I left a life in court. I never wanted power, only to have a happy and productive life, marry the right girl, and give my family the best life I could. It is all I have ever wanted," finished Aarik.

Orchid thought for a second, "You realize that there is a strong possibility I must embrace that part of my life. I might not be given a chance. This war will make my country realize that we no longer have the luxury of living the way we have been living. There must be someone making alliances with trading partners and defending our borders. I am the only known noble blood. If you are hinting at what I think you are hinting at, and that is us being together, then we might have to accept responsibility for who we are. That being said, it makes a strong alliance between our two countries." Orchid said, not believing the words coming out of her mouth. *Oh, that's it, Orchid take the romance right out of that man's sails,* thought Daylphine.

Orchid was quiet; Aarik did not need to be an empath to know what she was feeling. She was now feeling the strain of her duties and began to realize that her life was no longer her own. He himself had to overcome these obstacles when he was younger, but he had been educated in this way of life all his life. Here was a girl that only just now found out that she was of noble birth, and up till now, had taken it all in stride. Even now, she was making decisions on what was best for her country instead of what she actually wanted.

"Orchid, I would follow you to whatever path you wanted. If it is in the best interest of our relationship that I assume the throne so we together can rule our countries as one, then I will happily dethrone my mother," he said, chuckling. "I was supposed to take the throne when my father died, and I shirked my responsibility. So, legally, it is my duty to do such. I do not know what I am asking, Aarik; I don't know what my future holds. I do know it will be better with Daylphine, Dayla, Serephine, Maple, and of course, you by my side. With friends at my side like that, I do not believe there is a challenge we cannot overcome."

"We are close to home now, Orchid," said Daylphine through telepathy.

Orchid looked and could see the mountainous skyline far in the distance. "There is land Aarik," Orchid said. Aarik looked ahead of them but did not see anything.

"He cannot see it yet," Daylphine told Orchid.

"You can now see through my dragon sight," Daylphine continued.

"Where?" asked Aarik.

"You will see it in a moment," Orchid added.

"How can you see it?" asked Aarik.

"Through Daylphine. More and more of our abilities are transferring over to each other. I have her abilities of sight and hearing, and she has picked up my empathic abilities and my sense of touch, and I think, taste. When you talked into my ear, it caused tingles; she felt that. As she said before, we do not know if a feeling like happiness is from her or from me. It is all confusing but amazing, just the same. We are ourselves, but then again, we are each other. From what I have gathered, other riders don't go this far of a transference. They gain thought, and that is it. Telepathy is needed to fly, but she and I are completely turning into each other. It is actually scary, and neither of us knows what to expect. Maybe it is because we are both royals, and being like this makes us more powerful than the other riders because we need to fight off challengers for that spot; I really do not know; I am just guessing here," said Orchid.

"I can see the land now," said Aarik. "Let's just let our relationship take its own course, at its own pace."

"Yes, I want more than anything to be with you, to love and protect you, and yes, to be my wife and my queen. I want all of that and more, but I understand more than you know of the situation we are in and the dangers that it brings. I also know how powerful your dragon is and how skillful you are. Together you two are nightmares for the enemy, a formidable army all on your own. You will survive this coming battle; I am sure of it." With that, they were flying over some tall and jagged mountains.

Daylphine started heading for a large non-active volcano. They flew higher to clear the peak. The two dragons were side by side now. As they went over the top of the volcano, there was a huge area that took up several hundred acres. There were huge ancient trees, grassy fields, and even a several-acre lake. At the far end, there was a large cave; in front of that cave was a circle of stone pillars. Daylphine was heading straight there. There were dragons everywhere, hundreds of them, lying around in the sun and communicating with each other. As Daylphine and Bril came into view, all eyes were on them. They landed near the stone pillar and stopped.

Drakk took the lead at this point. "He needs to announce us," said Orchid to Aarik. "You need to dismount; we will be presented as rider and dragon, then I will dismount too." Aarik got down off of Daylphine. Drakk approached a small gong which was mounted by a brass chain, hanging inside a stone and brass arch. Next to that arch was a much larger gong and arch. Drakk picked up a brass rod with a ball at the end of it made from animal hide. He struck the gong three times, then went down on one knee and bowed his head.

Daylphine's mother appeared at the entrance of the cave; next to her stood a noble-looking woman wearing tight-fitting black leather and a long flowing red cape; clasping the cape was a gold and silver broach with a jade stone that was half the size of Orchids fist. She had never seen such a beautiful stone. Circling her head was a beautiful silver and gold crown with another jade stone. It was not gaudy; it was very tasteful. It just looked like thin colored threads winding around the jade. As tiaras go, it was exceptionally beautiful, and so was the Queen.

Orchid thought that if she wore a symbol of royalty, a tiara like Queen Alora's would serve the purpose. Orchid now looked at her stunning mother. She was the largest of any dragon she had ever seen. Well, that was not much; she thought she had only seen dragons as of today; she smiled to herself. A thought from Daylphine came to her head that Mother was the biggest and strongest dragon in this colony. She was massive; she stood eight meters tall, and her length was 40 meters. Her wingspan was, if she had to guess, over 43 meters. She was black in color with emerald and silver streaks. Orchid accessed Daylphine's memory and found the information she was looking for; Mother's breath was an acid that was flammable, and electricity would catch the acid on fire.

What a devastating attack, thought Orchid.

On top of mother's head was a huge crown of gold with a jade stone, twin to the stone that was on Queen Alora's broach. The crown that she had first seen on Drakk's shield. Mother and Queen Alora were looking at her. Drakk stood up.

"My Queen Alora, My Queen Dalinda (Noble Serpent), may I introduce to you a newly formed pairing who has already withstood the wiruthwix after only two hours of flying. I will let them explain what else is happening to them; it is not my place."

Queen Alora spoke up, "You may proceed, sir Drakk." Drakk walked to a large kettle that the small gong striker was resting in and pulled out the larger striker.

He walked to the big gong. He hit it three times. All the dragons and riders that were lying around started to gather around. Drakk had walked up twelve stairs to get to the gong; he now spoke into a horn. "MY QUEENS, HONORABLE DRAGONS, AND RIDERS OF DRAKCONIA…. I have a pairing to announce and present to you. MAY I PRESENT CAPTAIN ORCHID OF ARTISTAH, A HIELFLANDER AND ROYAL BLOOD!" Cheers went up; the sound was deafening, sounding like a hurricane as the cheers from hundreds of dragons and riders cheered their approval.

"AND HER DRAGON, OUR VERY OWN PRINCESS, FORMALLY FIRST SISTER, NOW KNOWN AS DAYLPHINE! A RECORD WIRUTHWIX OF ONLY 2 HOURS AND OUR FIRST PARING OF 2 ROYALS!" If Orchid thought the first cheers were loud, she was definitely mistaken, and being surrounded by mountains because it was like being in a bowl made the sound twice as loud.

"Daylphine, Orchid, present yourself." Orchid dismounted and walked toward the two Queens. This is it; she telepathed to Daylphine. "Orchid..." said, Daylphine, "I'm glad I am paired with you."

"Daylphine, I am honored and very proud to be paired with a most beautiful dragon both inside, spiritually, and outside physically," countered Orchid She could feel Daylphine blush and filled with pride. Orchid walked to the two Queens; she could feel the ground give behind her and knew that Daylphine was following.

She reached the two queens and kneeled on one knee. Daylphine stood next to her and lowered her head. (a dragon's way of bowing) "My Noble daughters," said the Dragon Queen, Dalinda, "you two are very impressive. A wiruthwix on the same day as your first flight. Yes, very impressive indeed. Orchid, put your forehead to mine, please." Orchid did as she was asked. In an instant, as the two heads touched, Orchid could see in her head a beautiful mountainous area with thousands of dragons.

Dragons of every color, size, and shape. In the dream-like vision, she could even see Budhulug dragons. Then slowly, the vision turned dark. Hunters of all different races were killing the dragons. Orchid could feel herself crying uncontrollably as the dragons were slaughtered. She even saw Hielflanders hunting the Budhulug.

She heard Dalinda in her head, "It is okay, darling, it's okay. That was your people long ago, not you, but something you should know. Your people had abilities that no other race had, and that was the ability to communicate with us like no race before. There is a reason we wanted to make contact with your race, but after the tragedy with the Budhulug, you can understand our reluctance. Our seer saw this moment in a vision. You, my lovely daughter, Orchid, will restore faith and bring harmony to both our races once more. Your kind will become riders, and we will set up a new colony in Hielflander, and there shall be peace." Orchid was still crying, although now it was tears of hope and joy. "My child, Daylphine, come join us, touch heads with Orchid and mine. It is my honor to welcome you both into my royal house as heirs to the throne and possibly rulers of a new colony. Daylphine, I am immensely proud of your choice. Through this union, there will be much good. The lives of the dragons and people you touch will be changed forever. I bestow upon you the title of Princesses and heirs to the throne of Drakconia. There will be a royal proclamation to all of Drakconia, and our emissaries will spread the word as well. You are the future of our nations. Your lives will be forever entwined with each other. You join the thousands of riders before you as eternal pairs. One major difference, though, is that you are the first ever Eternal Royal Pair. You, my precious Daylphine, you are my only daughter. I am glad that I gifted you to this young lady. I had a feeling that once you two met, there would be an instant bond. Still, the choice was yours to choose or not to choose. Now, go change the world. Together you will learn more about yourselves, and the trials you will face will no longer be alone; you will have each other." Orchid and Daylphine lifted their heads and looked at each other.

Orchid was now crying for both of them as dragons do not cry tears; they do, however, feel pride, and the pride Orchid was feeling right now could not have been all hers. They were both so happy that Orchid thought they would explode. Queen Alora then addressed them.

"Congratulations to you both. I am sure you will be a fantastic addition to our Family. We have grand expectations for you and know you will far achieve any and all our expectations. We are anxious to see who this bold new enemy is and are in your debt for giving us time to prepare."

"Aarik, please step forward," stated Dalinda.

"Hey," Orchid said to Daylphine in telepathy, "how come she can speak?"

"What makes you think I can't?" Daylphine answered. "I just use your voice because it's much more fun."

"That's just not right," Orchid said, laughing. Aarik went to one knee before the two Queens. "Aarik, has Your Queen given you the troops you will need?"

"Yes, my lady," Aarik replied, "Good, Good, now. Is there anything you need from me? What made you finally get on a dragon's back?"

"Well, my lady, I am here to ask permission to court your daughter," said Aarik. "You want to court Daylphine?" asked Dalinda.

"Well, your majesty, they are one and the same now, are they not?" Aarik retorted. Orchid and Daylphine burst out laughing, which caused Queen Alora to lose it, and also caused Dalinda to start laughing. Orchid was laughing so hard that she did not realize there was frost mist coming out of her nose.

"OH MY," said Dalinda. Everyone was looking at Orchid; it was now not just a mist but actual frost. She felt Daylphine trying to control it, and it soon stopped. "When did that start?" the dragon Queen asked.

"Well, like most things today, this is a new one. However, I did shoot Daylphine's breath from my fingers," explained Orchid. "Yeah, and sent me flying off the back of Daylphine. This is all new to us, too," stated Dalinda. "But I am very interested to see another pairing with a Hielflander."

"If I may suggest," interrupted Drakk, "Serephine and Dayla would be great candidates. Not only are they almost as good as Orchid with a bow, but they have also already been in the air; Serephine flew with me, and Dayla flew with Donush."

"I see," said Dalinda. "Get two unattached dragons and take them back with you; see if they choose them as riders. Drakk, you know it must be their choice."

"Yes, my lady, I do know that," answered Drakk.

"Also, sir Drakk make sure you find first hatched females."

"Yes," answered Drakk again.

With that, he asked to be released so he could conduct the queen's bidding. With Drakk gone, attention came back to Orchid. "Orchid," said Dalinda, "can you please back up a little and concentrate on releasing Daylphine's breath from your fingers?" Orchid did as she was asked and backed up. The moment she started to concentrate; frost started coming out of her fingers. 'More', she could hear the queen say. She concentrated more; the power now was showing lightning sparks, everyone moved to the side.

"Release it!" yelled the Dragon Queen. Orchid released it, and it flew from her fingers and into the mountainside; a ball of ice formed then exploded, electricity flew everywhere, and pieces of rocks, dirt, and ice shards also flew. The two Queens looked at each other. "My daughter," said Dalinda... "what is going on here? Orchid, my baby did that hurt you in any way?"

"No, mother," Orchid said, trying the term of endearment on for size and liking it.

"Show me your hands, please, Orchid." Dalinda looked at Orchid's hands; there was no physical sign of trauma.

"That's amazing," Dalinda said.

"Darling, do you trust me?" asked Alora,

"With my life, my lady!" answered Orchid.

Queen Alora took a dagger from its sheath and then took Orchid's arm.

She pressed the point into the skin, and the moment it touched, Orchid could feel her skin; it felt like it was alive; the Queen pushed harder but could not penetrate the skin.

"Very interesting…" Dalinda said.

"You are almost all dragon. If you start growing a tail, you have gone too far," stated Daylphine out loud. Everyone had a nervous laugh as if to say *hey, it could happen.*

Chapter 16: Dragons for my friends

"Orchid," said Queen Alora, "would you follow me, please?"

Orchid did as she was asked. They proceeded into the cave. Daylphine and Aarik stayed outside with Queen Dalinda.

"So, what is going to happen to her?" Aarik asked Dalinda? "Will she be able to live a normal life? A life with me and maybe a child or two? If we have said child, will we have to sit on an egg?" Dalinda and Daylphine laughed at that.

"We don't know, Aarik," said Daylphine. "We do not believe things like that will be affected, but don't count on it."

"I believe it is all because Daylphine and Orchid are connected mentally," stated Dalinda.

"Your child will not have that connection. Good because if he comes out with a tail and scales, the kids at school will have a wonderful time," said Aarik.

Daylphine started laughing until he unleashed a breath of frost and sparks. "I believe the teasing would stop then," said Daylphine. The three started laughing. Dalinda saw that Aarik was worried.

"Captain," she said, let us take this all one day at a time. "We don't know what we don't know, and until we do know, that will be the case."

"I understand that," said Aarik, "but we are about to subject two more Hielflanders."

"I am worried about them too! Well, I suggest you ask the girls first, see if they are willing before we give the dragons the opportunity to choose them," answered Dalinda.

"Yes, my lady," replied Aarik.

At that moment, Orchid walked out of the cave she was completely transformed. She was wearing black leather pants and a purple silk tunic that fit her perfectly. She had on blue armor, her hair was straight down, and wisps of it around her face were flying in the wind. She had on a sky-colored blue cape with bright white streaks and white fringe. Upon her head was a tiara identical to the one on Alora's head. The tiara she wore was a symbol of a dragon colony Princess.

Aarik was floored; even Daylphine was stunned. "You called me pretty," Daylphine said to Orchid. "You very much look the part of a princess now!"

"I totally agree," Aarik managed to say. Dalinda bowed her head, acknowledging the princess.

"That tiara belongs on your head, my daughter! You are very elite; there are very few female riders and only one royal one. Be proud the both of you! You have made me immensely proud. This day would never come, I thought. Now, go put the fear into our enemies. Make them wish they never crossed those mountains!"

With that, Orchid mounted Daylphine and pulled Aarik up behind her. She took one last look at Mother. "Be careful, daughters; when you get back, we will have a proper feast and coronation." Daylphine backed out of the way and took to the air. They circled around, looking for Drakk. They found him at the far side of the large lake. He was talking to two dragons. One was dark black with light blue under the scales. The other was crimson with black highlights around each scale. Drakk waved at them as they landed and walked over to him.

"Wow!" Drakk said after looking at Orchid. "Sorry, forgive me, my lady, and your forgiveness Aarik. I meant no disrespect. It's just …" Aarik filled in the missing words, "Beautiful? Gorgeous? Pretty? Cute? Yes, and she is mine!" he said, laughing! Drakk was laughing, too, "You better watch it, Aarik; she may zap you again!" Everyone laughed, except for the new dragons; the inside joke was over their head. "Are we ready to head back to Landia?" asked Drakk. "Let's get to it; there is a feast to be had!" With that, they took to the skies.

Dayla was with Serephine. "Did you like flying?" she asked Serephine.

"I did. I must admit I am jealous," Serephine answered.

"Me too," Dayla agreed.

"How do you think she is?" asked Dayla, worried.

"She was pretty shaken up when she left. I know, but she is the strongest of us; she can manage it. Can you believe we have had a Queen for a best friend all our lives and did not know it," stated Serephine.

"Well, to tell you the truth, I think I kind of did know that," answered Dayla.

"It didn't come as a big shock when I found out," she added. "Yeah, me too," Serephine continued. "I was standing there in the throne room, and it all spilled out. I got emotional because it was my friend, but like you, I thought to myself that I kind of knew that. I don't want to lose her."

"I still want her to be part of our lives," Serephine was starting to get emotional.

Just then, the dragons all started getting restless and looking south. Dayla emotion-checked the closest dragon to her; she found excitement and pure joy. It was then she heard the familiar buzz of Daerwen. Before they reached Landia, Maple had sent him to Dragonfly with an update; he was now returning. A few minutes later, he came into view. Maple walked over to the two girls and said, "Well, let's see what my sister has to say."

Daerwen flew over Maple and went buzzing around the riders and dragons. The riders were like children; they were very emotional. The dragons were purring very loud, a sign of approval and respect. Daerwen was uncontrollable; this was the first time in decades that he had seen creatures that were kin to him. He flew to one dragon, a frost dragon. He put his head up to that dragon's head. He hovered there. Then the next dragon, he did the same thing. It was only a 10-second thing, but he did it to every single dragon and let the riders pet him. Daerwen was incredibly happy; at last, he was with his kind. After each dragon and rider was met, he flew to Maple.

He buzzed around her but flew to Dayla. He put his head on Dayla's head. In a few seconds, Dayla heard him in her mind. She started repeating everything he told her aloud. "Dragonfly has sent four hundred sprites to the southeast of the main camp. Oaken Ash is in charge there, eight hundred directly south, and Gigi is in command there. And four hundred to the Southwest Ashen Oak is in charge there. All the Satyrs have now met up. We have many spies watching their every move. Dragonfly has one thousand sprites heading to Triangulus. She is with them. There are five hundred druids, five hundred brownies, still in hiding in the forests waiting for orders." Daerwen took his head away from Dayla's. Serephine pet Daerwen and put her head up to his.

"Hi, Daerwen, I'm Serephine, I am sorry, but I just had to talk to you."

"Hello, Ms. Serephine; it is nice to have your acquaintance." Serephine giggled like a schoolgirl. Dayla smiled. "I hope to be able to talk with you more in the coming days," said Daerwen. Serephine said, "Me too."

With that, Daerwen flew to Maple. Everyone heard dragon wings beating and looked to the sky and saw four dragons flying; two had riders. It was Orchid and Drakk coming back. As they landed, all eyes were on them. Drakk got down first before Aarik. Then Drakk announced Orchid to the Riders and Dragons.

"Hail Princess Orchid and Princess Daylphine of Drakconia." All riders that were not mounted went to one knee; all dragons bowed their heads. Daerwen hovered for a few seconds, then, like an arrow, flew directly to Orchid. As he got closer, he could see the jade tiara of a Drakconian princess, he approached her, and she held out her arms. He flew into them and placed his head on hers.

"My lady, what has happened?" Orchid told him all that had transpired with Wiruthwix and Daylphine when Daylphine spoke to him through Orchid. "Daerwen, I am so blessed to be able to see you. It has been a dream and a wish of mine as far back as I can remember." Daerwen answered back, "It is an honor, princess." Orchid spoke up, "Soon, Daerwen, soon your kin will be recalled to Hielflander, and a dragon colony will be established. It is the wish of the dragon queen Dalinda and Queen Alora."

"You princess, you will rule there, will you not?"

"Yes, Daylphine and I will rule that colony and maybe Prince Aarik."

"This is the best news ever," said Daerwen. Just then, the smell of grilled meats and vegetables assaulted her nose, and her stomach growled. "I am famished," she said. She dismounted and then realized everyone was still bowing.

"Rise, Riders, and thank you." She looked over to Dayla and Serephine and smiled; they, too, had bowed. She went over to them. Dayla looked at her in her new Drakconian clothes and blue armor. Then she wept a tear when she saw the crown.

"So, it's official now," she asked.

"Yes, for Drakconia anyway. We will have to figure out the best strategy for approaching our country about me being a royal. We need to talk," said Orchid.

"About what," asked Dayla.

"This concerns you too, Serephine. You see what has happened to me, how Daylphine and I have bonded. This is not a temporary thing; this is for life. We are now one in almost every way. Because we are empaths, the dragon bond is stronger; my mother, queen Dalinda, wants to make you riders as well." Serephine jumped up and down, and Dayla was staring at her.

"You must understand some things, though. Your life will never be the same once you are bonded; it is for life. You and your dragon might not bond, or they might not choose you. You must be ready for that too. But it starts with a choice to ride when asked or not. We need to see what happens if it does, however. We don't know if the power I now have is because Daylphine and I are both royals or if it's this way with all Hielflanders. Long ago, the dragons were going to seek us out. They wanted to unite with us as their riders. Then tragedy struck, and we hunted them down well, Daerwen's kind anyway. We hunted them almost to extinction. So, the dragons went into hiding. Now that opportunity has presented itself in a different manner, like me being a royal, they want to unite with us once again. They want us to build a thriving colony in Hielflander. So, now that you know what is expected of you and the changes that COULD happen to you physically like this," she started shooting frost from her fingertips Dayla, and Serephine gasped, "and you know what your responsibilities will be, will you accept the offer from a dragon if she did ask you?"

In unison, both said, "YES!"

"You remember how I had to present myself? Well, after the feast, two dragons will approach you, if they stare at you stare back. If they bring their head down to you, nuzzle-rub her head. Because we are empaths, you might be able to speak to them straight away. If you get chosen, we will all go fly and start our scouting missions, okay?"

The food was ready, and Drakk Announced to let the festivities begin. Everyone ate and drank and ate more. It was a fun and enjoyable time. There was Grilled Duck, chicken, goat, lamb, and Elk. Loaves of fresh bread, and butter, several different kinds of cheese, and winter vegetables were also grilled. Orchid spent most of her time with Aarik; they were holding hands and acting like a couple already. Serephine was with Drakk, and there were more than a few sparks there as well. Dayla was with Maple and Lindale.

Midway through the feast, the queen, Aarik's mother, appeared; the duty officer announced her. Orchid and Aarik approached her. Aarik bowed and Orchid curtsied.

"Lady Orchid, I see you now wear a crown," she said disdainfully.

"Where did you get it? It takes more than a crown to make a Princess." Drakk, who had come from behind them, spoke up.

"She is a princess of Drakconia; you will treat her with the respect that title gives her, or our countries will have issues." Aarik then also spoke. His voice was caring and calm, but at the same time, firm and strong. "She is also the possible future queen of Northland and my wife."

"After this conflict is taken care of, I will assume my place as king of Northland, and If she will have me, I will make her my wife."

Queen Anora gave him a hard look; twice in the same day, she had been talked down to by underlings; first, the pretense princess and now a Drakconian guard. She had had enough. "So, you think it will be that easy, do you? You think you can just send your mother your QUEEN packing?" she screamed. "We will see about this! Guards arrest this man," she pointed to Drakk.

Before any could move, Serephine had drawn her bow and moved in front of him; next to her came Lindale with her sword drawn. The scariest thing was Orchid; her blue eyes went cold, frost formed from the tips of her fingers, and her lips went blue; sparks of electricity danced over the blue armor she wore.

When she spoke, it was with authority! "You will not touch this man. If you mean to arrest this man, you will defend your own lands. I will not risk my dragons or our riders defending your country."

"Drakk mount Bril!" Drakk did as he was told. "Anora, the choice is yours!" "Stand down! Yes, stand down," Aarik emphasized authoritatively. Calling her by her name without title was a way of stating that she was an equal. This infuriated Anora! The royal guard was there, and Aarik spoke to them now.

"Royal guard, I am Aarik, Prince of Northland, Captain of the Guard, and general of its armies. Son to King Aamon and heir to the throne of Northland. We have an enemy at our doorstep; my mother, the queen, wants to squabble with our allies, the same allies that are now prepared to die defending us. She carries the burden of my father's death and the weight of the struggles and responsibilities of ruling our kingdom. Therefore I, Aarik, will relieve the queen of her responsibilities as Queen, and once this conflict is over, assume the throne. Meantime, take my mother to her chambers. Make sure she is comfortable, that all her needs are met, and to which she is tended. Also, keep her under guard; she is not to leave her to chambers."

Guards looked at each other, not quite knowing what to do and whom to follow when one of Aariks lieutenants... Devin came for the queen; several men got more courage seeing him take the lead and assisting him in escorting the queen to her chambers.

Aarik turned to the girls and Drakk, "Please stand down; I am sorry for my mother's behavior." The girls withdrew their arrows, Lindale sheathed her sword, and Orchid took control of her frost and calmed herself down. Drakk released a long breath that he had been holding. He looked at Serephine, "My darling, thank you for defending me." Serephine wanting to break up the seriousness of the situation, said, "I wasn't letting anything, or anyone get in my way of having my own dragon!" Everyone laughed and calmed down.

The time had come, though, to see if the dragons were ready to pick a rider, as Dayla and Serephine stood away from the crowd. Two dragons approached. One was black with a light blue highlight around each scale and a light blue underbelly. The other was a crimson red with black highlights around each scale and black underbelly. The crimson one approached Serephine but then moved to Dayla; the black one approached and went straight to Serephine. She got within two feet of her. She sniffed at her beautiful shiny black hair. The intake of air, then a big exhale. Serephine stood perfectly still, but inside, she was gonna burst.

She used the same technique she used with Daerwen. "Please, pick me," she said to the dragon. "Is that you speaking to me? Black-haired, Blue eyes we match. I am black and blue too!" Serephine replied, "Yes, it is me, and we do match." Dayla was interacting with the red one. She was excited; she knew the odds were that she was a fire dragon. She was extremely interested in this one. The red dragon went up to Dayla and lowered her head to be nuzzled. The red one had chosen. Then the black one lowered her head. "I choose you as my rider," the dragon said to Serephine. "And I accept," Serephine answered back. "I am First Born sister, and what might your name be?"

"I am Serephine of Artistah. Thank you for picking me, First Born." Dayla was still as a post. A girl's voice rang out in her head. "I choose you as my rider if you will have me."

"Of course, I accept; you are so beautiful; my name is Dayla. I am from Artistah. I am the First Sister of Drakconia," the dragon answered.

"How is it we can talk already?" First Sister asked.

"We are empathic," stated Dayla. Orchid and Daylphine are doing much more together than using telepathy. "Let's give them some competition."

"I like that idea," First Sister said back. "Come, let's fly." Dayla mounted First Sister and saw that Serephine had mounted also. All riders were now mounted, in fact.

Orchid looked at Aarik, "I'm sorry, Aarik," she said, "but I now have a station. I am responsible for Drakconia, above my feelings for you. You were in the right, my lady; my mother was not! I will meet you in Triangulus. I will ride with my cavalry and leave all other troops here. I will also leave my most trusted to guard my mother." Orchid nodded; she told Daylphine to get to the clearing. As they were walking away, Aarik yelled, "I'll miss you!"

Orchid did not answer.

Chapter 17: The Reconnaissance Mission

All riders, including Drakk and the girls waited for the princess to take off first. Daylphine took to the air. They had been in the air for ten minutes heading south when Orchid heard Dayla in her head.

Are you okay? Orchid asked. *How are you doing this?* she added.

The same way I converse with my dragon, I just concentrated on you. You and I have a strong tie and history. I thought it would work because of that, Dayla replied.

"Can you hear me?" asked Daylphine.

"I sure can, Daylphine," Dayla responded.

"I can too," chimed in First Sister.

"Okay, okay, okay, it's getting really crowded in my head," stated Orchid. "Yes, Dayla, I'm fine. I just needed to get away from that woman."

"Her lands are in danger, and all she thinks about is her position, nothing for her people or that some might die in the coming days! I pray that I never get that way!"

"I will not let you," said Daylphine. "I wonder what Hielflander tastes like," she added.

Orchid ignored her and said, "That's rude, you know. It also doesn't work with us; I can still hear your thoughts!"

The skies were filled with dragons and riders, all following Orchid's lead. She started heading towards the Triangulus fortress. Serephine and First Born were doing great; it was as if they had been flying all their lives together.

"So…" Serephine asked, "what is our breath weapon?"

First Sister answered, "It is wind and ice shards."

"Woah, can we try?" begged Serephine.

"Sure, let's break formation and go down," First Sister said.

They headed for a stump left out in the open. First Born got close enough, and at the last second, went into a hover and let her breath go. Hurricane-force winds escaped her mouth. The stump was pulled up from the ground a little, and then was penetrated by close to twenty-five ice shards. They heard wings behind them and moved just in time to see flames coming from First Sister and more wind to fan the flames, they had to move out of the way for Daylphine and Orchid, as three arrows hit the stump, then frost, and electricity.

They flew past the stump. Orchid turned 180 degrees and faced the rear and shot a bolt of ice from her fingers. It hit the stump with such force, that the stump came the rest of the way out of the ground, then sparks, then an explosion that sent sparks, ice shards, and wood in every direction. Orchid flipped herself back around and kept flying.

She heard Dayla in her mind say, *that was amazing, very deadly, but amazing all the same.*

"How does she do that?" asked First Sister.

"We are gonna find out," said Dayla. "Hahaha," they both laughed.

Orchid started to gain altitude, she made a directional adjustment. "You know you were right back there, right?" Daylphine asked Orchid. "Furthermore, you acted like a princess. You stated your point; you used Authority, not too much Authority, just the right amount. The queen is not used to having people talk her down or disagree with her. You were very harsh with Aarik, though. He did not deserve that. He does not want to be king, yet he just did it for you. He backed you up against his mother, and he loves you. I know that, and I do not even have to use our emotion check on him."

"You are right," answered Orchid. "I love him too, but I have too many other things going on that... Unfortunately, he is down on the priority list. My lands and people that are counting on me must take priority."

"Yes, I agree with you, Orchid. I just think we need to include him and keep letting him know we do not want to lose him! I, of all people, well, I am not a people .... or am I? Anyway, I know your every emotion. You are falling hard for this guy, and I cannot blame you. Now, what is your plan or battle strategy?" Daylphine asked, changing the subject.

"Well, I want to see what troops we have at Triangulus, and from there, we will split up. We will divide into thirds, once we know that the fort is well-defended. I think we should take out the Satyrs with one major strike. This will free up all the troops we have trying to box them in if the main army is not clear of the mountain pass. Well, then we can jam them up there."

"Well, that sounds like a great start," Daylphine said.

The flight did not take long from there, as they circled the old castle walls. There were Hielflander archers on all outer and inner walls. There had to be close to two hundred on guard at this moment, with hundreds more on the ground. The outermost walls stood 10 meters high and were a mile and a half if you were to walk around it. There was a large metal portcullis and a river that flowed around the outer walls with a drawbridge.

Orchid could see repairs and greasing taking place so that, when needed, the bridge could be pulled up, and the portcullis could be dropped down, barring the way. Hielflanders could easily shoot across the river to the other side of the walls. The second wall was slightly higher, running a mile around. Then there was the Keep, which rose to 60 meters into the air; it was surrounded by the final wall.

Orchid landed near the bridge and dismounted Daylphine. She started walking towards the castle when she heard Dayla cry out and pass out on the ground. Serephine jumped from her dragon, and she passed out too. They were both curled up in a fetal position as well as their dragons. *The Wiruthwix*, she thought. The joy in her heart started to swell. Dayla and Serephine were going to be Reborn! She could feel Daylphine getting excited.

"It's true, and it is because you are empaths that the bond is so strong," said Daylphine. Dayla felt like she was in a cramped space; she was wet but warm. She felt love coming from outside of her confinement. She heard, in her mind, a voice speaking to her. She did not know the words but felt encouragement. She then tried to get out. Serephine had the same experience; she could feel her mother encouraging her.

After half an hour, they both broke free and ran to their dragons. Soon, everyone was around them. Serephine named her dragon first. "The name I give you First Born is Iizmonahven (Icewind in Drakconian)." Everyone clapped. Dayla was named Ixenmonahven (Firewind). When the ceremony was over, Orchid headed to the castle with Dayla and Serephine on her heels.

"Dayla," called Orchid, "find out if anything is needed, find out if Dragonfly is here, and also, find out who the lead role of the Hielflanders is, please. I want all the information I can get so I can produce a plan. I want to be back in the air in no more than an hour."

"Okay," said the girls, heading out to do her bidding.

Orchid walked toward where the people were working, repairing the chains and gears to the drawbridge. "How is it going? Will it be operational soon?" she asked the workers.

The three Hielflanders and one sprite turned to her and then immediately fell to one knee. "That's not necessary under these conditions," Orchid said.

"Who are you, my lady?" asked a Hielflander female.

"I am Orchid of Artistah, Princess of the Drakconian Dragon Riders."

"You are from Hielflander?" the woman asked.

"I am," Orchid answered.

"My lady, this bridge is already operational. We are just putting more hog fat so the metal can absorb it. It was pretty rusted. As were the chains, but it's much better now and soon will be even more so."

"Thank you, what is your name?" Orchid asked.

"I'm Hannah, my lady," the woman said as she curtsied.

"Hannah, take charge. I want you to do your best to get the bridge and portcullis working at its best."

"Yes, my lady." Orchid turned around to walk away when she heard,

"My lady?" Orchid turned. Hannah's eyes were watery and glassy. "You make us very proud." Orchid smiled and said, "Thank you." She started to walk off again, then turned back around.

"Hannah, how much of that fat do you have? Will there be extra?" Orchid asked.

"Quite possibly," Hannah answered.

"Keep it. I may have a use for it."

"Yes, my lady."

Orchid headed over the bridge. Orchid walked into the courtyard. Everyone she walked by noticed her and went on one knee. Sprites, Hielflanders, and even the other dragon riders. She saw a large stage-like area and walked over to it and took center stage.

"Gather around everyone," her voice was not quite loud enough. She was about to ask a male Hielflander when she got an idea. She said it again, but she used Daylphine's Dragon's voice. Everyone jumped in fear and did her bidding. In a not-so-forceful voice, she started,

"Countrymen, sprites, Riders of Drakconia! I am Orchid of Artistah, Princess of the dragon riders s. First, I want to thank you for your hard work. We have five hundred or more cavalry riders, pike men, and a few swordsmen. We have two dozen dragon riders, I do not know what our total numbers are, but more are coming every day. I have two Lieutenants: Dayla and Serephine. Captain of the guard, Drakk of Drakconia. Dragonfly, princess of the Tree Realm, and coming with the cavalry is Prince Aarik of Northland. Our lands have been invaded by a large group of Satyrs. Yes, you heard me right, Satyrs. But I believe they were just a diversion. I think that the real target was Northland, and that the real army has not shown itself. I am about to fly out, and I and the dragon riders will scout the whole country if we must. The Princess of the Tree Realm will be in charge here. Working on the gate and bridge, I put Ms. Hannah in charge. If she asks you for a hand, consider that it is me asking. Lastly, do not worry about bows, curtsy, and other formalities here with me; we are all together in this."

From the back, someone started clapping, and someone else yelled, "About time we Hielflanders had a leader!" Cheers went up.

Orchid was blushing as she turned to walk off stage only to see Dayla, Serephine, and even Drakk and Dragonfly clapping right along with everyone else, blocking her from walking off the platform. Orchid put on her serious face and said, "Riders, let's go!" *Her life was now never going to be the same. There was no going back from this.*

It's okay, she heard Daylphine in her mind. ***We have each other, we have Dayla and Serephine, and we will be starting a new colony here in Hielflander. We will work on keeping our new life as normal as possible.***

Dragonfly took her arm and said, "I'm proud of you. Your bloodline is strong in you. Even without pursuing your own throne, it found a way to show itself, and now you are a Royal Rider on a Royal Dragon. Simply amazing!"

"Drakk told me that you recorded the fastest Wiruthwix," Dragonfly said, shaking her head. Orchid interjected, "Dayla and Serephine were the same days as well. It is because of our empathic ability we are thinking."

"Yes," continued Dragonfly, "but you being chosen by a Royal Dragon is no coincidence. And to have a rebirth that fast with a royal is even more of a rarity. I know you know Queen Dalinda has had many riders, some for years, but it never triggered the inner being to bond in that way. Therefore, she has never been eternally attached, yet here her daughter did it with her first rider. This is incredibly special. I look forward to seeing all that you two accomplish," she stated.

Orchid nodded and asked, "You have everything you need, right?"

"I'm going to do a quick scout, then attack the Satyrs so we can free up all the troops we have posted trying to box them."

"Good plan," stated Dragonfly.

With that, Orchid called the girls, and they made their way to their dragon mounts. They mounted, and took to the skies. Below, the Hielflander archers watched as they flew out of sight.

Chapter 18: A Winged Attack

Orchid and the other riders flew into a "V" formation. Orchid was the lead, Dayla behind her and to the right, and Serephine had the left side. Behind Serephine flew Drakk. They were heading toward the campsite they had attacked a week prior. As they drew near, Orchid felt danger.

What is that feeling? I don't like that feeling, thought Daylphine. **You don't like it because it's DANGER!** said Orchid using telepathy.

"Oh, that makes sense," stated Daylphine.

"There must be something over there. Let me concentrate." Orchid slowed her breath and concentrated on the area in front of her; her brain immediately went red. **There is a large force down in those trees and some in that outcropping of rocks. I think we are too high and have not been seen.**

Orchid concentrated on Dayla and said, "Dayla take a half dozen riders, fly around that outcropping of rocks, and come up from behind them at fast speed. Hit it with all you got."

"Yes, ma'am," Dayla said as she fell out of formation, pointed at five riders, and did a 180-degree turnaround. The five followed her. Orchid now concentrated on what was ahead of them. She sensed deception and cruelty. She messaged Serephine, saying, "Serephine take Drakk and eight to ten riders. Fly around and attack those trees from behind."

Serephine answered, "Yes, my lady, I sense a very large force, like a hundred or so."

"I do, too," Orchid answered. "Stay high so they do not sense us; we will wait here. Once you are clear of the trees, fly high because we will be coming in and attacking them from the front when you are done."

"Understood," said Serephine. Serephine pointed to her eight and Drakk and flew vertically up another few hundred feet, then flew west and around.

The hovering was a little strength-sapping, but it was necessary. There Daylphine said, "Orchid looks to the east; here comes Dayla,"

Flames, wind, and ice hit the stones and Satyrs came flying out of the rocks. Orchid could see Dayla firing arrow after arrow. Each one was a hit. Satyrs were stopping to take a shot, only to get shot. In a matter of seconds, it was over. Then a loud roar was heard as a hundred Satyrs left the trees and charged, only to be attacked from the rear. It was now Serephine's turn. The riders were all in a single side-by-side line; the dragons were using their breath weapons. Serephine was letting arrows go. As the riders flew over, they angled up. Orchid saw Serephine flip around and let more arrows fly. Then she saw something that intrigued her.

An arrow left Serephine's bow; there was a large ball of ice at the tip. The wind was making the arrow fly so fast. Orchid had to really concentrate on it. It hit the target so violently, causing the ice to explode, with shards hitting the targets next to it. Orchid now put the last of the riders, including her, into the fight. She shot an arrow while concentrating, noticing an electrical current forming on the metal tip. Letting it go, the arrow went straight at a target.

The lightning from the arrow divided into three and hit three separate targets. She then threw a large ball of ice from her fingers; it hit the ground and exploded with electrified chards of ice, taking out half a dozen or more Satyrs.

"That was amazing," said Daylphine. "We need to work on that more."

All dragons and riders were now engaged in the fight; the battle lasted over an hour and was now done. They had landed all the Dragons and searched the fallen.

"Well, it will be great if they keep dividing themselves like that," said Orchid to Dayla and Serephine as they walked up to her. "Check the other riders to see if anyone is hurt, please." Dayla and Serephine Did as they were asked. Drakk came up to her,

"My lady, that was incredible! Congratulations on your victory". "Thank You, Drakk but this much loss of life doesn't feel like a victory," Orchid said. "Dayla and Serephine returned; we have a few minor injuries to the riders. The dragons are uninjured."

"Good," stated Orchid. Drakk, "I would like you and your riders to stay here. Put a few on patrol and hide the rest in the same forest they were hiding. If anyone comes to investigate what happened here, you know what to do;"

"Yes, ma'am," answered Drakk. "Also, give the orders to attack anything you see while on patrol." She added.

"Yes, ma'am," answered Drakk again.

"Dayla, Serephine, will you ride with me, please?" They both ran to their dragons.

They flew back up into the air and headed west. Orchid took Daylphine high into the air. Till they were just a speck to people on the ground, she flew west for around 10 minutes, then headed south. They had been flying for about half an hour. Orchid, using telepathy, told the girls to hold up; she was going down to take a look.

With that said, she went down in a big spiral. As she descended, she was looking for the original camp. They got lower, and she saw the smoke from the camp ahead. She stayed out of bow reach and flew over the camp.

"What do you think?" Orchid asked Daylphine.

"I think there are not much more than three or four hundred."

"Exactly," said Orchid, "and the group we just attacked could not have been more than two hundred maximum. That means we are missing close to one thousand. Go back up," she said as she got back up with her friends. "There are only like four hundred down there," she told them. "That means the others are on the move, most likely the West."

"Dayla, head back to Drakk; attack the old camp here, then bring the riders to Micah's place. If we are not there, head to Artistah; Serephine and I will try to locate them."

"Yes, ma'am," answered Dayla. She whipped Firewind around and headed towards Drakk.

"Okay, let's go find the missing army, Serephine!" Icewind and Daylphine were flying side by side. They were searching with their eyes and their empath abilities. Orchid was also using her new dragon sight. Soon they were flying around Micah's house. ***Nothing looks amiss,*** Daylphine said with telepathy to Orchid. *Except that there is no smoke coming from the chimney. The stoves should be getting hot in preparation for an evening meal. Also, the sheep and goat herds are gone,*" stated Orchid. *Land over by the house, please*, Orchid thought in her mind, knowing that Daylphine was reading her thoughts.

Daylphine landed near the house. Orchid dismounted and walked to the door. She drew her sword, then proceeded to knock. There was no answer, so she knocked again, this time calling out, "Micah? Harmony? Lily……Ecco? It is me, Orchid." She sensed that there was someone in the house; she felt fear and mistrust.

"It's me, Orchid. We came by the other day and had a meal with you; it was me and Dayla…" She heard Harmony's voice now.

"Orchid?" The door opened, and Harmony threw herself on Orchid; she was crying hysterically.

"They took them… They took my parents and brother," she said in between sobs.

"I'm sorry," said Orchid patting Harmony on the back. "Don't worry, we will get them back." Harmony looked up at Orchid; her eyes got big, and she froze. "Orchid, why is there a tiara on your head?"

"Because she is a princess of Drakconia," said Serephine.

"Don't worry about that now, hun," assured Orchid. "Let's go get your family back."

"How?" asked Harmony

"Okay, don't get scared at what I'm about to show you. They are my very special friends, okay?" Harmony looked at her but said nothing.

"Daylphine, Icewind, come here, please." The two dragons came from around the side of the barn where they were hiding. Harmony's mouth dropped open. She stared in amazement at the two beautiful dragons.

"Are my eyes deceiving me?" she asked. Daylphine came up to them,

"You may touch me if you wish," she said out loud to Harmony. Harmony touched Daylphine for a few seconds, then just hugged her and started crying.

"Hey hey hey," soothed Daylphine, "it's okay…"

"You don't understand..." said Harmony, sobbing. "I have seen this in my dreams one thousand times. I have never told anyone because I thought it was crazy."

She moved over to Icewind and started rubbing her too. Icewind just purred. Orchid smiled and said, "Well, you are about to fly on one."

"Go get some really warm clothes on, it's a little chilly up there." Harmony took off for the house.

"Any ideas how to get them back?" asked Serephine.

"When we have our full force, it would not be that difficult, but it's just us right now. With only one hundred sixty arrows between the two of us. Why would they take prisoners?" asked Daylphine aloud.

"I do not understand that either," said Orchid.

Harmony came out of the house and up to the dragons. She had a nice fleece-lined leather overcoat over leather slacks, a linen shirt, and a wool sweater. Wool gloves and knee-high leather fleece-lined boots.

"Well, you look nice and cozy," said Orchid. "You're going to ride with Serephine and Icewind, okay?" Harmony nervously nodded but yet looked excited.

Orchid mounted up, and so did Serephine. Harmony paid attention to the way Serephine mounted and followed her lead. She snuggled in behind Serephine putting her arms around her waist. Serephine could feel Harmony's heart beating fast against her back. Daylphine took to the sky, followed by Icewind. Icewind, using telepathy, spoke to Serephine, *How is she doing? A future rider, possibly?* To Serephine and Icewind's surprise, Harmony answered, in thought, to both of them, *Oh, I sure hope so!*

How did you do that? asked Icewind.

"I heard your question in my mind, so I just answered using my mind," she said simply.

"It was as if Hielflanders were supposed to be our riders all along," stated Icewind. "I am extremely impressed with your race," she finished. The girls flew following the tracks that led toward Artistah.

Dayla reached Drakk and his riders and conveyed Orchid's orders.

"Drakk, Orchid wants us to attack the camp and then meet her at Micah's farm or Artistah if they are not there." Drakk gave her a quizzical look.

"There are only 300 or so left; the others are gone," stated Dayla. A look of concern came over him. "I'm sure she will be alright," said Dayla, "but all the same, I think we need to hurry."

"Agreed," said Drakk. "I don't like our new princess not being guarded."

Chapter 19: Round One

Daylphine, Orchid, Serephine, Icewind, and Harmony were flying toward Artistah when Daylphine spoke up but really did not have to say anything.

"There is that dangerous feeling again."

"Yes, I feel it. Go higher till we see what it is." Daylphine started going higher, and Icewind followed her lead. About two kilometers down the road, they came across a battle. It looked like about one hundred seventy-five or so Hielflanders were holding off the bulk of the Satyr army. The Hielflanders had archers down and wounded; the battle looked dire. On the Satyrs' side, there were dozens wounded or dead. Even so, it was only a matter of time before the Hielflanders were overrun.

"Serephine, protect Harmony as best you can, and fight your way through. We must distract them away from the Hielflanders, taking out as many as we can."

"I brought my bow," answered Harmony, "I will fight from here with you and Serephine." "Please, my lady Orchid," she begged.

"Very well," answered the princess.

"ATTACK them from the rear, Serephine use your ice arrows for maximum damage. Dragons, use your breath weapons!"

Daylphine took an angle at the rear of the army. Orchid focused intensely on her fingers, concentrating as hard as she could. One hundred feet to her left, she saw Icewind and her riders. Daylphine let her breath weapon go; ice and electricity froze and shocked a dozen or more Satyrs.

Orchid let her attack go. A beach ball-sized ball of ice left her fingers; a lengthy line of frost stayed connected to the ball. The ball was growing as it descended towards the ground. Once it hit the ground, an electric explosion shattered the ball into thousands of electrically charged ice shards, making a huge explosion. The entire Satyr army heard that and looked back to see two massive dragons attacking the rear.

too many of them. Serephine and Harmony had joined Orchid now. The devastation left the Satyrs retreating once more. However, once again, they were lining up just out of bow reach for another charge. Orchid checked on Daylphine; she was sleeping, and the healing herbs were doing their work. *This was not gonna be good,* she thought. The archers were exhausted, and arrow supplies were dwindling. The Satyrs might break the lines this time. Icewind still had not gotten her strength back. This was going to be fought all on the ground.

'HERE THEY COME!' Orchid shouted.

I'M HERE! Orchid heard Dayla in her head! **EVERYONE GET READY.** Orchid shouted. **MORE DRAGONS ARE COMING. WATCH YOUR SHOTS!**

The archers were re-energized; they were searching the skies. Within minutes the Satyrs started to charge. Orchid glanced with her dragon and noticed a long line of dragons descending from a high cloud. "All archers hold till I tell you to make every shot count," she ordered. The dragons and riders started attacking, then Orchid saw movement coming from the north. There were more Satyrs coming now.

Something was not right though. The armor was different; it was Aarik and the light cavalry. "Now," shouted Orchid, "hold second, Volley!" Arrows fired, and each one was deadly, finding its mark. Aarik's troops were now engaging. The Satyrs were in total panic. "Fire second volley and hold." A second volley left the bows, and a hundred or more Satyrs fell. The only escape possible was to the South. Dragons were attacking from the East Hielflander archers from the west and Aarik from the north. The Satyrs were in total chaos.

"FIRE!" shouted Orchid. "Then cease!" Between the dragons and Aarik's troops, she did not want any accidents happening.

"DRAW SWORDS PROTECT THE HIGH GROUND!" she ordered. "Healers tend to the wounded." Orchid saw that not everyone had made it. There were several dead and it saddened her. The Satyrs were refusing to surrender, and therefore, were being killed by either dragons or Aarik's men. She finally started to breathe a little easier. One more check to her mental conscience told her Daylphine was still asleep and okay. She sighed with great relief. Dayla came running to her and grabbed her in a hug.

"I'm okay, Dayla," she said. "We saw Daylphine all laid out; we thought the worst! What happened?"

"She is fine; she is sleeping. She was hit with an arrow that went into her soft spot, she was getting tired, and her normal ice shield was getting weak. I think the more we use our dragon's power, the less they have to use. I was throwing big ice balls so as to affect as many as I could with one shot. When we have time, we will need to test it out. To see just how much is too much."

Another 40 minutes later, the battle was over. Harmony came over to Orchid and said, "My parents were found tending to what is left of our herd. They are okay, and so is my brother Ecco."

"You are still incredibly young, Harmony, but I love what I saw here today. Will you take a walk away with me, please?"

"Of course, Lady Orchid."

The two walked away, talking. "Harmony? Did you like flying today?"

"Oh yes, I liked it very much," answered Harmony. "Would you dedicate your life to becoming a rider?"

Orchid proceeded to tell Harmony of the responsibilities and the things that could happen in the transference. Harmony then said, "I am already speaking with Icewind, and I just spoke with Bril." Orchid was extremely impressed. "So, are you ready? It is your choice."

"I'm ready," she said.

"Then wait here," said Orchid. The princess walked to where the dragons were. As she passed, the dragons lowered their heads, and riders saluted her with closed fists to their hearts and bowed heads. She came to the fast messenger dragons.

"Anyone who wishes a Hielflander rider?" she asked. All three looked up at her.

One was a dark red dragon; she picked her. "Go see if you want her; she is incredibly young, but she is proving to be very skillful. I know your messenger dragons are young too; that is why I am giving you a chance."

"I will go see," said the red dragon.

She went over to where Harmony was standing and stared at her. *So... you want to be a rider,* thought the red dragon. *"Yes, I do,"* stated Harmony to her.

"You are very beautiful, Harmony," said the dragon.

"Wow, and you already can communicate with me?"

"I am the Second Sister; what might your name be?"

"I am Harmony, Of Artistah," she said. The Second Sister lowered her head, and Harmony had a nuzzle.

"Let's fly." And away they went; the riders and other dragons cheered. Drakk explained something to Orchid, "You realize that that dragon is so young that she only has one breath, right?"

"Yes," stated Orchid, "I'm testing and pairing different combinations. Harmony is half my age too, yet she picked up talking to a dragon as if it were a random person on the street."

Chapter 20: The Royal Secret is Out

"So, Drakk, did you take out the other group?"

"Yes, my lady, but we lost one dragon and rider. We burned them as our way to honor the dead."

Orchid's heart sank. "Daylphine got hurt as well," she stated.

"This is war, my lady; these things happen. They died doing what they loved to do, and they died together. Every rider wants to go that way because life without your dragon is unbearably lonely," Drakk said.

"Do you think we can send for more riderless dragons?" Orchid asked.

"You are the princess," Drakk responded. "Just give the order, and I'll dispatch a messenger to the queen."

"I want to start the colony with experienced riders, and this will give them plenty. Also, I want to choose some of these fine archers here. Then once a suitable place is found, we will build a training ground, and Drakconian riders can come in groups here to learn archery and train up their skills."

"That sounds like a great plan, Orchid. How many do you want to start with?"

"Let us bring fifty first. Have them come here," Orchid answered.

"Very well," answered Drakk. He then headed to one of the messenger dragons, a green one. He gave her the message, and away she flew.

Meanwhile, Orchid headed back to the high ground. Once again, she found a high place with which to talk to the archers.

"Citizens of Hielflander, I am Princess Orchid, I am a Hielflander also! I was born and raised a little way from here in Artistah. I have been chosen to be the Princess of the dragon riders; I fly with a RoyalDragon princess named Daylphine! Thank you to those of you who helped and tended to her wounds. Now, we have won this fight!" There was loud cheering and clapping. "As you see, Hielflanders and dragons make a very powerful combination!" More cheers broke out.

"I have sent for more dragons; they should be here in the morning! I am looking for fifty volunteers. These two ladies here will make a list, and the first fifty will not be the last. We will keep the other names for later. We will be starting a colony here. Dragons have been wanting this relationship for thousands of years. Due to an unfortunate accident, we started hunting them down and killing them. Specifically, a dragon species called the Budhulug. This made the dragons that you now see, go into hiding until now. Because we have empathic abilities, we have a stronger connection with these beautiful creatures. It was wrong of us and against our nature to hunt them down. That was the past and cannot be undone. Now is the future, and Hielflanders will take the honored place of flying on and with dragons!"

More cheers erupted. A pudgy little man moved to the front of the crowd.

"Captain Orchid! May I see you for a moment?" the little man asked. Using telepathy, Dayla told Orchid that the man was the one giving her trouble at the council. Therefore, Orchid ignored him.

"So, the choice must be yours. If you choose, however, you choose for life. A bond between dragon and rider is an eternal bond, a sacred bond. Once Serephine and Dayla get your names."

"MISS ORCHID!" the man said more forcefully. Again, Orchid ignored him.

"Once they get your names, I will meet with you here." There was a loud cheer again.

Orchid walked to the pudgy man. He took an angry tone with her. "DO YOU KNOW WHO I AM?"

"Yes, you are from the Council. Now answer me this, do you know who I am?" asked Orchid.

"You are Orchid of Artistah, and you are letting this Captain Orchid thing get to your head! I dismiss you at once!" She was about to lose her temper when a knight walked up behind the man, grabbed him by the shoulder and spun him around.

"How dare you speak to the Princess of Drakconia and future Queen of Northland in such a manner! I should have you imprisoned!"

"Sir Aarik," the little man said, trembling. "And if he doesn't imprison you, I will," said Sir Drakk.

"You just insulted my princess!" Everyone started moving to one side as Daylphine walked to Orchid.

"Shall I eat him?" asked Daylphine aloud so everyone could hear. "I'm famished." The pudgy little man fainted. Orchid started laughing, then ran to Daylphine and threw her arms around Daylphine's neck!

"Aarik, Drakk, take this man to that large tent over there. Please, I will address him in private."

They both picked up the little man and carried him to the tent. The line to sign up to be a rider was over seventy-five already.

"Well, that looks successful," stated Orchid.

"Are you okay, Daylphine?"

"Yes, yes, I am fine! But I am hungry."

"Lieutenant Donush?"

"Yes, my lady?" Lieutenant Donush answered.

"Take some riders for a hunt. I am sure my dragon is not the only one hungry," Orchid ordered.

"Yes, my lady, right away," answered Donush.

Orchid walked toward someone she saw in the crowd. "Orlagül," she called to the man. "Yes, my lady?" he answered. "Please, I have a chore for you."

"Of course, my lady, anything," he stated. "Can you ride quickly back to Artistah and bring me my genealogical records, please? Four generations should be enough."

"I will be back in half an hour." With that, he was off. The records were kept in a large brick building that functioned as the town office. Orchid got something to eat and slowly headed to the tent where the pudgy man was being kept.

Aarik had him seated in a chair, with him on one side and Drakk on the other.

"First, tell me your name," asked Aarik,

"I am Councilmen North," the pudgy man stated proudly.

"You were," stated Orchid as she came in.

"You have no right or authority here," the man said smugly.

"Don't I?" asked Orchid

"Right now, I am the only one with that right. Am I not, Mr. North?"

"This has gone on quite long enough. Untie me, good sirs," North said.

"Answer me this, Mr. North," asked Orchid. "Do you think you vouch for all the council? Do you think you have the deciding vote? Or maybe you just think that since you are the oldest member, you oversee our country! I have news for you, Mr. North."

As if on cue, Orlagül walked into the large tent and handed Orchid a large book. He opened it to a particular page. Orchid took a brief look, smiled, and asked Orlagül to show it to Mr. North.

"See anything of interest in that book Mr. North?" The little man studied it for a second, then gasped.

"Ah... I see," said Orchid. "You know your history. What does it say, Mr. North?" he mumbled incoherently.

"Did you lose your voice all of a sudden?" Orchid asked.

"You are Hielflander Royalty," he said.

"So, what is my title now?" asked Orchid. "I am recognized by two countries here and one at Triangulus as a royal. So, do I have the 'right' now?"

"Yes, I guess you do," stated Mr. North.

"Is that how you speak to your queen?"

"I mean, my lady," he rushed to say. She smiled. "Feed him to my Dragon," she said, winking at Aarik. The man went limp in the chair as Aarik and Drakk chuckled.

"You have been spending way too much time with my mother," Aarik said, laughing.

"I was scared for this guy," added Drakk.

"Orlagül, I thank you for providing the truth. If you could keep these records safe for me, I would appreciate it very much. I also have a bigger task for you!"

"My lady, anything," he replied.

"Please, can you arrange the council meeting?"

"I will be there first thing in the morning. I will send messengers at once," he answered.

"Thank you. You were an immense help," Orchid said, smiling at him. "Orlagül... You know I was only kidding about feeding him to my dragon, right?"

"Yes, ma'am, of course, I knew that. You love your dragon. That man would give her indigestion for a month," he said with a straight face. Aarik and Drakk completely lost it. They were all still laughing when a rider came running into the tent. "My lady, Harmony is back, and she is in rebirth!" They all went running to the field.

Orchid saw Drakk grab a chalice and dagger and headed toward Harmony, then to Second Sister. Just as before, the wound healed, and then at the end of the birth, Harmony ran to her dragon and embraced for an awfully long time. Then Harmony named her dragon Melody. Many who had signed the paper had witnessed this. Some were solemn, some crying happy tears. Orchid was the first to hug her.

"You have made me proud," she said to Harmony. When Harmony left Orchid's embrace, she was swallowed up by her parents. Orchid left to let them have their moment. As she started walking away, she noticed the parents moved to Melody and started nuzzling her.

Aarik was waiting for her. "The dragons are being fed, food is cooking for the troops, and I am waiting for my orders," he said.

"I want you and your men to stay here tonight. I think I will start building a training ground here. Tomorrow, I will fly to the capital and meet with the

Council. I will announce who I really am and see what happens. I would like your company if you do not mind. I also would like Drakk with us as well. I will leave Dayla and Serephine in charge here," Orchid said to Aarik.

"What about Mr. North?" asked Aarik.

"I will tell the council tomorrow that I have stripped him of that honor," stated Orchid nonchalantly.

"Then, my lady Orchid," Aarik said as he took her hand and brought it to his lips; he gave her hand a soft kiss and said good night.

Orchid headed to the medical tent. She went in and checked on the thirty or so wounded Hielflanders; she talked to every one of them and then to their healer. "If you need anything, just let me know," she said. Poppy looked at her and replied, "My lady, you need to sleep; we have this under control."

As she was walking back to the fire, Dayla, Serephine, and Harmony approached her. "My lady," said Harmony, "they have set up special tents for us; they were wondering if we would be together or if you require your own space. The tents could sleep about eight comfortably."

"Well then, let's all share and get some sleep," said Orchid.

In the morning, Aarik, Drakk, and Orchid headed to the capital. It was a chilly morning; Orchid had her dragon armor and was covered by a warm fur cloak. Drakk was in his usual leathers, and Aarik was in his queen's guard armor, with a warm wool cloak around him as well. Orchid had gone to the medical tent and visited with the wounded again before she headed to the capital. "Good morning, Aarik," said Daylphine.

"Good morning, dear," said Aarik, which made both Daylphine and Orchid smile.

The flight to the capital was about 40 minutes. They landed near the stables and walked over to the main building. They entered the building and walked into the main chamber. The council was waiting for them. Orchid took center stage.

"Honorable members of the council. I am Orchid of Artistah. I also have a new title, and that is Princess of Drakconia! I have called for this meeting as a way to communicate what has been going on in my time as captain. I have made allies with Northland. Here with me is the Captain of the Royal Guard and Prince of Northland, Aarik." The council members bowed. "Next to him is the Captain of the Queen's guard of Drakconia, Drakk. The crown you see on my head is from the two queens of Drakconia, Queen Alora and Queen Dalinda. I am paired with a dragon for eternity, and I bring a message of hope. We are also aligned with the Princess of the Tree Realm, Princess Dragonfly.

"To understand the message I bring, I must give you a small history lesson. Lesson one, long ago, our people were companions with a dragon-like creature called the Budhulug. They were giant dragonfly-like creatures with the head of a dragon and the tail of a scorpion. Due to an unfortunate accident, a little girl was killed while her Budhulug was trying to defend her from a bear. The people in this council back then turned on the Budhulug. Hunting them to the brink of extinction."

"At the same time, flying dragons were going to reach out to have Hielflanders be their riders. Then the hunts began, and the flying dragons went into hiding. They turned to Drakconians to be their riders. Queen Dalinda was curious as to how life with us would be different; because of our empathic ability, she thought that the bond between dragon and rider could be much stronger. I was an unknowing participant in this test. The Queen entrusted her daughter, the first-born daughter of the Queen, to fly with me and test her theory.

"Daylphine, as her name is now, and I flew for 2 hours; immediately, we were conversing using something called telepathy. When we returned, we experienced something that takes most Drakconians weeks to accomplish. It is called the Wiruthwix, or rebirth in our tongue. This bonding is very sacred and only happens if the rider and dragon are spiritually connected. As Daylphine and I landed and the moment I stepped off of her, the rebirth began. This was a record time. Never before had there been a rebirth that fast! More recently, it has happened three more times. All Hielflanders. Dayla, Serephine, and most recently, an incredibly young Hielflander, Harmony. I have requested fifty more dragons from the queen; they shall be here today. My plan is to pair those fifty dragons with fifty Hielflanders.

"You must be wondering why I would do this. I only have the authority till the end of this campaign. Orlagül of Artistah has in his possession my genealogical records, which have been seen by these honorable men here and Mr. North. I am the descendant of Hielflander Royalty. This attack on our lands leads me to believe that we need one person in charge again. One person that would keep up with allies and trading partners. One person that would unite our villages in time of need. I am asking for your blessing in this. The Drakconians would like to build a dragon colony here in Hielflander. I will start this colony with the fifty volunteers we have assembled south of Artistah where dragons, Aarik's cavalry, and Hielflander archers defeated close to one thousand Satyrs attacking our land."

With that, cheers erupted in the hall. "Mrs. Silverman? Can you come here, please?" Orchid asked. Mrs. Silverman walked up to Orchid; she bowed and looked her straight in the eyes.

"Mrs. Silverman, I dismissed Mr. North. He was getting too big for his britches. I will, however, trust this court to make the decision on and about me! If you agree with me as your queen, then so be it. I will do my best to live up to my responsibilities. If you choose not to accept me, then after this campaign, I will move north to Landia or Drakconia. I will, however, request the fifty riders as payment for securing our borders. I am Princess to Drakconia and quite possibly the future Queen of Northland. By claiming me queen, we unite three countries. Drakconia already requests trade with our country. They want bows and arrows for their riders."

"I will leave you now to make a decision." Clapping started, and Orchid, followed by Aarik and Drakk, left the hall and went outside.

"Well said, my lady, very well," stated Aarik.

"I agree with Aarik," said Drakk.

"Well, we will see," said Orchid. Clouds were coming into the sky, and the loss of sunshine made it seem a little colder. The three walked to an inn and sat at one of the tables that were empty. A man took their orders and went to fetch their food and drinks. Nothing to do now but sit and wait.

Chapter 21: The Council Decides

The food was tasty and eaten amazingly fast. They were now sitting and sipping on hot herbal tea when a young man appeared at the door and looked around. He spotted them sitting and approached the group. He looked at Orchid and bowed.

"My lady, the Council requests your presence at your convenience."

"Thank you, we will be there shortly. Inform them, please," stated Orchid. The young man bowed again and stated that he would inform them.

Aarik went to the innkeeper and paid for the meal with a gold coin, and started to leave when the innkeeper said, "Sir, that is way too much. I cannot accept this." Aarik turned around and looked at the keeper. "My fine fellow, it was a fine meal. The pumpkin pie was especially good, the fire in the fireplace was very warm and took the chill from my bones, and the tea relaxed me, and that, my good sir, is priceless. Please take the coin you have earned."

The keeper did not know what to say except, "Thank you so much. You and your friends are welcome anytime." With that, the three walked back to the tall building and the hall of the council; as they entered the council chamber, the one hundred sixty or so council members dropped to one knee as she walked in.

"Well, this is a good sign," whispered Aarik to Orchid.

"Maybe," she whispered back. Mrs. Silverman got to her feet as Orchid walked up.

"My Lady Orchid, I have been elected to be the spokesperson for the council. We have a few questions to ask before we give you our vote count. First question, what makes Hielflanders so much more different than the Drakconian riders?"

"Good question," answered Orchid. She concentrated on her hands, and immediately frost and electric sparks started forming from her fingers, and a frost mist started spewing from her nose. The crowd gasped. Then Orchid turned it all off.

"We Hielflanders have a much better connection with the dragons. Drakconian riders can communicate telepathically, and there is a strong love and bond. Hielflanders actually start becoming dragon-like, and our dragons actually start to learn our empathic abilities. She can call upon my abilities, and I can call upon hers."

"Aarik, draw your dagger." Aarik did as he was asked. She continued, "Now, try to penetrate my arm with your dagger." Aarik reluctantly did as she bid him to. The people stared in amazement as Orchid's skin hardened and Aarik's dagger could not draw blood.

"Daylphine and I are separate, yet we are the same. I know her thoughts, and she knows mine. These changes have only happened to Hielflanders so far. It is as if we were the perfect match all along. Drakconians will always be the keepers of the dragons, but we were meant to be their riders."

"Then it is with honor I give you our vote," stated Mrs. Silverman.

"Of 162 members present today, you got 162 votes to be our Queen! Of the 162 votes, there were 162 votes to strip Mr. North of his title. Of the 162 votes, there were 162 votes to build a dragon colony here in Hielflander and 162 votes to see your dragon." All laughed at that. "Well, she is out by the stables. She just told me to tell you she expects food tributes," said Orchid laughing, and so did everyone else. Daylphine telepathically said to Orchid, *why are they laughing. I was not kidding*, which made Orchid laugh harder.

Aarik walked next to Orchid and said, "She just told you she wasn't joking, didn't she?" Orchid smiled at Aarik.

"Yes, you are getting to know her pretty well."

"It is not hard," Aarik went on. "She is you, and you are her."

The crowd made it to the stables, and 162 people saw something they had not seen in their lifetimes. There was already a crowd there. Darian Horseman was keeping the crowd under control, his daughter Tara was dancing around Daylphine, and Daylphine was playing with her, swishing her tail and going in for nuzzles.

Orchid walked up to Darian, he started to go to one knee when Orchid bear-hugged him. Darian started blushing.

"Thank you for looking after them, Darian."

"They are magnificent creatures. I never in my life thought I would get to meet them in person," he said.

"Well, soon you will see many more, and I hope to send you to Drakconia to learn from Drakconians how to care for them. So, you can teach this new skill to other Hielflanders," said Orchid.

"Well, one thing is for certain," said Darian. "We will need bigger shovels." Aarik laughed.

"Hey, that's not nice," said Daylphine out loud.

Darian laughed more and said, "It's nothing to be ashamed of, Lassie. We all go!"

Everyone was now laughing. Orchid walked to Mrs. Silverman and took her hand and walked her to Daylphine. She could feel her old history teacher fill with excitement. As they approached, Daylphine lowered her head for a nuzzle. Mrs. Silverman was ready to give her a warm nuzzle.

Dayla, Serephine, and Harmony were getting the fifty volunteers ready for their meeting with the dragons. Thirty-five of the fifty were females, and the other fifteen were males. They took them to the makeshift range and watched them all shoot. All were satisfactory, and a few were astonishingly good. This pleased the girls. They chose the first ten to go through the picking process and then waited for the dragons to appear.

Dragonfly was inspecting the defenses and the fort. Most troops were sleeping inside the keep, where it was warm and cozy. There were stacks of wood to keep a good fire going. There was also a large fire going on in the dining area, and of course, the kitchens. Rosters had been drawn up and chores were handed out. Everyone had duties. If you were not on guard duty, then you were either eating, resting, or performing your other assigned tasks. Things were running pretty smoothly. Earlier in the day, they were flown over by a very large number of dragons heading south; only one dragon had a rider.

This bodes well for Orchid, Dragonfly thought.

"Princess, princess," the shout came from Ashen Oak. "My lady, we captured a prisoner in the forest," he stated.

"A Satyr?"

"No, my lady. You must see for yourself, he was spying on the fort…"

"Show me," Dragonfly ordered. She had sprites hiding in the forests just for something like this. They walked out to pass the bridge over the river mote. Dragonfly saw three sprites and one of Aarik's men bringing a figure that had his hands tied behind his back. His skin was a greyish color, his face was sunken, and he wore a camouflaged cloak. He stood about five foot ten inches tall; she knew right away they were in trouble. The creature they captured was an Elf, a Dark Elf, to be exact.

Dark elves were mysterious; they dabbled in dark magic, and they were fairly good archers and swordsmen. Most of them had left for the far east of the mountains after they were defeated by the High Elves around a thousand years ago. Dark elves, or Drow as they are called, are connected to the evil Goddess Loith. They are traditionally evil. Ever since their defeat, they had not been seen. It looked like Orchid was right; the Satyrs were a diversion. The real enemy was about to show themselves.

The men dragged the elf into the keep.

"Keep him in a lighted place; do not let him into the shadows," Dragonfly ordered. Maple and Lindale came into the room; they had arrived earlier with the foot troops Aarik had sent from Landia. "Ah, just who I wanted to see, Lindale. Can you please retrieve your lute?" Lindale smiled, knowing what exactly was going on in the princess's mind. "Yes, ma'am, right away."

She went to the corner near the fire where she and Maple's things were and grabbed her lute. She walked back over to where the Drow was tied up. She then took a seat in front of the Drow, who, up to this point, had not uttered a single word. Lindale smiled at him, then started strumming the lute. At first, she started singing in elvish, a beautiful tune that put the Drow at ease, but then the Druid spells started coming out, which made him start to chant in a dark tongue. He was trying to shield himself. Lindale smiled again and switched the tune, to which the room itself started illuminating, getting brighter and brighter; and every so often, she went back to the druid spell.

The light was causing the elf pain; however, the spell was starting to work. He was still resisting, however, but Lindale did not seem to mind. She kept right on playing and smiling at him. Her voice was that of the mythical sirens that lured ships to their deaths. To those that were watching and did not harbor dark thoughts, the music was delightful and enjoyable. To the Drow, this was torture. This went on for a while until the Drow started nodding like he was asleep, but his eyes were still open. The tune stayed the same, but Lindale was now singing questions.

"Who is the leader of the Drow," she repeated this over and over in elvish, then druid, and back to elvish. In a monotone voice, he answered, "The Ruler of the Drow, King Havoloch." Dragonfly was writing the information down, and Lindale kept playing. "What are your army's numbers?" Again, switching from elvish to druid. "Eight thousand," he answered, everyone gasped. Lindale herself was trance-like so as not to disturb the rhythm she was playing. "Tell me more, please." Her voice was so hypnotic and beautiful that the Drow had no idea that he was even answering her.

"We have powerful mages, archers, siege engines, Minotaur ax men, spearmen, and swordsmen." Because of the spell he was under, he could not lie. "What is your objective?" "To take Hielflander and Northland."

"I see," sang Lindale. "You must be so brave," she kept singing. "We will have our revenge on the High Elves!" There it was, the final objective. With that, the tune changed, and the Drow shut his eyes and went still as a post. The music slowly faded and then ceased. Dragonfly looked at Lindale. "Well done! WELL, DONE!" she said to her. Lindale smiled and said, "That was fun."

"Oaken Ash, get as many torches as you can find, hang them in every available space and chain him to a wall," Dragonfly instructed.

"Yes, my lady," he answered as he went to do her bidding.

"Maple? Send Daerwen to Orchid with this information. She needs to know we need more troops."

"Yes, ma'am, a lot more," Maple added. Maple went outside, retrieved Daerwen, and released him to find Orchid.

Chapter 22: The Colony Gets Started

Orchid, Aarik, and Drakk had just returned back to the battlefield. There were large piles of bodies in a field, and they were being set ablaze by dragon's fire. It was the only humane way of disposing of the corpses. Orchid did not like thinking about that. So, she went to the medical tent to check on the wounded. She was pleasantly surprised to learn that there were only two left in serious condition, ten that were just under observation for one more day, and the rest were sent home with a 48-hour rest period. She was walking around with Dayla and Serephine when she heard marching on the road from Artistah. There were close to a hundred woodsmen with axes and large draft horses marching toward them. Orchid walked to them.

"Can I help you men," she asked. The lead woodsman bowed and said, "My lady, our queen…We have come to help you build your dragon colony, training ground, barracks, dragon stables, and royal castle. We are here to start clearing out land and gathering trees from the forests, then replanting."

"Who put you up to this" Orchid asked.

"We are of our own accord," the lead woodsman said.

"What is your name, sir?"

"My name is Brock, my lady. We will have five or six hundred more workers coming. The word has gotten out that we have a queen. Everyone wants to be a part of it," the woodsman finished.

Orchid got a little choked up. Dayla and Serephine had smiles that took up their whole faces. The sound of wings interrupted them as fifty dragons all landed in a field close by.

The girls walked down to see the excitement. As they were walking, Orchid asked Serephine to gather the first ten riders from the list. Orchid walked to the dragons.

"Dragons, please stand side by side." The dragons did as they were asked. "You first, dragon, you will be number 1, next two, then 3 to ten," she instructed them.

"Dragons, this is your choice; you do not have to pick. I will send you one at a time if you do not find somebody, do not worry; there are plenty of choices. When ten of you have riders, you will fly with Ms. Dayla here for about an hour or two, then fly back here. There is a good chance that you will experience wiruthwix after your first ride, so land away from each other and give each other space."

"Yes, I said wiruthwix after the first flight. It has happened 4 out of 4 times. Dragons are matching and achieving things much faster with Hielflanders as their riders. So good luck."

Serephine had ten people, each fifteen feet apart from the next. Orchid sent a green female dragon first. It walked completely down the line choosing the very last person, and it was a female. They stared at each other, then the dragon went in for a nuzzle. The female Hielflander mounted her new dragon, and they walked away from everyone else. The second, a male frost dragon picked. The last one in line again was a female Hielflander. Thus, it went on till all ten were picked. Firewind and Dayla then took them in the air.

A similar thing happened to the next ten; the first dragon picked the last person, and Orchid thought that was a little strange. As long as they were all getting riders, she was happy. Serephine took the second group up. Drakk was preparing the knife and chalice. Orchid had a nagging feeling that she should send Aarik and his men to Triangulus, as well as all the Drakconian riders. She gave the order to Lt. Donush. He gathered up the riders and carried out his orders. There were still around 175 Hielflanders left, and she put them to the task of building the training area and helping with building the new colony. She knew that there were still more archers arriving every day at Triangulus.

The first group was now returning. Orchid's emotion-checked Drakk because you could just see that he was so excited about what was about to happen. His emotions were flying off the charts, so to speak. He was excited beyond measure; he was anxious, curious, and so happy that he could barely contain himself.

"Are you ready, Sir Drakk?" she asked him, using his title.

"I am my lady," he answered. The dragons started landing; Orchid had them stay mounted. She went to the green dragon, the one that had been chosen first. She called to the rider, "Rider, what is your name?"

"I am Donya of Carismah." Carismah was a village about ten miles west of Artistah.

"Donya, can you communicate with this dragon?"

"We can, my lady. What is your dragon's name?"

"Her name is Third Sister," replied Donya.

"Very well, Donya and Third Sister, let's see if we keep the streak of first-day wiruthwix going. Rider Donya, you may dismount."

Before she dismounted, Donya leaned into her dragon's neck and gave her a big hug. Orchid could tell they were talking with telepathy. Donya then took a deep breath and stepped off her dragon's back. She landed on the ground and took those two steps, then fell, as did her dragon. Orchid moved them somewhat together and went to the second rider. Drakk stayed by the first pair, ready to perform the blood ritual at the appropriate time. The second rider was a male, as was his dragon.

Okay, thought Orchid, *another unique pairing of our first males.*

"Rider, what is your name?" asked Orchid. "I am Aaron of Toptah (Toptah was a town near the capital)," he responded.

"Rider Aaron, can you communicate with your dragon?"

"Yes, my queen," he answered. The use of the title took her aback.

"Aaron, what is your dragon's name?" Orchid asked.

"He is the First Brother," answered Aaron.

"Very well, First Brother and Aaron, let us see how males do. Aaron, you may dismount."

"Thank you for this opportunity, my queen," he said. He patted his dragon on the head, took a few steps down the wing, and then jumped the rest of the way down. He took one step, then collapsed. Well, she thought males could do it too. Although, it was interesting that females seem to put a lot of emotion into the bond, like the hug Donya gave Third Sister. At the same time, the males had more of a macho-type male bond. I wonder what a male dragon and female rider will do. She did not have to wait long; the very next pair had a beautiful rider, with long flowing blond hair, and the typical electric blue eyes.

"Rider, what is your name?"

"I am Jasmine of Ursula," she answered.

"You look like an angel up on that dragon; are you communicating with your dragon?" Orchid commented.

"Yes, my queen," Jasmine answered

"What is your dragon's name?" asked Orchid.

"His name is Second Brother."

"Very well," said Orchid, "you may dismount."

Jasmine leaned in and hugged the neck of Second Brother, it wasn't as tender as Donya's had been, but there was tenderness there. Second Brother had responded by bringing his head around for a nuzzle. And to protect her from falling while dismounting. That was curious, thought Orchid, and emotion-checked the dragon. He cared for her already, she found. The next pair was another male rider with a female dragon. The dragon was another green dragon, and the rider was a strong-looking Hielflander, around 1.82 meters tall. Blond hair and blue/gray eyes.

"Rider, may I have your name, please?"

"I am Nerron, of Ursula my queen."

"And Nerron, are you communicating with your dragon?" asked Orchid.

"Yes, my queen," he answered.

"Rider Nerron, what is your dragon's name?"

"Her name is Second Sister, my lady," Nerron answered.

"Very well," Orchid said. "You may dismount." Nerron leaned in and gave the Second Sister a big, wonderful hug. She, in turn, turned her head around and rubbed him with her head making him laugh. Orchid emotion-checked him and found pure joy; he was so happy. This brought back the happiness she felt on her first flight. As he dismounted and touched the ground, the two of them fell into the rebirth. So, it was true in every instance the pairs went through wiruthwix after the first flight, and some bonds were very strong indeed. For the next 2 hours, she repeated the process for every one of the next forty-five riders. Drakk was a few riders behind her. Tonight, there will be another feast and a ceremony for the naming of the dragons.

Dayla and Serephine were talking with Orchid about the day's events. They were all so tired but really happy that things worked out and that Hielflanders were turning out to be the ultimate rider. Orchid stated to her friends that some Hielflanders were calling her Queen Orchid already. "That is because the council sent messengers declaring it to be so," said Dayla. "There is no turning back now." As they were talking, Gigi came marching in with around eight hundred troops, mostly sprites. Orchid walked over to her. Gigi was running to her at full speed but then saw the tiara and stopped two feet in front of Orchid.

Orchid swooped her up as she went down on one knee and gave her a big hug.

"So, what does the tiara represent?" Gigi asked curiously.

"I'm now a Princess of Drakconia and a Queen of Hielflander," Orchid answered.

"I am proud of you," Gigi stated. "We knew you were special." There was a commotion coming from the large field that all the dragons were spending time together on, and they looked to see Daerwen flying toward them. Daerwen flew directly to Orchid and relayed the message from Dragonfly, saying, "The princess needs us to return at once. The enemy has shown himself. Drakk, get all riders ready to fly. Gigi, I need you to take charge here. West of here is my village, please do not let anything happen to it. There is a Hielflander Brock with around one hundred men clearing trees, and soon we will be building a training center here, dragon stables, and my new home. Supposedly, there are six hundred more volunteers to help on the way. I do not want you to mistake them for an army."

"Yes, my queen," she answered, looking up at Orchid to make sure she wasn't mad at her for using the title. Orchid smiled, then bent down to hug her.

"You have 175 of my archers, do not forget to use them if needed."

"I have all this under control. Go see my princess," Gigi said.

All the Riders were ready. Orchid got on Daylphine's back, and away they went. Orchid was flying lead, Dayla on her right and slightly behind her. Serephine on her left, also slightly behind. Flying to Serephine's left was Drakk. To Dayla's right and slightly behind was Harmony. The rest of the fifty riders fell into place, forming a big "V" like geese, heading south for the winter. Two hours later, they were landing in the field next to Triangulus Castle.

Orchid called Drakk. "Drakk, will you please set up camp here, get the dragons comfortable and fed, hunt if you need to, and keep Daylphine, Icewind, Firewind, and Melody ready to fly."

"Yes, my lady, right away." Orchid, then called Dayla, Harmony, and Serephine. "Let's go talk to Dragonfly." They walked to the bridge. Orchid looked at the chains and gear and saw that they had a healthy amount of grease and looked to be in great shape. Hannah did an excellent job. They went under the portcullis and into the courtyard and took the stairs up to the keep. In the main chamber, they ran into Dragonfly.

"Girls come with me, please," she said to them as they entered the main chamber. They went to one of the back rooms where the dark elf was being held.

The girls walked into the room; it was very bright and warm, there were torches lit every two feet or so, and the fireplace had a roaring fire as well. At the center pillar, there was a creature; he was sitting in a chair, chained to the pillar with chains running through metal rings that were connected to his hands and feet. He was a pitiful-looking creature with grayish-colored skin, dark eyes, and light-colored whitish hair. He now looked up at the girls entering the room. "Is he what I think he is?" asked Dayla. "If you are thinking dark elf, then yes," answered Lindale.

"Why is it so bright in here?" asked Harmony.

"Dark elves can draw power from the shadows and dark places," stated Dragonfly. "They can be spell casters; most know a little magic, like wards for protection, and minor spells like hide in shadows and camouflage. It's best to keep them in well-lit places. It weakens them and renders their magic useless.

Lindale has used the magic of her own and found out some details for us," stated the princess.

"They have a standing army of around eight thousand," everyone gasped as she continued, "Mages, siege weapons, swordsmen, and Minotaur ax men; their main objective is neutralizing Hielflanders and Northmen, so they can proceed to their main objective which is Caras Galadhon (Fortress of the Trees). They seek revenge on the high elves for a loss they endured twelve hundred years ago, which in turn exiled them from these lands."

Orchid was stunned. Harmony spoke first, "We must warn the high elves and maybe find the extra men we will need to keep them from getting past us." Dragonfly approached Harmony. "Who is this beautiful young Hielflander," she asked with real amusement.

"I'm sorry, my lady, I am Harmony of Artistah," she said as she curtsied.

"What is in the water over there in Artistah that produces such quality beings," asked Dragonfly. The girls all laughed. "Harmony, you are correct," Dragonfly affirmed. Right then, Orchid interrupted, "The four of us will fly to Caras Galadhon."

"Princess, you have twenty Drakconian riders and fifty Hielflander riders outside. I have given them orders to set up camp, start hunting parties, and ready themselves for war. They are at your command until my return. We will get supplied with more arrows and provisions and head to see the High Elves. It is two days there and two back, plus the time we will need to convince the high court that we need their help. But understand, it will take some time till they can get an army gathered and be of any help here. I will dispatch a messenger to my mother—I mean Queen Dalinda and Alora. I will ask for all the riders we can muster; they could be here in a day to help."

"Don't worry, Orchid, I can cover here. I have already sent for the pixies and brownies and more sprites and tree elves."

"Lindale, can you cocoon our little friend?" asked Orchid; Lindale smiled so mischievously that the girls laughed.

"I'll take that as a yes," said Orchid. Lindale got her lute out. The elf started chanting in a dark tongue again and visibly shaking. Once again, Lindale sat in front of the elf. She smiled at him. The elf got more defensive and started chanting louder. Ever graceful, Lindale started playing. The dark elf fell to her spell faster this time. His chanting stopped. Her spell was causing paralysis, and his breathing went terribly slow.

The tune changed, and yellow threads appeared out of thin air and started wrapping around the paralyzed elf; then, more threads appeared and started wrapping themselves. Soon the elf was completely wrapped up like a cocoon. Lindale now slowed the tune, and the threads finished and disappeared from the air. "Please mount this butterfly on the back of Dayla's dragon. We will be taking him to the High Elves," stated Orchid. Everyone was chuckling at the butterfly remark. Lindale added, "Put him by the fire first; he needs to dry."

"Girls, have something to eat and tell me what happened south while he is hardening," said Dragonfly. Orchid and the girls were served a hot soup with a beef broth, chunks of elk, carrots, onions, peas, and wild potatoes, and served with hearty bread for dipping. It was a great meal that warmed the body and invigorated it. Orchid recounted everything that had happened since they left, detailing the battle and the addition of fifty new Hielflander riders.

Dragonfly was extremely impressed. "They all experienced the wiruthwix on the same day?"

"Yes, everyone after their first flight," answered Orchid.

"That is simply amazing," said Dragonfly.

"We will check on them when we return to see if any of them are getting powers like mine," stated Orchid.

"What powers?" asked Dragonfly. Orchid concentrated, and frost started appearing on her hands and mist from her nose.

"Oh my," stated Dragonfly.

"Yes, I am able to use Daylphine's abilities, and she can use mine. We are separate, yet at the same time, we are the same."

"Wow, I see," said the Elven princess.

"Is the guy dry yet?" asked Lindale. One of the sprites standing near the dark elf checked. "Yes, he is."

"Girls, we will need warm cloaks and bedrolls to take with us. Don't overburden us; take only essentials."

"Um, Orchid?" said Harmony. They all turned to see flames coming from her fingers. Then she turned it off.

"Did it hurt?" asked Orchid as she grabbed Harmony's hand. "No, I just started concentrating like you told Dragonfly." Orchid looked at Dayla and Serephine, they both concentrated and soon, firewind from Dayla and icewind from Serephine appeared on their fingers.

Chapter 23: Off to Meet the High Elves

The girls mounted up on their dragons. Orchid called Drakk and explained where they were going. She also ordered him to send a messenger to the Queens asking for all the troops they could send. She then took to the skies. This time they flew in a diamond shape, with Orchid in the lead, Dayla on the right, Serephine on the left, and Harmony directly behind Orchid. They wanted to get miles behind themselves before they stopped for the night.

"Orchid, I can see much better in the night with your night vision added to my dragon vision," stated Daylphine. Orchid gave it a try and agreed with Daylphine.

"We need to find a place to put down for the night," she told Daylphine. "Yes, I think we should," the dragon agreed. "How about there?" she said, looking at a small meadow surrounded by trees.

They landed, started a fire, and set up their bedrolls. They ate a bit of provision and were getting ready to turn in for bed when Daylphine spoke up.

"Girls, each of you, get comfortable under the wing of your dragon. We will face outward, so take an inward wing." The dragons formed a circle with their heads facing outwards, and the girls snuggled under the wings on the inside of the circle.

With a fire burning in the center, they all went to sleep. The next morning, Firewind went for a hunt and came back with an elk and a deer. They cooked the meat over the exceptionally large fire because it was now starting to snow. They ate as much as they could and packed a bunch as well. The girls ate deer, and the dragons devoured the elk. There wasn't any elk left over by the time they were done. When they were done packing, they all took to the skies again. Orchid and Serephine were pretty warm; it had something to do with their dragons being ice dragons that they could manage the cold; on the other hand, Dayla and Harmony were fire dragons which made them really warm too. The fire dragons gave off heat. So even though there was a frigid wind and snow, the girls were very comfortable.

They flew for most of the day, but the wind was coming at them, thus making the dragons have to fly harder, which tired them out. So, they were looking for a place to camp for the night. About an hour later, they landed near a river next to an open field that had a forest on the east side and also on the west side across the river. The girls gathered wood; then Harmony volunteered to see if she could find some food. Dayla stacked the wood to make a large warm fire. She had a bunch of birch bark and pine sap to start it, but it was all pretty damp. So, she concentrated, and soon there were flames coming from her fingers. She shot the flames over the small branches, and they burst into flames; she giggled as she added the small branches to the stack of large stuff.

Guess I'll never need flint and steel again, she thought. Harmony came back into camp with a large branch across her back. Serephine ran to help her; six exceptionally large salmon, each twelve to fifteen pounds, were stuck on the branches that were sticking up. "Wow, you did good little one," said Dayla.

"Little one?" asked Harmony, and playfully acted as if she was hurt.

The fish were already cleaned, and Harmony had already found some seasoning herbs. The fish were put on sticks and stuck in the ground near the fire. The deer meat was given to the dragons, and Icewind decided she wanted to fish too. "Okay," said Harmony, "I'll go get you some, little one watch and learn," said Icewind.

Icewind walked into the river right there in front of the camp; she went over where a pool was and jumped really hard and at the same time blew her ice breath; two salmon jumping to get out of the way froze in mid-air. Icewind grabbed them with her mouth and walked back to shore. Everyone clapped. "That was amateurish," said Firewind. She went to the same pool that Icewind was at and breathed fire until the water started to boil, and three more fish bubbled up. "Look, and already cooked too," said Firewind.

Everyone laughed and clapped. Firewind took a bow. Daylphine headed to the water; Orchid knowing Daylphine's thoughts, had a big smile on her face. Daylphine went to an area that was slowly moving and then breathed her shock only over a large area, twelve salmon, twelve trout, a few smaller fish, and a few eels jumped out. All were stunned, and the girls hurriedly collected them all. They all agreed Daylphine won the contest. The dragons and the girls ate until they thought they would pop. They were sitting by the fire, drinking herbal tea, talking, and joking around. They had become good companions, both the dragons and the Hielflanders, as a group. They loved each other's company.

"What do you think the High Elves will say, Orchid?" asked Harmony. "I do not know much about them, to tell you the truth. Only that I am descended from that royal line; we are only bringing news and a prisoner."

"Speaking of the prisoner, shouldn't we feed him?" Daylphine asked. Lindale put him in a hibernation state. "The cocoon will provide all he needs. I really love Lindale, she is very pretty and so mysterious, and the things she can do with that lute are so magical," said Harmony.

"She had a tragic life," stated Orchid.

"Lindale was different," Orchid began to tell a story. "She was okay with a bow like most Hielflanders, but she dominated with shield and sword. Her parents lived near the druid forest. One day while picking herbs and berries, Lindale ran into one of those druids. She was a youngling too! The two of them played till it was time to go home. The next day they found each other again and soon became good friends. The druid's name was Lully, short for lullaby.

"Soon their parents found out and set a meeting to meet each other. It happened on a warm summer day. A picnic was planned, and the two families met; they were neighbors by golly, and they should know the parents of their child's friends. At the picnic, the two families had such an enjoyable time that they ended up being remarkably close neighbors. A few years later, while Lindale was in the woods playing with Lully, a fire broke out and killed all of Lindale's family. Her parents and brother, only a few months old. Lindale was still pretty young, like 17 years old. Lully's family adopted her, and she grew up with them. They were enchanted with her voice and always made her sing for them. They loved her like their own. They hired a mage and a spell crafter to teach her how to infuse spells into her songs, handcrafted a special lute, and gave it to her as a gift on her 18th birthday. The Number 21 is a special number to the druids; it is the 21st of the 6th month for the summer solstice and the 21st of the 12th month for the winter solstice. Lindale was born on the summer solstice."

Everyone was just quiet. "Over the years," Orchid continued, "she has learned many spells; you never know what spell she will produce next. I once saw her call a swarm of bees to attack a bear that was in an elven berry bush just so she could get to the berries herself."

Everyone had a good laugh. Harmony stated that she wanted to learn that spell; she was addicted to elven berries too. Everyone admitted to loving elven berries, as well.

"Okay," said Orchid, "we need to get some sleep; tomorrow is a big day." They slept under the wings of their dragons again as it made them feel safe and secure. Daylphine had told them that this is how they looked after their younglings after they hatched.

The morning came; there was a covering of snow on the ground, yet the girls slept warm and cozy. Dayla started a fire the quick way(using her fire hands), and they cooked up the leftover fish that had been cleaned the night before, but not cooked. There was enough salmon for two servings each for the dragons. The girls had plenty of trout. With breakfast eaten, they all got on their dragons and took off. They were close now and would be there by midday meal. The snow had stopped during the night, and there were clear skies and little wind.

However, it was below-freezing temperatures. Still, the girls were not suffering in that area. An hour later, they crossed over into the High Elves Territory. One more hour to Caras Galadhon. They landed about half a mile from the castle, dismounted, and then waited for the guards to approach. They had left their bows on the dragons and only had their short swords at their waist. Eight guards on horseback came at a gallop. The guards, observing no signs of hostility, slowed down and moved closer. Orchid was adorned in her royal armor and a light blue cape, which had a hood. Removing her hood, Orchid revealed her tiara adorned with the jade stone. The guards dropped to one knee. "Captain, I am Orchid of Artistah, Princess of Drakconia, Queen of Hielflander, and dragon rider of Princess Daylphine of Drakconia. Daughter to Queen Dalinda, I wish to see your king and queen; we have important news and bring a gift."

The guard captain said, "Right away, my lady. I will arrange a meeting."

"That would be appreciated," answered Orchid. "And can your men carry that yellow object there."

"Yes, of course, my lady."

"Will our dragons be safe here?" Orchid asked.

"Yes, my lady, quite safe."

"Very well, let us proceed."

They walked to the castle and entered the main chamber. There, they were told to wait till they were announced. The four girls waited. They looked around and admired some of the tapestries that showed momentous events in the High Elf's history. One even showed the battle with the dark elves. The captain returned and stated that the royal couple would see them now. The girls walked in, followed by the captain and two guards carrying the cocoon. Orchid walked in front of the two sitting on the throne; then she went to one knee. The captain announced her,

"My king and queen, may I introduce to you Orchid of Artistah, Princess to Drakconia, Queen to Hielflander, dragon rider To Princess Daylphine, daughter to Queen Dalinda." She then ""The last descendant of Queen Amakir."

The king stood up.

"I am King Galadur, Descendant of Amakirs', Twin Sister Anastasia, which makes us cousins. We knew you existed. You are written into our royal genealogy charts. We keep track of such things in case something was to happen to us. We have not been blessed with offspring as of yet. Yet you say that you are Queen of Hielflander?"

"My liege, I am sorry to interrupt," said an older elf from the main hall, "we received this from a Hielflander rider this morning." The king took the scroll offered to him and looked at the seal. "Hmm... from your Council." He broke the seal and read the scroll, and he chuckled; it was an edict stating that "Orchid of Artistah, descendant of Queen Amakir, was voted to be the new Queen over Hielflander. A coronation and crowning will be scheduled after the conflict."

"What conflict?" the king asked. Orchid caught the royal couple on all that had happened up till this point, leaving out the part of the new enemy.

"So, any idea what or who this other enemy is?" the king asked.

"Yes, we do," answered Orchid. "My lord, may I use your court wizard for a minute and a few guards?"

"Of course," the king replied. A messenger brought them in a few minutes later. "Guards bring forth the cocoon," ordered Orchid.

"We are being attacked by a giant butterfly," the king joked.

"My lord," Orchid continued. "He was caught spying on the ancient fortress of Triangulus. Wizard, he is under a bard's spell cocoon and in hibernation."

The wizard laughed and muttered, "Good spell."

"Guards, be ready," Orchid cautioned.

The wizard started chanting, and the cocoon started dissolving. As the face cleared the threads, the king and queen gasped. Soon the cocoon disappeared. "A dark elf," stated the king.

"My lord, the same bard that put him in that cocoon hypnotized him as well, and under hypnosis, she interrogated him. There is a force eight thousand strong on the east side of the Travallah Mountains, an army of dark elves, Minotaur axe men, siege weapons, and mages. Their final objective was retribution for the war twelve hundred years ago. The first objective is to neutralize Hielflander and Northland."

"You will not be alone, my cousin; we will muster our armies and march through night and day. We will rid ourselves of the enemy once and for all. Fly Cousin, fly back to your people. We will be there in no more than four days."

"May I hug you, my lord?" asked Orchid.

"Only if I get one, too," said the queen. They all hugged.

"Cousin, if you don't mind me saying," said the king. "You are strong-willed and make our ancestors immensely proud, I'm sure. What you have accomplished in such a brief time, then left your army to warn us, is very admirable. We are in your debt. We will not fail you." With that, the girls left the dark elf with the high elves. They got their dragons and started the flight home.

Chapter 24: Preparing for War

Dragonfly was checking in on all her charges when she was approached by a royal messenger from the nature elves. The message read that all were in place at Travallah Valley. She smiled. Dragonfly and the princesses of the Tree Realm had come up with a strategy. They had gathered around sixty or so mountain trolls and marched them to the Travallah valley. Then they were going to march to the top of the north and south mountains of the Travallah Pass. The pass was seventeen miles long, a valley that cut right through the Travallah Mountains with 3000-meter peaks on its north and south side of the valley. The valley was only about a kilometer wide, give or take. But in some places, it was only maybe half a kilometer. It was these places that the Mountain Trolls were to be placed. They were to drop and roll large boulders and stones down on the invading army.

Hoping to cause an avalanche and block their progress or take out as many enemies as they could. Dragonfly had thought of this plan. She now had twenty-five hundred Hielflander archers; they were occupied making arrows, watch duty on the walls, and hunting. Although now carts of vegetables, fowl, and livestock had also been brought from Hielflander and Northland and the Tree Realm, they had fresh eggs, pork, and other salted meats and fish. Food was not an issue at the moment. Along with the Hielflander archers, she had five hundred pikemen, five hundred axe men, five hundred swordsmen and seventy-five dragon riders, and over three thousand Tree Realm folk. Two dragons had flown south to the Travallah Sea and brought back a large black and white whale; the fat was all melted down and mixed with the hog fat that they had. That was poured in strategic places in front of the castle on the opposite side of the moat river. Also, substantial amounts were used in the Travallah Valley.

The meat from the whale fed the dragons. On the roof of the keep, which was flat, there were seventy-five archers posted whose sole purpose was to attack any enemies that might be flying. Dragonfly was comfortable with the setup, she knew there would be things she didn't think of, but she had to let that thought go. She was not worried about a victory; she was sure they would win. It was the cost she was worried about—the cost of lives and the grief of those that survived.

War was a horrible thing that really only ended in tragedy on both sides. Where normal beings were taken from their peaceful lives and made to do such horrible things, just because someone who is in command wants something or thinks he or she has been wronged. And it will be the farmers, woodsmen, fishermen, and innocent that will pay the price.

"My lady," her thoughts were interrupted. "Yes, Ashen Oak?"

"My lady, over five hundred dragon riders have arrived, and the two queens among them. They brought tons of food from the sea to feed their troops and tons more to help feed the armies. My lady, we just might live through this."

"I never doubted that," Dragonfly replied. "But I was worried about the casualty numbers. The more we outnumber them, the fewer casualties we should have, though. If Orchid is successful, we will have at least one and a half times the army they do."

Aarik was out training his men. "My captain?" It was a young lieutenant. "Yes, Donavan?" he replied. "Sir, I have some disturbing news," the young lieutenant answered. "It's about the Queen."

"What is it, man? Spit it out!" said Aarik impatiently. "Sir, she took her own life. She poisoned her own wine and asked to be taken to your father's tomb below the castle. She was left alone, the men not wanting to disturb her while she was there; when they checked on her, she was lying across his tomb dead."

Aarik's heart was up in his throat. "Thank you, Donavan. I know that was difficult news for you to deliver, stay here and get some food. I will talk to you when I return." Aarik headed toward the Dragon Field, where he found Drakk. "Drakk, will you fly me to Landia as fast as you can?" asked Aarik.

"What is it?" Drakk asked.

"My mother is dead. I need to return."

"Of course, let's go get Bril," answered Drakk. "Bril is over by the queen; let's go." They ran to where the queen and the dragon, Bril, were. Drakk went up to Queen Alora and told her the news and got permission to take Aarik to Landia. Aarik and Drakk both jumped on Bril and headed toward the capital of Northland.

Gigi was supervising the building of the main barracks. However, she did not like to see trees being used. She understood the importance of this structure, and they were also using stone as much as possible. Gigi gathered all the children that had come with the families to build the colony. The women were collecting and bundling thatch for roofs; the men, of course, were chopping and sawing trees. So, Gigi got all the kids together and sat them down on the ground.

"Hi, kids. Does anyone know what race of people I am from?" "A faerie," said one child. "A Brownie," said another. "A high elf," still another guess. "A pixie," said another. "No, she's too big to be a pixie," said one of the kids who already answered. "A… a… a Dragononyan woman," said another, unable to say Drakconian. Everyone giggled, including the little girl who said it, saying, "That's a hard worrrd."

A little girl in the back with long beautiful blond hair and those Hielflander electric blue eyes said, "You are a sprite." "That's right; I'm a Tree Sprite." The other kids groaned because they guessed wrong. "Can anyone tell me what tree sprites do?"

"You cast spells," said one. "A mage," said another. "You fly; no pixies fly," yet another. The same girl that guessed before answered, "You help things in nature like plants grow."

"That's right!" Gigi said excitingly.

"Aww," everyone else moaned again because the same little girl answered. One little boy said, "It's not fair; she is way too smart; her mother is the teacher."

Gigi giggled and asked, "Do you see what the men are doing to that beautiful forest?" The boys got excited. "Yeah, they are chopping down trees and stripping bark and small branches," one of them answered. "No, I mean to the forest." All the children looked to see big stumps; they looked ugly. All the kids looked sad. Gigi asked, "Do you want to see some magic?" They all cheered. Gigi started walking to one of the stumps, and all the children followed. Gigi took a metal spike and started digging a hole in the middle of the stump; when the hole was big enough, she dropped in a seed. She then covered the seed with dirt and poured water from her water skin over the dirt.

All the children were as quiet as could be and watched her every move. Gigi smiled. She then placed her hands on the dirt, closed her eyes, and started chanting in elvish. She kept repeating the same thing. Soon the sprout came slowly up between her fingers; it grew and grew. The children at first gasped, then started jumping up and down and squealing with delight.

"Do you all want to plant new trees?" Gigi asked. All the children squealed again. Gigi handed a seed and spike to every child. The last child was the teacher's daughter. "What is your name?" she asked the little girl. "I'm Daisy," the little girl said. "Daisy, are you going to plant one?"

"Yes, please," she answered. Gigi gave her a seed. Daisy headed to another stump and dug her hole, put the seed in, and covered it with dirt. "Good job Daisy," Gigi said. Then Daisy put her hands on the dirt and started repeating the chant perfectly in elvish. Gigi was amazed. Daisy kept going, never getting frustrated, just kept saying the words in a monotone voice, Gigi was going to tell her that it was something only tree elves could do when she saw Daisy smile and a sprout came up through her fingers, but Daisy just kept her eyes closed and kept chanting.

She finally stopped and opened her eyes. The smile took over her entire face as she squealed and laughed.

"You did it, Daisy! You did it," Gigi exclaimed. The new tree stood almost a foot tall. Daisy ran to Gigi and hugged her. "How did you do that?" she asked, "I have never seen anyone, but tree elves do that."

"I am sorry, Ms. Gigi. When you were chanting, I...I...I know it is not nice, but I emotion-checked you, and you were using love—real, true love—for the trees. I do not know if it is the spell that does it or if it's just the love you give it. It may be both, but I just copied you," she answered. Then she quickly added, "Please don't be mad."

"Honey, oh sweet child, I would never be mad at that. You did great. No wonder you answered all the questions right today; you are a great student! Let us go do all the other trees." Daisy giggled as she and Gigi ran, going to each and every stump and making them grow. Later that evening, she went to another project. Gigi had shown respect to the Satyrs by burying the ashes of the dead, then planting the seeds of hundreds of wildflowers and encircling the area with stones. This will stand as a memorial to the Satyrs who fought here. She said a prayer to Atta, the Father of the gods.

Lindale was heading to get something to eat. She did not feel particularly good; in fact, she was in a grouchy mood, and she didn't know why. She was always in a good mood and never cross. "Oh well, food always cured everything," she told herself, trying to be positive. She ate, and that did not help, so she went to her corner, rolled herself up in her bedroll, and fell asleep. When she woke up, she was home; her mom and dad were alive. How can that be? She ran to them, only they burst into flames and started after her while they were on fire, she was screaming trying to get away. She ran into the woods, only to see hundreds of dark elves attacking the sprites. It was a slaughter; her heart was racing. "Where are the dragons?!" she exclaimed as she pulled out her sword and charged! Her first swing took a head clean off an elf, then another; she was fighting for her life, two or three at a time, using her shield to protect her left while attacking the right. They were coming at her from all sides, and she was killing them as fast as she could, but they kept coming; there were dead bodies all around her, yet they still kept coming; she kept fighting.

Maple had enough to eat. She was getting tired and headed to the corner where Lindale and her stuff were kept. As she drew near, she saw Lindale already in her bed roll. That was odd, she thought; Lindale was usually a night owl, the last to go to bed. She bent over to get her bedroll when she heard Lindale moan a little. She took a closer look now; there was sweat all over Lindale's face. She rushed to her and tried to wake her, but it was no use. She was burning up. Maple ran to get her sister. Dragonfly came running to Lindale's aid. Dragonfly wiped Lindale's forehead and affirmed that she had a bad fever. Dragonfly then lifted Lindale's eyelid to reveal black pupils where her beautiful emerald ones had been. Her suspicions were correct; she was under the dark elf's spell. "Maple, get me some clean rags and hot water, and find me a druid, fast!" she screamed.

Maple ran to do her sister's bidding. Dragonfly was frantic. She was using a counter spell, but it didn't seem to be working. Maple announced upon returning, "The druid went to fetch the necessary items and will return shortly." "I don't know if *SHE* will be!" replied Dragonfly. "We are losing her." Dragonfly chanted another spell; it became very bright. She repeated it, and it got even brighter. "Only way to beat darkness is with light," she stated. The druid came running in.

"My lady, what is it?" he asked.

"She is under a dark spell. She interrogated a dark elf this morning. I think he threw a shadow spell on her," she replied.

"A shadow spell? Let us see what we can do."

He took out some herbs from a bag; he started mixing them to make tea. Maple brought more hot water. They mixed the tea and said a counter light spell over it. They sat her up and made her drink. It was pretty much just forced down her throat because she never woke. The druid then took a cloth and dipped it in hot water, put some mint and sunflower petals along with a yellow ribbon and a few marigold flowers in the cloth, and folded it in thirds. Then she put it on her head. Both the druid and Dragonfly started chanting in druid. They kept up the counter spell for an hour. Finally, the druid said only time would tell now if we got to her in time.

Orchid, Dayla, Serephine, and Harmony landed in the field, which was now called Dragon Valley. They dismounted and a messenger ran to her.

"Lady Orchid?"

"Yes," Orchid answered.

"My lady, I have dire news for you," the messenger said.

"Carry on then."

"My lady Captain Drakk and Aarik have flown to Landia. Queen Anora took her own life out of grief for her late husband, it would seem." Orchid gasped. "Also, my lady Lindale is fighting for her life in the keep. The Princess Dragonfly is tending to her."

"What happened?" questioned Orchid.

"I do not know, my queen," he said.

All four girls ran to the keep. They saw Dragonfly tending to Lindale. Orchid rushed to her side. "What happened?" she asked frantically.

"We think the elf put some kind of shadow spell on her, and it is so powerful we have not been able to help her. We are doing the best we can. Orchid look," Dragonfly explained as she lifted Lindale's eyelids. Orchid saw the dark void where Lindale's' beautiful emerald eyes once were. She gasped. It took everything she had to hold it together. Dayla and Serephine did not do so well; they saw her eyes and lost their composure. Harmony was trying to console them. Orchid went outside. She could feel anger welling up inside her. This was her fault; she made Lindale put the cocoon spell on that filthy elf.

She heard a voice in her mind, *Bring Lindale to me...* It was Daylphine. Orchid turned to Dragonfly. "Bring her to Daylphine; she is in front of mother, um, I mean the queen." The girls picked up Lindale and took her to Dalinda. Next to the queen was the orangish-colored dragon that was used in the blood rituals. "Lay her here," the queen said. The girls laid Lindale down at the queen's feet. The orangish-colored dragon approached Lindale and sniffed her. It instantly shook her head. "This is Amber; she is a very special dragon." "Everyone shield your eyes." Amber breathed. Lindale was bathed in pure light. Even through her hands, Orchid could see the brightness of the light. The light went on for several minutes, then stopped. Orchid bent down and opened Lindale's eyelids again, they were still dark, but some tinge of green was returning. "Make an awning here and leave her. We will tend to her; it is the least we can do," the queen said.

"Yes, Mother," said Orchid. She broke protocol and got up and held her mother; it was then she lost her composure. Dalinda was just soothing her. Everyone was crying now. "My daughter, you do not always have to be that strong; this is a close friend. It is okay to grieve. She is not gone yet, my girl. We will do everything we can, okay? Amber's magic is not only pure light, but it also has anti-magic capabilities as well. It will work as a counter spell, but it will take time and a few more applications. Now wipe those tears. It will be all right."

Aarik and Drakk were just now arriving. The guards at the gate greeted them somberly. Lt. Devin met them in the main hall.

"My condolences, my captain," he said.

"Thank you, Devin. Where is she?" Aarik asked.

"The court Vizier had her placed in the throne room on the viewing slab."

"There will not be a viewing, not until this attack is over. I know it is protocol, but these are trying times. We have a dark elf army with minotaur axmen, and the army is at least eight thousand strong!"

Devin looked at him and said, "Captain, you took less than two thousand."

"Yes, but we have five hundred dragon riders from Drakk. Orchid has another fifty-three Hielflander riders fifty-four, including her. There are close to two thousand Hielflander archers, around two thousand tree elves, then another two thousand pixies and brownies. So, we have a formidable force, and Orchid flew to the High Elves at Caras Galadhon. Good chance she will get more troops from there."

"Devin, I trust you. Hold down the fort, when I get back, you will be my captain," Aarik concluded.

"THANK YOU, sire. It will be an honor."

"You deserve it. Devin, do we still have those copper horse water troughs?"

"Yes, sire, I am sure we do."

"Grab a few men and bring my mother to the courtyard. Then fetch one of those troughs for me, please. I have an idea." Devin went to do his captain's bidding.

"What are you thinking of doing?" asked Drakk.

"I'm gonna feed her to Bril," said Aarik jokingly.

"I won't allow that," said Drakk.

"Relax, Drakk; I'm gonna have Bril freeze her solid, then have them take her down to the catacombs next to my father; she should keep for a few days."

"Good idea," agreed Drakk. They laid Queen Anora in the copper trough, and Khelek-Bril froze her solid. The guard then took her down into the catacombs and let her rest there, where it was much cooler. Aarik then ordered two thousand more men to march on Triangulus. Then he proceeded to fly with Bril and Drakk back to the Triangulus fortress themselves.

Dayla, Serephine, and Harmony decided they were going to fly a reconnaissance mission to Travallah Pass to see if the Drow were on the move. Orchid thought that was a promising idea. She could use the information on the pass. So, the girls provisioned themselves with more arrows and some food. It was early in the morning, the day after the dragons started taking care of Lindale. They checked on Lindale before they left, then got on their dragons and headed southeast. It was an uneventful flight to the pass. Once they got there, Dayla had them spread out and go higher.

Travallah Pass was eight kilometers long, as mentioned before. The first three kilometers were at about a 10 percent grade going up. The pass itself was at 4700 feet elevation to start this grade increase. So that added 2820 feet of elevation at the end of the three kilometers; the top of the pass was fairly flat for two and a half kilometers, then a 15 percent grade going down three kilometers. Dropping 4210 feet to the Travallah Valley. The downward drop would be extremely dangerous with heavy siege weapons, armored men, and horses. Being attacked from the skies while making that decent would be terrifying. Dayla was all about making this journey for the dark elves as terrifying as possible. The girls were now very used to flying and using telepathy with each other. They were staying in constant communication with each other, dragons included.

Icewind had taken a motherly role with Melody; it was kind of cute. Of course, Melody was the fastest flier, so when they needed to get word back to the fort, it was Harmony and Melody's job to get it there fast. Dayla saw movement on one of the cliffs; she ordered the others to just circle; she was going in to investigate. She thought it was a herd of elk. Firewind and her headed down, descending in a large circle. Once again, there it was. As she rushed toward it, she focused on an emotion-check, but it was too late. She heard a boom, and a net swiftly shot out of the pine trees, enclosing them. They were in a free-fall into the large, tall pines.

Chapter 25 Dangers of Being a Rider

Dayla was thrown off Firewind, although, at the last second Firewind put her under her wing before the net closed around them. They hit the trees hard, and when they hit the ground, Dayla rolled out from the wing; they were both unconscious. Dark elves grabbed Dayla and tied her hands behind her. They also tied Firewind's mouth shut and her legs together. They tied Dayla to a post that had metal rings and secured her. She was tied tight, and small branches and firewood were surrounding her. She could smell oil and animal fat as well.

One dark elf, slightly larger than the four others, spoke to her. "So, you thought you would burn us with your dragon, did you? We are going to burn you instead. Then we will eat your dragon. It has been centuries since we tasted dragon." Dayla did not say anything; she was checking on Firewind. *Are you okay?* she asked in telepathy. *Yes, my shoulder ... well, wing will be sore,* Firewind answered. *Can you fly?* asked Dayla. *I believe so,* answered Firewind. *Let us hope the girls help us get out of this mess. That was stupid of me. I should have emotion-checked before we dove in. Don't be hard on yourself; you thought it was just elk,* said Firewind; Dayla started trying to reach Harmony telepathically. *Harmony, can you hear me?* She concentrated harder. Then she heard Serephine, *Are you okay? I sent Harmony to get help. Good, they have some kind of weapon that shoots nets, do not get too close. Are you in danger?* asked Serephine. *Not at the moment. Head down the pass, Serephine, don't get too close but see if you can see more of those contraptions, use your empathic abilities and dragon sight.*

"So, what are you?" a dark elf interrupted, "you are not Drakconian. What are you doing riding a dragon?" Dayla still did not say anything. She was trying to think of a way out of this. "Won't talk, eh? Let us see if you can scream," he said as he threw a torch at the wood surrounding her. The flames leaped up; she could feel the heat. This was it; this is how it ended.

Orchid was beside herself; she was pacing the ramparts when she saw a single dragon returning from the direction of the pass. She used Daylphine's sight and saw it was Harmony. *Harmony is everything, okay?* she asked mentally. *Orchid, Dayla, and Firewind have been shot down!* Orchid heard Daylphine in her head. *Get ready to jump on, flying below the walls you jump on.* She saw Daylphine coming, so she timed it and jumped from the walls. She landed right on Daylphine's back and slid into her riding position. She could see about forty dragon riders following, mostly Hielflanders. "Do not get close to the cliffs," said Harmony. Orchid looked at the riders and noticed Dalinda with Alora as a rider. She heard her in her mind. *Only here to observe,* said Dalinda. *Thank you, Mother,* thought Orchid. *You are most welcome, my daughters.* Orchid started thinking that she really was enjoying having this relationship and a mother again. *Yes, she is an awesome mother stated Daylphine, I was very lucky. Yes, you are, and thank you for sharing her with me!* stated Orchid.

The flames started getting higher, and Dayla was shocked that she did not feel pain. She did feel the rope around her hands and feet burning, and soon she was free. At first, she did not give it away. She saw them all laughing at her; the larger one said, "I guess she cannot talk or scream." Dayla thought it must be her bond with Firewind; she was immune to fire, *Haha, okay well now to take out the trash, she was mad, very mad that they just tried to kill her and were now kicking her dragon, and one of them was bringing a big ax to kill her.* That's it; she stepped out of the fire, and blue flames were coming from her fingers. The dark elves stared in amazement. She aimed and took out the one with the ax.

When the flame bolt from her fingers hit him, it launched him in the air and back 10 meters. Then letting the flame and wind do their terrible work, she swept it over the other four; the flame was as hot as a metal forge. Blue flame fanned by the wind. All four caught aflame instantly. They screamed as they poured their water supply over themselves, but the flame was too hot, and the water turned to steam instantly. Within seconds all of them were dead. She ran to Firewind and burned the rope off her legs and mouth.

"Firewind, can you burn that net contraption, please," asked Dayla.

"My pleasure," answered Firewind. Dayla checked around the camp. She explored the paths and looked at the tracks. From what she could tell, this group had been posted here, meaning others would not be coming up to relieve them.

There was a large latrine dug in the ground, so she dragged the bodies to the big ditch and threw them in the filth. Then using a flame wind from her fingers, she burned it all to ash in seconds. She heard wings and turned to see Daylphine and Orchid coming in. Orchid jumped from Daylphine before she even landed and ran to her best friend and hugged her so tight, she couldn't breathe.

"I thought the worst," said Orchid.

"Well, it almost was," said Dayla, then proceeded to tell Orchid how they were gonna burn her alive, but the flames did not affect her.

"Well, they had an effect on your new clothes," Orchid said. Dayla saw for the first time that her shoes, pants, and shirt were no longer there. All she had on was her leather armor, and that also was in bad shape. Orchid went to her pack and pulled out the new armor that Dayla had given to her and her old set of clothes and handed it to her.

"That's good to know," said Orchid. "About fire not affecting you. Let us take out all of these contraptions and get our mountain trolls up here." Serephine came in and landed. "There are twenty more, ten on the north side and nine on this side." "Harmony?" called Orchid. "Yes, ma'am?" she answered. "Take a message to the Nature Elves. They are staging on the south side of the exit of the pass. Tell the elf Queen Aredhel that I want them to start marching and to split the trolls in half and have her put half of them on the north side and half on the south side. Have them prepare tactics that we discussed. She will know what you mean."

"Yes, ma'am, on my way." With that, Harmony and Melody were off. "Okay, as for all of us, let us clear the mountains. Dayla, take half of them to the north; the rest with me; let's clear the South."

With that, they took off. Dayla talked to her squad. She chose another dragon, a green dragon with choking gas and acid breath. It would fly over at a height and drop it and let gravity take its toll. Then, when they were all choking, came in and used bows and other breaths. Orchid's plan was to make beach ball-sized ice balls and bomb the entire area. And taught a few other

Hielflanders how to do it so they all could bomb their area. A few hours later, they were all safely back at dragon field, laughing and telling others of the experiences that had happened when a dragon was seen coming in, two riders the sentry reported. "It must be Drakk and Aarik returning," Orchid thought.

Lindale was still fighting dark elves; her arms were so sore she could barely swing her sword. She remembered training with a sword master, and he was teaching her to control movement and conserve energy when in big battles. She now put those lessons and techniques into practice. Then her mind moved to her druid spell teacher. Teaching her how to infuse spells into just about anything, not just her lute. She started singing; her sword became light as a feather, then her shield also. Then she changed the tune, a fierce, strong tune; soon, she had the strength of a mountain troll. She kicked at the wall of dead bodies that surrounded her. They toppled over, crushing several dark elves. She moved into the open again, only to see more elves coming to attack. Again, a tune changed, and a bright light emanated from her sword, she concentrated harder, and the light grew brighter. She felt dizzy and collapsed to the ground. *They finally got me,* she thought. *At least I took out close to two hundred; why didn't the dragons help?* It was then she saw it, a black dragon. It was glowing and coming for her. Then, all went black.

Amber, the dragon, was applying another dose of light to Lindale, the queens had just returned, and the Hielflanders were excited about a victory they had over the dark elves in their first skirmish, clearing the mountain tops of the net throwers. Lindale moved for the first time in a few days. Amber called Queen Alora and Dalinda. They came running along with Orchid, Dayla, Serephine, and Harmony. Now known as the Hielflander Four.

"My lady," Amber began; "Lindale started moving. She has been humming every now and then. Also, her sword is glowing. She has had fitful dreams, but about an hour ago, it seemed to change. She is still dreaming. I just do not think it's dark dreams anymore." Alora moved her eyelid up and saw beautiful emerald green eyes, the eyes were bloodshot, but the darkness was no longer there. Alora touched her head, and it was no longer burning up. She wiped it with a wet, cool cloth all the same, and Lindale sighed slightly but did not wake.

"She needs rest," Amber said, "but this is all good. I will bathe her in the light once or twice more just in case, but I think it is safe to say she will make a full recovery."

"Harmony?" called Orchid. "I have a task for you early in the morning. I need you to take two or three Drakconian riders with you and head south and tell Gigi to bring 80 percent of her force to the entrance of the Travallah Pass; tell her to collect Ashen Oak and Oaken Ash and their armies too. Choose your riders now and tell them when and where to meet you."

"Yes, my lady," Harmony answered. Harmony ran off to get it done. Dalinda looked at Orchid. "So young yet talented beyond measure, and already an expert rider," she said to Orchid. "Yes," agreed Orchid. "She is even amazing to me. I was watching your kind today; they are incredible riders. They have taken to this like they have been doing this for a lifetime and the close bonds with their dragons. They genuinely care for one another. I have no doubt they would die for each other, each and every one of them. It makes me…" the queen's voice trailed off. "Makes you want to try again to have a rider?" asked Orchid. "The only proper rider would have been you," answered Dalinda. "I have given that honor to Daylphine, and I am glad I did so. I do not think you understand the impact you two will have on the world, not only here in these lands but all over Tarsus. The union of Hielflanders and Dragon kind will be the union of Tarsus. Once this battle is over, the word will spread like wildfire. Races will be united and swear loyalty to you! No one will dare oppose you once you have a standing army of eight hundred to a thousand riders. With us at five to eight thousand supporting you, and an army of several thousand in Northland. Our three countries united under one crown. Speaking of which, Drakk, can you retrieve the blacksmith, please?" Dalinda uttered.

"Right away, my lady." A few minutes later, a very dark and huge Drakconian came to Dalinda. "Orchid, meet the lord of the forge, our smithy, and a dear friend, Mathius Smith."

"My Queen," he said. Orchid thought he was talking to Dalinda, but she was mistaken; he was looking directly at her. "Mathius, can you show the queen what we have been working on." The smithy showed Orchid a sketch of a beautiful crown with three stones in the front. The stone in the middle was as white and pure as the light in the picture. To the right side was a beautiful jade, and on the left was an aquamarine. Orchid knew the meaning of it all.

"The center stone was a diamond; it was to represent the North Star, which was the Hielflander flag, a dark blue background with the North Star at the center top. It symbolized Hielflanders being steadfast and consistent in who they were as a people, like the North Star. Always caring for each other and never faltering. The jade was, of course, Drakconia. The aquamarine was the stone of Northland, the country on the sea. The crown itself was three types of gold. Three strands, rope-like in appearance, braided in a full circle around the head. Yellow gold to represent Drakconia, White gold to represent Hielflander, and rose gold for Northland. The two crowns, one from Northland and the one you are wearing, will be melted down and made into your new crown so a little bit of each country will be always with you," said the smith. Orchid was emotionally overcome. "You will make us proud, my daughter," Dalinda said.

Aarik came to where Orchid and the Queens were standing by, and he was accompanied by Drakk.

Chapter 26 The Shadow Lord

Queen Aredhel of the Ruling Elves, gathered her armies. She had two thousand pixies, one thousand elves, two thousand brownies, and sixty mountain trolls. The mission was to follow the animal paths up to the mountain cliffs and collect boulders and huge stones and get them ready to throw them down on the dark elf army or to cause an avalanche to stop them from going further. For the pixies, it was easy just to fly up; five hundred of the brownies were mounted on the backs of ferrets. It would be quite simple for them to be great climbers and have good night vision. It was getting the walking brownies and the huge, clumsy trolls up there that posed a problem.

Just then, a dragon rider patrol flew by to make sure all was well. Queen Aredhel enlisted their help. This made it much easier with ten dragons. Three trolls were put in each site with several hundred little people (pixies, brownies, and elves) supporting them. The trolls were on the task of gathering huge boulders to throw down on the army in the valley, causing an avalanche or blocking them from advancing. The pixies, however, were making harnesses; they would fly the ferrets with their riders to the enemy army for night operations. They would chew through ropes on the siege weapons, chew crossbow strings, anything to make mischief.

Serephine was leading a scouting patrol; it was her, Harmony, and eight Hielflander riders. Dayla was getting some rest; she was scheduled to fly another patrol later in the evening. As they were gathering the things, they would need for the patrol, Queen Dalinda called them over.

"I have a gift for you riders before you take off," said the Queen. "There are some colored gearboxes over there," she said, pointing to a few dozen boxes a few yards away. "You will find leather pants and tops, the clothing of a proper dragon rider. There are also leather armors that are to match the color of your dragon. These armors are enhanced to use your dragons and your abilities. For instance, the blue will use a layer of ice to protect you when danger is nearby. So, when your dragon charges up her underbelly defense, your armor will charge as well."

The ten riders ran to the large footlocker-type boxes and started getting new gear. Dalinda told them to each take three. Serephine spoke up, "This will be the only thing allowed for you to wear while on duty. This is your uniform; we are all united together in this. Go to the keep and change." Everyone went and got dressed and stowed away their extra clothes. Then they came out of the keep and back next to their dragons. Serephine walked up to a female rider she knew as Onyx; she had named her dragon Onyx as well.

The dragon was a large male dragon. He was almost solid black with streaks of white. The rider, Onyx, was of average Hielflander height of 1.80 meters, long, shiny black, wavy hair, and yellowish-brown intense eyes. She was very muscular, having trained with a bow from a youthful age. When asked why she named her dragon the same name as hers, she replied, "We are one and the same are we not? No reason to confuse people."

Everyone thought that made perfect sense, especially that the dragon was black. Some other riders named theirs the same way as well. Serephine went to a barrel and picked out an apple, and took a bite, and the lesson began. Serephine slowly walked fifty paces from the group. "The reason your armor is the color it is, is that it is made with dragon scales. You see, as dragons grow, they replace scales, sort of like we replace our first and second sets of teeth. The Drakconians take those hard scales and shave them, and those shaved scales are worked into the leather. Your armor is also double-layered. In between the two layers is a bronze plate. It's not that thick but can help you from being injured." Serephine turned away from the group, but in a flash, she spun around and threw the apple at the rider Onyx. There was a sonic boom, and the apple blew up in a hundred pieces. Dragon Onyx's breath was sound waves. But the sound wave was not from her; it was from rider Onyx.

"So, what just happened there?" Rider Onyx flinched and got ready to defend herself. The armor perceived it as an attack and defended Onyx. "Why am I telling you this? I know some of you are young and like to play practical jokes on each other. While wearing this armor, that would not be a great idea." Some of the girls started to laugh nervously as understanding hit them. They also started looking around at the different colored armor, knowing what the breath weapons were and imagining the consequences of the breath on them.

"Okay, enough of that," stated Serephine. "Let's get on patrol." The night air was cold, and the smell of snow was in the air. Along with the armor, there had been great thick fur cloaks, fur-lined leather gloves, and wool hoods to line their leather helmets. All the team thought they looked good, and they were warm and comfortable. The ten riders took off into the night to patrol the Travallah Pass. There was another squad that was patrolling the valley.

Orchid went to Aarik. She took his hands and looked him in the eyes. "I am sorry, Aarik, my condolences." She saw in his eyes that he was putting on a front. He was hurting but had not let it out yet. She emotion-checked him and found two dominant emotions: the first was anger, and the second was loss. He looked back at her, "I'm not going to tell you my feelings because I know that you already answered that by emotion-checking me. So, I will just say that she was my mother, no matter what."

"Aarik," Orchid said, questioning, "I care about you, and I know what it is like losing a mother. Do not shut me out because I can read your emotions. I am here as a friend and probably the next woman and chapter in your life." As she said this, she kissed him lightly on the cheek and ran her fingers through his hair, then walked away. Orchid gathered up the rest of the Hielflander riders and had them pick out their armor and riding clothes. She then called a meeting and went over the same things that Serephine had gone over with her patrol.

An archery range had been set up days ago, and the Hielflanders were teaching the Drakconian riders how to shoot the bow. Hundreds of bows and practice arrows had been brought for this purpose. The Drakconians were not as good as the Hielflanders, but they were getting better every day and were diligent in learning and open to coaching. They could see the advantage of having many more attacks than just their three javelins. Drakconians had not been in an encounter like this. The javelins were for hunting, more or less. So, they practiced at the range and the other range, which was further away. This second range was for attacking from the air. Overall, it was what you would expect to see and at fort preparing for war. The Drakconian smith had also worked countless hours in the last few days on harnesses that could hold eighty arrows on each side of the dragon. This would give each rider one hundred and sixty arrows each, a devastating thought.

Serephine, Harmony, and the patrol were now flying high over the invading army. With dragon vision, they could see the distance but were way out of range for the enemy to fire anything at them. Serephine was just routinely doing her duty when she felt sick to her stomach. Icewind felt it too. **Something was not right down there,** she telepathed to Icewind. *I feel it too! It feels dark and full of danger,* said Serephine finishing Icewind's sentence. Harmony was then heard, **hey, something is very scary down there.** Icewind laughed, **must be true,** she said. Serephine answered, Harmony, **we know we feel it too!** Serephine then emotion checked; she concentrated extremely hard because it was a long way down. She immediately felt cold and dark, fear took over her, and her heart rate started racing. She then passed out. The new harnesses that the smith had made had a safety strap that kept the rider from falling off in case of being shot. Serephine was strapped in, so it was safe. Icewind called to Harmony. **Serephine is down; do not emotion-check! Head back to the fort now.** As she said this, she saw a pixie fly up to them. The pixie flew to Serephine, then saw that she had passed out and flew to the ear of Icewind.

"It's the Shadow lord. We came across him last night! He is pure evil! You must get her back to the fort as fast as you can. We lost a bunch of brownies and pixies last night on a night raid."

Icewind turned and headed to Triangulus. The pixie found a place in one of the quivers and stayed on. The rest of the patrol followed Icewind and turned around. Icewind flew faster than she had ever flown before. Even Melody had a challenging time keeping up with her. As they drew closer, Harmony reached out to Orchid. *Orchid, Orchid Serephine is down; we are about to land now! She needs help fast!*

Orchid was watching the Drakconians practice archery; Aarik and Drakk, and even Dayla, were with them when she straightened up! "Serephine is hurt; Icewind is landing her now," she blurted out. They all looked up to see the patrol returning. They all ran to where the dragons were landing. Orchid reached Icewind first; she unhooked the safety strap, and with the help of Aarik, took her off Icewind.

"What happened?" she asked in a frantic voice. A pixie came out of one of the quivers. It surprised everyone. "She had a run-in with the Shadow Lord," the pixie stated

"Who are you?" Aarik asked.

"I'm Wasp," said the pixie. "We were on a night raid last night; we encountered a mysterious dark mist around an exceptionally large tent. We went to investigate when several brownies got sick and then passed out. We took them out of there, but they did not make it."

"Quick!" Orchid screamed. "Get her to my mother and Amber!" Drakk, who was in total panic, picked her up and ran to the Queens.

Everyone followed, including Icewind, who made all the onlookers dive out of the way. They made it to Dalinda, and Alora was there too. Drakk ran to her and explained the situation. Amber came running and bathed Serephine in pure light. Serephine was burning up with a fever. It was almost the same as Lindale but looked much worse. Serephine's face was contorted in pain, her muscles were cramping, and her heart was running fast. Orchid checked Serephine's blue eyes to find black orbs instead. Icewind then collapsed next to her. Orchid screamed. Drakk was sitting with his legs crossed, crying and rocking Serephine in his arms. Alora had never seen him like this. *He really loves her*, she thought.

"We need time," said Amber. "Lindale has recovered, and I believe Serephine will too. Icewind will be tied to Serephine's fate. I detect pure evil. Pixie, tell me all you know about this Shadow lord." Wasp began, "We were in the camp about three hours before sunrise. We were almost ready to go when we noticed that several of the brownies that had gone looking for mischief had not returned. I sent a few pixies to fly around; when they reported back, they stated that there was a large tent that was giving off an awful aura. It was surrounded by shadow mists and it tried to suck you in. Most of the pixies were able to resist it, but the brownies were not able to. We flew them back, but they were too far gone, and our healers could not help them."

"It sounds like Kardama," stated Amber.

"There's more," continued Wasp, "the dark elf king is possessed; this Kardama, if that's his name, is the true leader here."

"Amber, what do you know about this Kardama?" questioned Orchid.

"He is an ancient evil, a dark force. Where he goes, only death and destruction follow."

"This is all starting to make sense," Amber continued. "He was the one pulling the strings one thousand two hundred years ago. He wanted these lands in shadow. The High Elves were the ones that thwarted his plans. Now, all in his wake will feel his wrath. One thing is different; however, Hielflander is not unarmed like last time and now has matched with us dragons! The High Elves will be here in a day or two. Northland stands with us, and so does the Tree Realm. We are not alone in this fight. We need but to hold them in the Travallah Pass."

"How will we take him out of the picture?" asked Aarik. "We can't get close," said Dayla.

"We will have to get as high as we can and drop fire and ice balls and lightning storms; Onyx can use sound waves to cause an avalanche down on them. Arrows themselves will not be accurate, so we will have to charge them with our breath weapons and let them fly. Everything must be done from a distance."

Drakk was inconsolable, he had Serephine in his lap, and he was gently running his fingers through her shiny long black hair. There were still tears streaming down his cheeks, and he did not attempt to hide them. Alora tried to comfort him, but he just kept stroking Serephine's hair, humming an old Drakconian child's lullaby, and rocking her as Amber kept dousing her with light. Orchid could not watch; it was too upsetting. She did not need to emotion-check him; it was clear to see that he loved her very much. In such a brief time, they had built something magical. It hurt her to see her friend Drakk in such distress, not to mention one of her best friends in that condition.

She went to the range and started shooting. Bull's-eye! Bull's eye! Bull's eye! She just kept firing arrows as fast as she could. There was no more room in the center of the target she was shooting at; every arrow she fired now knocked out two or three arrows that were already there. Her vision was getting blurry because she was crying. Tears were falling freely, but she just kept shooting. Someone came behind her and put their hand on her shoulder. Dayla took the bow from Orchid's hands and just held her. Both girls were crying now when they were swallowed up by Aarik's arms and two dragons that were very close by. "We must be brave," said Aarik. "Amber will heal her. Be positive, okay?"

A familiar buzz came to their ears. It was Daerwen; he flew to Orchid and used telepathy, *Orchid, I need to show you something I found on my patrol! It is particularly important. It is a colossal cave through the freshly dug mountain. It is how our dark elf spy got here. We all assumed he came through the pass. But I found footprints and followed them. It led me to a colossal cave, one big enough to move fifteen people abreast. Or five or six on horseback. I must tell Dragonfly I will be back soon. Then I will show you the way.* Orchid explained what she had just been told by Daerwen to the others.

"Dayla, please get fifty Hielflander archers dressed in armor, and two quivers each, grab water and provisions for three days just in case, and muster them back here."

"Yes, my queen," Dayla answered and ran to do her bidding. Calling her by her title did not even faze Orchid; she guessed she was starting to get used to it. "Aarik, I need you and fifty swordsmen with shields and twenty-five pikemen."

"Yes, my lady," acknowledged Aarik, and he went to conduct her orders. *Daylphine, get Firewind and Melody and Harmony and meet me at the range, please! I'll see you in a minute,"* Daylphine answered in thought. Orchid ran to the Keep, got her gear, and got ready. She headed back to Dalinda and Alora, and explained what she was doing, then bent down and kissed Serephine on the forehead and Drakk on the cheek. "Watch over her, my Captain." There was no reply; it was as if he was in shock. Drakk just stared straight ahead and rocked Serephine and hummed. The two queens told her to be careful and wished her luck.

Chapter 27: Spelunking

Orchid made it back to the range. Everyone was there and ready. Orchid noticed Onyx; she was standing at attention in the group of archers. Dayla had asked for volunteers and got more than she needed, and Onyx had been one.

"Onyx, can you call your dragon, please? We are going to march, but I want Onyx, the dragon, 'Onyx,' to fly with Daylphine, Melody, and Firewind. I want them close, but I might have an idea. I'll know better later."

Onyx called Onyx and explained the situation, and they all started marching, with the exception of the dragons; they flew above, watching over the troops. It was a 3 kilometers hike to the cave. When they got there, everyone was amazed at how huge it was.

"Daerwen was right; it could easily hold fifteen troops side by side!"

The entrance of that place was massive, and for its size, was fairly well hidden. It was carved out of stone and earth. There were structural pillars holding the load and keeping it from collapsing in the places where there wasn't much stone. Large stones carved from the very cave were used as well to keep collapses from happening too. "Alright then, Dayla, Harmony, Onyx, and I will lead. Then Aarik, I want the swordsmen in five rows, ten across. Then will be the pikemen. Pikemen, your job is to protect the archers, Understood?"

There were mixed shouts of 'Yes, my lady' as well as 'Yes, my queen,' dragons in the rear. They all lined up and started to march as quietly as a group this big could. They got back a few hundred yards when they saw torches along the walls on both sides.

"I believe they are planning to attack us on two sides," stated Orchid to her captains. "Yes, it would seem so," answered Dayla. "While we are concentrated to the South where the Pass is, they attack from the north with a separate army. Maybe even have ways to bridge the river and attack the castle directly. They would be remarkably close to Dragon Valley, though," she thought out loud.

"If they attacked at the Pass first, then all the dragons would be in the air and they could surround us. Okay, everyone, hold up. Harmony, Dayla, Aarik, and I will go ahead and scout. Onyx, you come with us too," added Orchid.

Onyx joined the girls and Aarik. "Why are you so interested in having Onyx?" asked Dayla. "Imagine what her breath weapon can do to the cave?" answered Orchid. "Oh," answered Dayla, "I MEAN OH!" as she thought about it a second longer. As the walls came tumbling down, she giggled.

"Stay close to the north wall and away from the torches as much as possible. Dayla, Harmony, and Onyx, use your shadow ability and night vision."

They all hid in the shadows, Aarik doing the best he could, which, if Orchid had anything to say about it, she thought he did very well. After about an hour of walking in the shadows, they heard faint voices. They kept advancing and soon were on the outskirts of a huge chamber. There was a large bonfire in the center and dozens of tents and bedrolls scattered about. The chamber itself was circular, about two hundred meters in diameter. The ceiling was 20 meters high, with a shaft heading straight up to the sky to let out all the smoke.

The cave continued heading east on the opposite side of the chamber. Orchid was in awe of the total size of the thing, not to mention the artisanship. It was a humongous undertaking. "This chamber could hold a thousand or so troops waiting on the word," whispered Aarik right into Orchid's ear. She nodded her head. Onyx hit Dayla. "Look," she whispered, "there are people in those cages over there." Dayla and Orchid looked in the direction Onyx was pointing and saw some exceptionally large cages.

There were four of them. Two on the north side of the cave entrance they were on and two on the south side. Each stood about 2 meters high and about 4 meters wide and 35 meters long. Orchid could make out some people in the cages but not clearly. "Hielflander prisoners," asked Harmony, remembering the Satyrs taking her family. "I do not know! You guys stay here. I am going in for a closer look." They all nodded.

Orchid using her shadow ability, slowly inched her way closer, stopping to emotion-check to make sure the coast was clear. As she drew near, she gasped! Another race she had never seen before. In the cages were dozens of dwarves. So that's how they dug all this; they used dwarf slaves. *We have to free them*, she thought. She slowly but methodically started stepping closer, staying in the shadows. As she got within a few feet of them, she listened to the conversations going on inside the cage.

One dwarf was saying that now that they were through to the other side, there was no longer a use for them, and they would be killed soon; even the women and younger dwarves held the east camp. Most agreed with him. Orchid came into view.

"Not if I get you out first," Orchid said. There was a gasp.

Then one dwarf spoke up, "Where did you come from, lassie, and what are ya?"

"I am a Hielflander, a race between Northland and the High Elves," explained Orchid.

"Aye, whatever that means," answered the Dwarf.

"I think I heard one of the shadow elves say something about High Elves and Hielflanders," said another one.

"What is your name?" asked Orchid to the second one who talked.

"I'm Rat," he said.

"Rat?" questioned Orchid.

"It's kind of a nickname, lass because I tunnel like a tunnel rat."

"Oh," Orchid replied.

"Where are the guards?" she asked. "Mostly towards the middle, some sleeping, and some on those alcoves up there," answered Rat.

Orchid looked up to see several alcoves with which to post archers. "Okay, hold on a minute. I will be right back."

"Lass, we appreciate what you are trying to do, but there is no way you can get this lock open without making noise that will attract all of them," Rat said.

"Don't worry; I'll be back," Orchid replied. As she moved back into the shadow, she heard the excitement in the cage. Orchid snuck back to her team.

"Okay," she whispered, "there are about twenty-five dwarves in each cage, which makes sense; if you need to dig tunnels, why not get the best diggers there, right?"

"So, I'm going to free the two cages to the south. Dayla, you take the two to the north. Aarik, you go back and bring all the troops here. Position all my archers on each of these entrances in the shadows as much as possible. Once we free them, send them all the way back to the entrance. Tell them to hold up there till we return. If the alarm is sounded, have the archers open fire and have your men block the Drow from going back that way."

"Yes," answered Aarik. "Good plan."

"Dayla, use your fire fingers to melt the locks, then send them all this way, making sure to tell them to stay hidden as much as possible. Let's do this," Orchid said as she started back the way she had just come. Dayla took the north side. Orchid got back to the cage.

"You guys ready?" she asked.

"We were thinking while you were gone, if they find us missing, they might do something to our women and children outside."

"Don't worry, Rat, we will make sure they don't touch them," stated Orchid.

"We?" asked Rat.

"Yeah, I brought an army. My friend is freeing the two cages to the north."

"Lass, this is the first chamber; if you came from the west, there are two more chambers further east. The furthermost one was pretty full of soldiers last time I was down that way."

"We will free you one chamber at a time. So, do you want to be freed?" Orchid asked.

"Aye, Lassie, we do." Orchid took her hood off to see the lock better; there were gasps.

"Lass are you royalty?" asked Rat.

"Aye, lad," she said, giggling. "I am Queen Orchid of Hielflander, Princess of Drakconia and the dragon riders and future Queen of Northland."

"Lass, that jade stone is quite valuable."

"I wouldn't know," stated Orchid.

"Hand me that handpick, please, Rat."

"Hey, Rat, a queen just said please to ya," said someone from the back.

"Shut it, Fats," answered Rat.

Orchid, the troops are all in position, said Harmony through telepathic means.

"Okay, do not be alarmed once the lock is broken. All of you head west; there is an army up there at the entrance. There are fifty very well-trained archers that will watch over you. Once you make it outside set up there, we will meet back there after we free all of your kin."

"Rat…"

"Yes, Lass, I mean my lady?"

"Stay with me, please," ordered Orchid.

"As you wish, ma'am," answered Rat.

"Here we go." Orchid started concentrating on the frost; she held the lock and started freezing it. There were several gasps from inside the cage. With one hand, she held the lock so it would not fall, and with the other, she hit the lock with the handpick. The lock popped as easily as that. She then opened the door.

"Run," she whispered. "Rat, let's go get the other cage." Rat told everyone to get ready in the second cage and also said he would explain later, then passed down the orders to head west and not be alarmed by the army up ahead. With that, Orchid froze the lock, and this time Rat hit it open and swung open the door. All the dwarves ran by her, the majority thanking her. Rat and Orchid followed the last one up the hill to the awaiting army.

"Rat, do you speak Drow?" Orchid asked him.

"Of course, I do; we have been at this for 65 years!"

"What?" Orchid questioned.

"Yes, I am 34 years old; I am the second generation of my kin. I have never even seen a Dwarven settlement other than this one!"

For some reason, this made her angry.

"When I say 'now', I am going to want you to yell in Drow that the prisoners are getting away, so we can see where they are," she said.

"Aye," answered Rat. Dayla and Harmony showed up at about the same time as Orchid. "Harmony, when my new friend yells, I want you to fire a fireball right at that bonfire. Light this place up as much as you can. Dayla put the tents and bed rolls on fire. Harmony, after you hit the bonfire, start shooting at those alcoves up there," she said, pointing at one. "There are archers up there, so hit them hard and blow them off that perch."

"Yes, my queen," answered Harmony.

"Rat, how solid is this chamber?" Orchid asked.

"Solid rock. This took almost fifteen years."

"Thanks, Onyx. Follow Harmony's lead fire with a small explosion but big enough to knock them off those perches," Orchid said.

"Yes, my queen," Onyx answered.

"Now, Rat!" ordered Orchid. The dwarf screamed in Drow. In half a second, there was movement in the chamber. Then a huge explosion in the bonfire; there was another explosion, and two Drow screamed as they fell from the alcove on fire. Then another explosion as three more were knocked from an alcove on the south side; that one was Onyx. Other Drows were cut down by the other archers; some Drow had three or four arrows sticking out of them, having been targeted by more than one archer.

"Suffer, you filthy no-good demons!" yelled Rat down at them. In six or fewer minutes, it was all over. Rat dropped to one knee and said, "My Queen; I do not know how to thank ye."

"Well, Rat, it is not over. I want you to guide us all the way," answered Orchid.

"After what you just did for me and my kin, it is the least I could do," he answered back.

Orchid emotion-checked the entire chamber. It was clear.

"Firewind, Melody, go down there and Torch everything, especially those siege weapons over there," she said. The two dragons started moving up from the back. Rat saw them and almost peed in his pants.

"What in the sandstone is that?" he shrieked. Everyone started laughing.

"Those are fire dragons, Rat," said Orchid.

"And you ride those lasses?" he asked.

"Yes, they fly in the air," Orchid answered.

"I'll be a piece of slate," said Rat. Melody and Firewind went to the center of the chamber and started breathing fire and fireballing everything. Once the flames died down, Orchid and her army moved on. They started traveling down the east side of the chamber and into the next cave heading east. About 3 kilometers in, Rat signaled them to go stealth.

Within five minutes, they started seeing the light, then the archers moved into the shadows and crept to the edge of the chamber. There were more dark elves here; the chamber was identical to the first. Dayla went to the cages to the north again and Orchid to the south. Dayla made it to the cages first but noticed a single guard fairly close by. She was in the shadows, and no one else was close. She sent an arrow at the wall, using the wind to move it faster. It crashed into the wall hard, making a crashing sound that was not overly loud, but he heard it and got up to investigate. She pulled out a blunted arrow and hit him in the head with it. It knocked him out cold. Dayla then went to the cage door and told the dwarves who she was and what was going to happen, and where they needed to go.

She melted the locks and let them escape; she then did the same to the other cage. By the time she got back up to where everyone else was, Orchid was already back. Orchid had a new plan for this one. Aarik's troops were ready.

Rat yelled, "The dwarves are escaping!" Onyx let a full-fledged sonic boom go, and this stunned most of the elves. Then Aarik and his troops charged, while the archers thinned the herd, and Harmony and Onyx took care of the high perches. There were close to one hundred dark elf troops; they were no match for the Orchid's group, though.

And 20 minutes later, the battle was over. The third chamber went pretty much the same way. "Okay, my queen," said Rat, "it's three kilometers to the opening last time I checked, which was three days ago. There were twenty-five hundred or more troops there."

"Okay, I want everyone to head back to the west side. Onyx, Dayla, Harmony, and I will go at this one alone," Orchid said.

Everyone started to object when Orchid said, "That's a command." They all turned and headed west. The girls headed east. An hour later, they were at the opening. It was dark out, and there were fires lit to give off warmth more than light. The smoky smell of the wood fires assaulted their noses. It was also colder. The sun had gone down, as Orchid had expected. Orchid and Dayla performed their rescue missions, and once all the prisoners were free and running west, Harmony sent a huge fireball into the center of the camp. The fire exploded into the night, sending up sparks and flames everywhere. Onyx sent shock waves that knocked people back, some of whom were on fire. Orchid was sending big ice balls that exploded with electrified shards. Dayla sent her flame bolts into wooden structures. They tried to take out as much as they could. Then Orchid yelled,

"Now!" And they all sprinted back into the cave; once in, Onyx stopped, smiled, and took on a very cocky attitude. Orchid smiled to herself; Onyx was getting increasingly confident. Onyx concentrated hard and then let out a sonic wave so powerful that the entrance of the cave collapsed.

"Okay, see you soon," she said. Orchid gave her a hug. "Okay, if you don't hear from me, you know what to do, right?" she asked her new friend. "Yes, Orchid, now go and hurry back." The girls assumed a jog and started the long journey back to Triangulus.

Chapter 28: Another Royal

The girls made it back to the west entrance and led the dwarves to the fortress of Triangulus. They got blankets, tents, and food for them and said their good nights. Orchid then met with her cousin, the High Elf King Galadur, who had arrived with his army while Orchid was gone. Orchid then checked in on Serephine, who was still in Drakk's arms. Then she headed to a quiet place to get a few hours of sleep. The next morning, she got Harmony and Dayla.

"Now, girls, I have a special mission for you today. I want you to escort the high elves to the Travallah Valley and start the assault. We will give you time to get there; then all the dragon riders will head to the east cave entrance and attack there, then we will attack the rear of the army attacking you. Having the High Elves should attract the main dark army to commit to launching an attack once they start up the east slope. I want you and three or four other fire dragons to go to the highest peaks and melt all the snow on those peaks. I want water, ice, snow, trees, rocks, and mud sliding down the mountain. All the trolls we have are occupying the lower peaks on the flat stretch of the Pass, so make sure not to harm them. That ought to slow the dark elves, and minotaur's, down. Leave eight hundred of our now three thousand archers here as a reserve. Keep the archers you take in the back or protected." Dayla and Harmony hugged Orchid, and they each wished each other good luck.

Orchid walked over to where they had set up the dwarves, only to find around two hundred of them dressed in armor and weapons like axes and hammers and a few swords.

"What's this?" asked Orchid seeing Rat.

"My lovely lady, I am so glad to see you again," Rat stated. "We have decided to march with the elves and King Galadur. We want to fight as a way to thank ye for saving our wretched lives." Orchid got a little choked up. "Rat, I did not free you to die. I really want you to have a life free of bondage. A life you really do not know anything about."

"Aye, Lass, but Dwarven Honor dictates that we must repay your kindness. My beautiful queen." Orchid blushed.

"Rat… promise your queen that you will return after!"

"My lady," he answered, "I will do my best." He bowed his head, and Orchid placed a kiss upon it.

With that, he led his men to join up with elves and to battle. Orchid watched twenty-two hundred of her archers' march in the same direction. Galadur had brought three thousand men. If her calculations were correct, there were now seven thousand troops heading to the Pass with close to three thousand already there. Aarik had come by earlier and wished her luck; he was now down there with his men.

"Orchid?" called Dalinda. "Can we talk?"

"Of course, mother," answered Orchid. "I need to tell you some disturbing news. It's about Lindale."

Orchid gasped. "Is she…"

"No, dear," Dalinda interrupted the thought. "Nevertheless, I need to tell you something. When Amber was tending to her, she caught a scent. I am just going to come out with it, dear, okay?"

"Please, Mother," answered Orchid.

"Lindale is a royal," stated Dalinda.

Is she related to me?" asked Orchid. Daylphine had come up behind her to hear this too.

"No," Dalinda replied.

"She is not Hielflander bloodline, nor is she Northland or High Elf."

"I'm confused," said Orchid.

"She is druid royalty. The man Lindale knew as her father was not. There were rumors that the druid elves wanted a stronger royal line to strengthen their position over the ruling elves in the Tree Realm." Orchid then saw that Dragonfly had joined the conversation. Dragonfly then took over the story. "We know that Lindale's mom knew about this and was probably promised something in return. However, we do not know if Lindale's father knew. There is more unsettling news. We believe that the fire that killed her family was probably not an accident. Everyone thought it was an unselfish act of them taking her in and treating her like their own was not really that; she did belong to them."

"Why haven't they come forth to claim her then," asked Orchid.

"She will become of age this summer solstice," answered the dragon queen.

"There is something I want to add," continued Dalinda. "A confession I want to make to both of you, my daughters," she said, choking up.

"I am old, an ancient dragon. I must admit that I am very ashamed of what I now will admit. I am jealous of the bond you have. It is something I genuinely want to experience. The only proper choice was for me to choose you, Orchid, but I gave that honor to my only daughter. For that, I am not ashamed, but once things started happening, I felt alone. Now I have the chance again. Lindale is a royal too. I am asking permission to choose her as my rider."

Orchid felt her heart swell like never before; she knew it was Daylphine mostly because she had the Hielflander emotion of crying for joy.

"Is Lindale awake?" asked Orchid.

They all found and approached Lindale, who was sitting near Drakk and Serephine, with Amber napping near, regaining strength. Orchid took the lead.

"Lindale, can we talk?" Lindale got up and approached the party.

"Of course, my lady," she answered.

"I don't know how to say this, Lindale, but I have some information to impart to you that is going to be exceedingly difficult to hear. So, brace yourself. I also have a particularly important question to ask you once I tell you the first part. So, while you were recovering, Amber detected a smell on you. You have royal blood," Orchid said.

"Are we related?" Lindale asked.

"No, we are not; you are half druid. That is royal blood," answered Orchid. It only took a second for her to put the pieces together. Tears were flowing down her face freely.

"The fire was... it was..."

"Yes," Orchid interjected, "there have been rumors throughout your life that it was all a setup. The druids wanted a stronger claim to the throne of the Tree Realm," Dragonfly continued. "This is why all the training with sword and shield and bard spells. They wanted you to challenge the throne. When this is over, the ruling elves and I will seek justice for what happened, but it was important you knew."

"I don't want anything to do with them!" Lindale yelled, sobbing. She put her hands in front of her face, and Dalinda came to her.

"Darling, I am so sorry," she said to her. "When I was in my dark dream state, I saw them, my parents; they were coming after me; they were on fire. They were blaming me. It was because of me!!!!" Dalinda lowered her head and nudged Lindale closer to her. Lindale lunged at Dalinda's neck and just held tight, sobbing. "This may not be the time for the other," Dalinda said.

"What is it?" asked Lindale through sobs and sniffles.

"Lindale, I am very jealous of my daughters' union. I have never had an eternal rider. The only appropriate rider would have been Orchid. I gave that honor to my daughter. Now I find myself with another opportunity. You are a royal. Would you care to be my rider?" Lindale stopped sobbing and looked at Dalinda; everyone knew she was emotion-checking Dalinda to see if she was being truthful. *Lindale, I choose you as my royal rider. It is your choice, however,* Dalinda telepathed to her. Lindale answered in telepathy as well. *Dalinda, Queen of the dragons, I choose you to be my Royal Dragon.*

Dalinda went in for another nuzzle, and then Lindale got her sword and her bow. The smith came and installed the quiver harness, and then Lindale stepped up on her wing and took the position of a rider on the queen of dragons. "I have been jealous of not being a rider too," she announced to her friends, wiping away the tears, and she was not the only one. In fact, everyone was in tears. Daylphine was so happy Orchid thought she was going to burst. Lindale's friends cheered and clapped for her. *I hate your stupid emotions,* Daylphine said telepathically to Orchid. *I have never felt this emotional as I have since I have been with you!* Orchid laughed.

"Well, let's go hunting, Drow," said Orchid. Everyone once again waited for Orchid to take off first. Then a hurricane almost started as five hundred and fifty dragons took to the air. Dalinda took her place on the right side of Orchid. They flew north past the cave a few miles, then up and over the mountains, then south on the east side Of the Travallah Mountains,

The main army had started heading east through the Pass. Dayla, Harmony, and three other fire dragon riders were in the skies, making sure the coast was clear. They also decided not to use the strategy of using the mountain trolls on the mountain tops. They were going to use them directly on the front line, throwing things down on the opposing army. Aarik's cavalry was the first row. The High Elves' heavy infantry was next, followed by Aarik's Infantry, then twenty-two hundred Hielflander archers. Then the trolls and last was the Tree Realm folk.

They were nearing the eastern slope, and the air support had signaled that all was clear. Aarik started his men setting up defenses like rocks and stones. The Hielflander Archers started taking up Defensive positions where they had a good distance view. Dayla and the other riders took off east, looking for the location of the dark army. They found them at the base. Just starting the 3 km hike up the slope. *Harmony, stay here and telepath to me when they are all on the slope then come help me melt snow. Okay, Dayla!* Dayla took off, signaling to the other riders to follow her. They found the perfect place to start a waterfall/avalanche about an hour later. *Dayla, they are all marching up, and you should know the Shadow Lord is with them! Okay, Harmony, get back here,* answered Dayla.

Harmony headed back, and all the riders started melting ice. Large chunks of ice broke and started falling down the mountain, but the flames were melting the ice as well.

"Look out!" yelled Harmony getting impatient. Everyone got out of her way, and Harmony and Melody sent a very large fireball at the peaks, then another and another. That was all it needed: water, ice, rocks, and trees came crashing down twenty-five hundred meters or so, gaining momentum as it fell. The riders flew higher, then back to the east, they wanted to see their handiwork.

The front line of the Dark army was marching at a pretty fast pace. Finally, they were going to fight elves again. Tonight, there would be a feast unlike any other they had had in their lifetime; dragons had been seen, and dark elves loved dragon meat. It soon started to get dark around the troops as a thick dark mist appeared to hide the dark elves' numbers and movements. Scouts had reported that an army awaited on the flats. The 3 kilometers stretch before the western slope downgrade, the army had High Elves leading it.

They also had several dragon scouts, so this mist would keep the archers from aiming at any one contact or letting the scouts see where they really were. They would be shooting in the dark. Then the ground started to rumble. Toknah, one of the dark elves' captains, asked his lieutenant,

"What is that?"

"I don't know, captain," he answered. "Earthquake, maybe?"

"Maybe," Toknah agreed.

The elves had great sight in the dark and the mist, but beyond that, they could not see that well in the light, and the sun was pretty bright. Then it hit them with a wall of freezing cold water; large stones rolled over them, trees knocked them down, and large ice shards stabbed them and knocked them down. Some were killed by the debris; some drowned, and others were washed down the eastern slope. The dark mist disappeared, and the carnage became visible. Then twenty-two hundred arrows took flight.

Orchid, on the eastern opening of the cave, now attacked with her dragon's breath weapons of every kind, hit the secondary dark elf army near the eastern cave entrance. The Drow were caught off guard. They were trying to dig out the cave. **Now onyx,** Orchid telepathically told her. The entrance to the cave exploded open as Onyx's breath weapon was unleashed from the inside. Rocks and gravel flew from the opening. Killing and injuring lots of the Drow. Onyx, the dragon came in, swooping toward the entrance when a perfectly timed maneuver happened.

Onyx, the rider, came running out of the cave, jumped on a flying stone, shot an arrow, and then took a second leap that gave her elevation. The third step was on another flying rock, and lastly, landing on Onyx the dragon and almost flying straight up to get out of range of arrows that were from the dark elves that were not in the direct line of fire from the flying stones and shockwave. *Show off,* said Orchid. Onyx laughed and fired a few more arrows.

All were hitting their intended mark. She then charged up an arrow like Serephine had taught her and sent that arrow at a group of elves that were bunched together. Her arrow exploded and launched three elves into the air. Showing off again, she hit all three elves with more arrows before they hit the ground, shooting three arrows at the same time. *She is amazing!* Daylphine said to Orchid. *She certainly is!* Orchid agreed.

The elves were now falling back. Half of their number lay dead or badly injured. After still getting pummeled with arrows and dragon breath, the somewhat orderly "fall back" turned into a panicked retreat. Orchid saw no downed dragons, and for that, she was very thankful. She then caught a glimpse of Dalinda and Lindale; they looked amazing together too. Lindale was firing arrows with accuracy, and Mother was using her acid breath. Orchid noticed that the riders were staying out of range for the most part, using speed, height, and gravity to deliver their deadly attacks. Flying down at top speed and launching breath and arrows, it had been 30 minutes or so now, and less than eight hundred elves were alive. Orchid sent a telepathic message to her riders, *Push them to the main body!* At once, the dragons started intensifying the attack. The elves, on the other hand, were now in a run-for-your-life mode. They were not even stopping to fight. Some had even dropped their cumbersome weapons, so they could run faster.

Slowly moving down the mountain, Aarik led his mounted troops, followed by the High Elves' forces. Following them were the archers of Orchid, as they called themselves, while the dark elves who were not dead or badly wounded, started regrouping. Fireballs came out of the sky and hit them; then, a dark mist filled the sky, and Dayla and company had no choice but to go higher. It was a successful way to take the dragons out of the fight. Aarik kept advancing. Arrows from the dark elves filled the skies, some hitting his troops, but most falling short because his troops were on the high ground. Then he heard the sound of arrows flying through the air as twenty-two hundred went heading in the other direction. The arrows blocked out the sky, and most hit the mark. The mist started covering the dark troops again. Aarik's mounted troops started moving abreast to close off further advancement; that line was strengthened by the mounted High Elves.

As for Aarik's and Galadur's foot soldiers, they kept advancing. Another fireball shot from Firewind, but it was off target. Firewind tried just using her wind breath, but it also was truly little help. A third volley of arrows from Orchid's quiver went into the mist, but it was hard to say if it hit anything or not. Then out of the mist came hundreds of shadow bolts; they tore into the advancing High Elves and Northland troops.

Two light orbs came from the High Elves forces that flew at the dark mist. It was a mage battle, shadow versus light. Then something unexpected happened. The brownies and pixies, thousands of them, went running by, heading for the dark elves. Aarik chuckled.

"What's so funny?" asked Galadur.

"The dark elves won't be expecting an attack from that height," Aarik answered. Galadur found the humor in that as well and chuckled too. "This is going to be a long day if we don't find a way to get through this mist," he said.

Orchids group was now down to only three hundred or so enemies. For the dark elves, it was terrifying. The dragons were flying up to a dark mist. ***Go above it!*** she telepathically told the others. There they saw and met up with Harmony and Dayla. Daylphine flew next to Firewind.

"What's going on?" asked Orchid.

"Kardama is causing mists and shooting shadow bolts, some kind of dark magic," answered Dayla.

"Harmony, keep the dragons up here, they need to recover a bit from our first fight. Dayla, come with me, please." Dayla and Orchid then flew down to where Aarik and Galadur stood.

"Any ideas, cousin?" asked Galadur.

"I have five hundred dragons standing by," Orchid answered. "We can have them just start dropping breath weapons on them."

"No, that won't work. The brownies and pixies are in there, and our foot troops are about to be," Galadur said. Orchid looked at the battle. "Well, there is only one way to stop the mist," Orchid said as she took off toward the front line. Galadur and Aarik looked at each other and then charged themselves; Dayla went after her. ***Dayla, help Galadur and Aarik. Don't let anything*** *happen to them, please.* ordered Orchid! Dayla answered in a sad, dejected voice. *Yes, my Queen.*

Orchid flew Daylphine close to the front and got ready to jump off.

"Stay close, girl. I love you," she whispered into Daylphine's ear.

"And you don't get hurt," she answered her.

"He isn't a weakling; he has terrible powers," Daylphine added.

"I know," agreed Orchid. Daylphine got close to the ground, and Orchid jumped off, strapping two quivers and her bow to her back and drawing the new short sword that she had picked up at the fort.

Into the shadow she went, using night vision and her emotion-checking to find danger. As she went in, she was attacked by a Drow, but she dispatched him in seconds, then another, and another. She was searching for the largest threat in her mind. There were lots of threats. And she even felt some friendly people, too, in the form of brownies or pixies. She reached out and caught a pixie in her hand and got a stab for her efforts.

"Hey, I'm friendly," she said to her. "Where is the Shadow Lord?"

"I am not sure," answered the pixie. *Well, that didn't work,* Orchid thought. She kept moving east; well, she thought it was east. A large sonic blast came from somewhere a little to the left of her. *That's Onyx,* she thought, *attacking the rear, so that should be east.* She made a slight direction change and dispatched two more attackers. She tripped over something, and when she reached out, she touched his face. The dead body was a High Elf; she had touched his pointed ears. After stumbling over his shield, she swiftly retrieved it with her left hand. Her entire mind went red, and she saw it coming for her. She got sick to her stomach, and her mind was swimming. Nevertheless, she held on to her shield and sword, ready for action.

Chapter 29: Light vs. Shadow

The first stroke slammed her shield so hard it sent tingles down her left arm. She could feel Daylphine helping her, trying to give her dragon strength. She swung from the right going left, but he was waiting for it. His great sword had a further reach and was massive. She felt him coming down for another overhand stroke and she sidestepped it, then spun with her sword arm fully extended. The blade hit armor. Kardama cursed as blood ran down his arm. He then performed a series of swings, beating Orchid back. The air got thick, and Orchid had a challenging time breathing. She lit up the sword with electricity and swung back. This caught him off guard and shocked him every time she lifted her sword against his sword or metal armor. It was more of an irritant than doing damage. She also knew the cold would not have an effect. She was running out of options and strength.

The mist was growing weaker, and archers started firing on targets. Dragons started using more precise weapons instead of the area-of-effect ones, and they were slowly gaining ground. The mounted troops fighting from horseback were working as well. But the casualties on both sides were pretty large. The Elven kind, with long, almost eternal life, lying dead next to the dirty, impure dark elves, made Aarik sick to his stomach. Dayla was flying, using her bow. She saw a High Elf knight get separated from the rest of his group; he was pulled from his horse. Dayla charged a fire arrow and shot it. The arrow caught a dark elf just as he was ready to come down with his blade. Dayla quickly cleared the rest of the area. The soldier was hurt, so she flew in close and jumped off Firewind.

She ran to his side. "Are you okay, Captain?" she asked. The knight looked up at her. "Are you an angel?" he asked.

"No," she giggled. "I'm from Hielflander." She jumped up and shot three more, getting ready to attack.

"Come on; we got to get out of here. I can't hold them off," Dayla said.

"Leave me, my lady, fair. I am injured badly," Said the knight. There was a heavy ground shake as Firewind came in and landed; she sprayed fire in a circle around them. Dayla then heard several explosions as Harmony started clearing out the crowd as well.

"Come on, Captain; my dragons can't do this forever." The young captain tried to get up but passed out from the loss of blood and the pain. Dayla caught him. Firewind laid down so Dayla could get on easier, carrying the young knight. Once she was aboard, Firewind took off, fanning the flames with her wings, forcing those Drow that were close to backing off. Dayla headed to the rear of the flats where the healers were and landed Firewind. Dayla ran to Poppy, the Hielflander healer.

"Poppy, help this captain, please." A High Elf healer headed to help. "He is one of ours," she stated.

"Yes, Poppy will help him, and you can too, please," Dayla said.

"Why, it's Captain Tristan," said the Elf healer.

"Tristan," Dayla said aloud.

Now, she could take time to see his face and features. *He was amazingly handsome,* she thought.

"This wound is too open," said the elf healer about a cut on his calf. "We need to seal it shut and get a blade heated. Cauterize the wound once I get everything sewed up, so it doesn't get infected." Dayla ordered everyone to stand back. She brought blue flame from her hands. The elf healer looked at her and said,

"Yes, that will work perfectly." She instructed Dayla where to seal the wound. Then placed Tristan in a cot and covered him, then she thanked Dayla, saying, "Come by later; when he is awake, I am sure he will want to thank you." *I just might do that,* thought Dayla. She stayed and helped the two healers with loads of wounded that were coming in.

Back at the battle between Kardama and Orchid, Orchid was being overcome by darkness. Then a thought came to her. She concentrated on the dragon, Amber. She then concentrated on her breath weapon. She was on the ground, with one leg underneath her; her left arm was up, protecting herself with the shield raised above her head. Every hit on the shield sent painful vibrations down her arm. Again, she felt Daylphine adding her dragon strength. Her right hand still held her short sword, but she was using that right hand to brace herself from falling completely flat on the ground. Pure light started coming from her fingers. Her armor started to glow, as did her sword and shield. Kardama staggered backward.

Orchid picked herself back up from the ground. She felt a surge of energy going through her. Orchid then started her own attacks. *Left and right, left overhand, roundhouse.* Kardama backstepped as he blocked. *Right, right, left, overhand, another overhand, roundhouse,* and that one made it through the defenses. Kardama screamed as her blade hit the exact same spot she had hit before.

Left, left, overhand, left, right, Roundhouse spin to the left this time! Another hit and scream from Kardama.

"WHO ARE YOU?" Kardama hissed.

"I am High Queen Orchid, Queen of Hielflander, Princess to Drakconia, and future Queen of Northland," she said in a tone that sounded like he should have known that.

"Do you yield?" she asked him. Kardama looked at her with contempt in his eyes.

"You are at a disadvantage; you are injured," Orchid stated.

Kardama laughed and said, "Minor scratches, girl." A surge of shadow reached out to envelop her. Orchid just concentrated more on the light, and the darkness dissipated before it even reached her. Kardama made a lunge at her, and his attack was an overhand swing from that mighty two-handed sword. Orchid took full force on her shield. She had braced herself with her legs, and as the sword hit her shield, she slammed the shield upwards, sending Kardama stumbling backward.

Orchid slammed the heavy metal shield once more, striking Kardama directly in the face. Kardama managed to stay on his feet, but blood was coming from his now broken nose and his mouth, where she had knocked a few teeth loose and broken another. Orchid felt fear coming from Kardama. From the corner of her eye, she saw two Gelkin—an imp-like creature—and a minor demon. They stood about three and a half feet tall, had red skin, and threw fire bolts from their fingers. Kardama had summoned a distraction.

Orchid charged her fingers with lightning and sent it at the Gelkin. It was much more powerful than she intended; it killed both on contact. Orchid was about to resume her attack when she saw a shadow serpent flying toward her.

She was about to fire a frost spell when she felt Daylphine. Out of the sky, she came and snatched up the smaller flying dragon. She lifted her shield to block another powerful overhand swing trying to split her head. Orchid had to put her emotions in check because she was about to totally go berserk! *Right, right, right, left, right overhand, crouch, upward stab*She felt the blade go under the armor and sink in all the way to the hilt. She twisted the blade and then withdrew the sword as Kardama fell to the ground. The mist instantly disappeared. Orchid could see that the entire army was now engaged in the battle. Orchid, however, did not have strength left. She looked over the carnage; there were dragons dead on the field as well as riders. Every group was represented by the wounded and dead, and dying. Orchid felt lightheaded, and then all went black. Orchid didn't know it, but Daylphine too had blacked out, hit a few trees, and tried to land but crashed.

Lindale and Dalinda were clearing out a small pocket of defenders. All of a sudden Dalinda felt queasy, *something happened to Daylphine and Orchid,* she thought Team Onyx was nearby, and Dalinda directed them to engage the defenders, and the royal pair went looking for her daughters. They found Orchid in an area northeast of where they were engaging the dark elves' defenders. Lindale jumped from Dalinda's back and ran to her friend. Lindale shook Orchid, but she only slightly moaned. Then she checked her for wounds or blood; she found a lot of blood over her hands and armor. But when she lifted her armor, she saw no wounds.

She turned and saw the tall, dark figure lying dead near Orchid. He had blood from a horrible wound at the bottom of his armor. She then saw Orchid's sword covered in blood.

"She killed the Shadow Lord," she said to Dalinda. "Yes, it looks that way. Is she hurt Lindale?" asked Dalinda. "Not that I can see we need to take her to the healers, though, then find Daylphine." Lindale picked up Orchid and got back on Dalinda. They flew straight to the healers and handed Orchid to a panicked Dayla. The royal team then went looking for Daylphine.

Dayla took Orchid and had two healers instantly by her side. They looked her over and could find nothing wrong with her. Amber had even sniffed her and found no dark infection, as they now called it, inside of her. Lindale had explained to Dayla that Orchid was responsible for killing Kardama, so Dayla explained it to everyone else. Dayla emotion-checked her.

"She is totally done in, no strength. Let's let her sleep," said Amber. When Dayla lifted Orchid's eyes just to make sure, she saw that her eyes were glowing; Amber checked as well.

"Hmm... how interesting. It's dragon light," Amber explained. "It sometimes happens during wiruthwix."

"But she went through that weeks ago," interjected Dayla.

"This is new ground," stated Amber.

Dalinda came back with two other dragons carrying Daylphine. Amber went over to her and asked Lindale to open Daylphine's eyes, Lindale stepped off Dalinda, and they both collapsed. "Great, not too good of a time for this!" stated Dayla. "Wiruthwix," stated Amber excitedly, "the Queen will have an eternal royal rider!"

Dayla checked Daylphine's eyes and found the glow there as well. More and more volunteers were coming to help the healers. There still was lots of work to be done; people to heal, dead to bury, and dragons to have their traditional burial. In the absence of Orchid, Dayla accepted the position of being in charge. Dalinda and Lindale were in wiruthwix, and Orchid and Daylphine were passed out. Alora saw to the dead and wounded out on the battlefield, and Aarik saw to his men. "Harmony," called Dayla.

"Yes, Dayla?"

"Can you gather the Hielflander archers? I want some kind of list of how many dead, wounded, and missing we have. When you get those numbers, do the same for the Hielflander riders. Please."

"Right away," answered Harmony.

Dayla then performed the wiruthwix blood ritual with the dagger and chalice. 30 minutes later, the wiruthwix was done. Dalinda was beyond happy. Lindale was crying. It was then -Galadur and Aarik showed up. They both saw Orchid at the same time and ran to her. Aarik saw all the blood and started shouting, "No, no, no! It's not her blood," stated Dayla, "its Karama's blood. She is the one who killed him." Neither man knew what to say.

"What's wrong with her then?" asked King Galadur. "We are not sure, but…" said Dayla. She lifted open Orchid's eyelid, and then Daylphine's, Aarik, and Galadur saw the glow in both their eyes.

"It's called Dragon's light. It happens to dragons sometimes when they are entering a new stage in their lives. This is a first with a rider," explained Amber. "We don't know what it means, only that it is happening to both of them, and I can detect no danger." Dayla interjected, "I am getting ready to start moving all badly injured to the keep in Triangulus. We have ten Nen Yaksi (a water yak, about the size of an elephant, approximately eight meters high, weighing around 4 to 6 tons, with a thick bony structure across his forehead, like a water buffalo, and thick shaggy long fur like a yak). I am going to have the dwarves build a large series of wagons connected to each other and harnessed to a Nen Yaksi to use as a transport. We should be able to transport enormous quantities of the wounded back there."

Just then, a light started glowing around Orchid and Daylphine; the light was so bright and had a humming noise. No one could approach them. Dalinda and Lindale took watch. Galadur and Aarik went to attend to other duties leaving orders to contact him the moment there was a change. Dayla started off to get some water and something to eat when she saw a familiar face.

She went over to the High Elf Captain. "Tristan, how are you feeling?"

"You were my rescuer, is that correct?" Tristan asked. "Yes, I am Dayla of Artistah, second-in-command under the new High Queen."

He said, "My lady," as he tried to get up. He could only sit.

"Heal, you were injured pretty bad," said Dayla.

"Yes, and I'm still pretty weak. I was told I owe you my life!" Tristan said.

"You were doing very good on your own," said Dayla. "You just got outnumbered."

"Were you riding a red dragon? Or was that my imagination?"

"Her name is Firewind, and yes, we are a team, rider, and dragon," stated Dayla.

"I would love to thank her," Tristan said. "I remember seeing flames keeping me from being surrounded just before I passed out. My last thoughts were…were…Ah never mind."

"Come on, tell me," said Dayla.

"Well, I thought you were an angel coming to take me to Eldamar."

"No, just a dragon rider to fly you to a safe place to be healed," added Dayla. "I am also glad to have done it, Tristan. Now get well, I have duties to tend to! When you are better, I will introduce you to Firewind."

With that, Dayla went to find something to do. As she started walking away, her stomach reminded her that she was hungry. She saw some food being handed out and went to get some cheese, an apple and half of a loaf of bread. She put Rat, the dwarf, in charge of building the wagons and told him her plan. She had to show him a Nen Yaksi because he did not believe her. She knew that he would get the job done. She then let Poppy in on the details. Poppy put together a large party of tree elves to head to the keep and prepare it to receive the injured. The dark elves were either dead or in full retreat mode since the Shadow Lord had fallen. Some, as is their own way, took their own lives. The dark elf-kind army had fallen. Orchid's first campaign and she was victorious.

Dayla wondered what was in store for herself now that this was soon to be over. She was a dragon rider, so going back to her provincial life and returning as a village hunter was probably not going to happen. Besides, Orchid needed her. Orchid needed Serephine and Harmony too. Dayla thought she could be an excellent archery instructor or a captain of the Riders. Orchid was going to be much too busy being High Queen, she thought. Well, only time will tell, she told herself.

Serephine was in a deep dark sleep. She kept hearing humming and sometimes singing. It kept the darkness at bay. All of a sudden, she felt anger, and she saw a dull light. For some reason, the light made her angry. She rushed to it and swung her sword. Wait, that was not her sword; she had never held a two-handed sword before. The person she was fighting was skilled. This made her angry. The opponent then spun, and she felt a pain in her right arm.

She attacked, and then her opponent fell. Then there was a bright light, and it blinded Serephine. Her enemy's armor glowed, as did her sword and shield. She did a series of swings then she felt severe pain in her stomach, up to her chest. Immediately the darkness left her, and she heard the humming again. She was being rocked like a baby, and the voice seemed somewhat familiar and peaceful. She opened her eyes and saw Drakk. He was somewhat asleep. She was lying in his lap. *This is comfortable*, she thought. She moved slightly. Drakk never opened his eyes but started stroking her hair and resumed the lullaby. She turned her head and kissed his hand. He was startled and then looked into her beautiful blue eyes.

"You're awake," he mumbled while yawning. "How long have we been here?" she asked.

"Three days, I think," he answered. "Where is everyone?" Serephine asked. "The Battle," he replied.

"You didn't go?" she asked him. "No, I wouldn't leave your side," he answered.

"DRAKK, you will get in trouble!" she stated. "I don't care," he answered. "I care for you more than I have ever cared for anyone in my whole life. I will take my punishment, but I was not letting you go through what you were going through alone."

"The darkness that had me was defeated. I think the Shadow Lord was killed," she told him.

"Let's hope those we love, new and old friends, are still living," said Drakk.

They heard the wings of a dragon coming toward them. Drakk looked to see the Dragon Queen Dalinda being ridden by Lindale. He sensed something was different. Dalinda approached him, and Drakk fell to his knees. Tears were streaming down his face.

"My forever queen, please forgive me," he sobbed. "My Sir Drakk, you have served me faithfully for many a year. Never have I ever questioned your loyalty." Drakk hung his head even lower, still sobbing.

"I only wish you would have been there for my… Wiruthwix." Drakk looked up and into Dalinda's Dragon brown eyes. He then looked at Lindale.

"Yes, Drakk, another Royal Wiruthwix. Lindale is a Druid royal blood."

"I ……I am sorry, my Queen."

"Drakk, it is a great thing that happened…I care deeply about you too, and I am so happy that you have found someone that you care deeply about. What happened to me was long overdue, and I am extremely excited about the future. What Lindale and I have is special, but so is the love you have for this girl. I know how deeply you care for her. I have empathic abilities now," she giggled. "I fully forgive you, but really an apology is not necessary."

"Where is Orchid?" asked Serephine.

"She is back at the Travallah Pass. Something happened to her and Daylphine after she killed the Shadow Lord. The two of them are glowing and are now surrounded by a bright orb. Amber does not detect any danger, but we do not know what is going on," explained Dalinda.

"Orchid? She killed Kardama?"

"Yes, apparently by herself," answered Lindale.

"I know," said Serephine. "I was kinda there. In my dark dream, I kinda accessed Karama's mind. She was surrounded by light at the end. Kardama was winning; he had beaten her; she fell backward, and Kardama was going in for the final blow. Suddenly, she was glowing bright her armor, sword, and shield started radiating the glow as well. She got up and started her own attack. She was a blur to me. I could not see who it was, but she became more confident, and fear was growing in Kardama. He summoned help, but Orchid dispatched them quickly. That scared Kardama even more. Then I felt a searing pain in my stomach and woke up in Drakk's arms. She is so amazing," Serephine said.

"We knew she was a special friend all our lives, but this…this is beyond all of our dreams. She… is…" Serephine was lost for words.

"Just incredible," Dalinda interjected. "She is the High Queen foretold by our seers before she was even born." "We, the Dragons, have waited for this prophecy for an exceedingly long time. Now that it's here, magical things are happening, like me after centuries getting my first Eternal Rider."

Back at the pass, the light surrounding Daylphine and Orchid started to fade, first around Daylphine. Her color had changed, whereas before, she was a light blue, she was now a very dark blue. Her body was hovering a few feet from the ground; without flapping her wings, it was magical. Then the glow started fading from Orchid. Her hair was the same color as Daylphine. Dayla looked at her. She, too, was hovering a few feet from the ground.

Chapter 30: The Reign of the high queen

Orchid came out of it, and she felt different. She was hovering above everyone, about four or five feet in the air. *How was she doing this?* She looked at Daylphine; she was a darker shade of blue. Then she noticed her own long hair was the same shade. Orchid saw Dayla looking up in amazement at her. Barely, the thought entered her mind about getting down to the ground when she started descending.

Did I do that? she thought. She thought of going back up, and then she started going back up. *Oh, this will be fun,* she thought. She descended back down and walked to her friend Dayla. Dayla dropped to one knee and bowed to her.

"My High Queen," she said to her. "DAYLA! You have known me all my life; you know I don't like titles!"

"Yes, my Queen, but you are now a High Queen! You are the highest-ranking official that there has ever been since we were a country."

Orchid looked out over the healers and soldiers, just wanting to catch a glimpse of her, but all were down on one knee and bowing their heads. "You may rise," she said. Then turned her back and went back to hovering and flew over and mounted Daylphine, and they both took off for Triangulus.

"You need to get over yourself, Orchid," said Daylphine. "There is no going back. We now have the responsibility of Tarsus."

"Dayla is my friend, my closest friend," Orchid said, "It just doesn't feel right making her do that and lower herself to me."

"Orchid, she does it to set an example. She still loves you more than ever. She just needs to stay professional while in the company of others. We must now surround ourselves with people like Dayla, whom we trust. There will be others that will try to press for their advantage. There will be those we cannot trust! We must stay forever vigilant!"

All this was making Orchid's head hurt. A few months ago, she was just out on a hunt. Now she was the High Queen of three countries. This is not a life she wanted for herself. **Then why did you choose me as your dragon?** asked Daylphine. *I did not think it would amount to all this!* answered Orchid. She felt that Daylphine at once was mad. *I do not mean us,* corrected

Orchid. Daylphine closed her mind, and they flew back to Triangulus in silence.

As they landed in Triangulus, Orchid once again hovered off Daylphine, and walked away, not saying a word. She did not understand why she was so mad; she just needed to calm down, she thought. It is just that this is all over now, and she was just exhausted. The threat was now over, and she could breathe, and more importantly, rest. The thought of the coming weeks was exhausting to think of: cleaning up, dealing with the deaths, accepting the crown, spending time with Aarik. That made her smile; Aarik would be the perfect distraction from all that happened and still was to happen. Once all settled down, she would like to explore the lands to the east of the Pass, just her, Daylphine and Dayla, Harmony, and Serephine. *Serephine! I need to check on her,* she thought to herself.

Dalinda approached her daughter Daylphine.

"How are you feeling?" she asked her.

"I am mad," Daylphine answered.

"Mad at whom?" her mother asked.

"I am mad at Orchid," Daylphine answered. "She does not really want to be Queen; she is afraid of all the responsibility. She got upset at Dayla for bowing to her!"

"Honey," the dragon queen started, "you have been a royal all your life; this was the life you expected for yourself. This was the life you were born to have and prepared for your entire life! On the other hand, Orchid had a good, humble, and simple life. She was a huntress. Each day, she woke up, had a meager breakfast, washed up, and put on the same clothes or a second pair of the same clothes while the first pair dried. She then went outside, packed her horse, and went into the woods to hunt for food for her village. Some days she had Dayla or Serephine, but mostly, she was alone. All this has been thrown at her in the last two months. Yet she never wavered. She united all the needed allies, and she conquered two enemies. She figured out the plot of the Shadow Lord, produced a plan, and defeated him."

"Daylphine, I am not sure I would have been any more successful at what she just accomplished. Darling, I have never been ruled. I have always been in charge. Before me was my mother. I, Queen Dalinda, gladly call Orchid High Queen, and my queen, and with that title is your title, High Queen of Drakconia. I will seek adventure with my new eternal rider, Lindale."

Daylphine looked at her mother. "Child, Orchid will have doubts, and it is then that you need to stand strong together! Now tell me why you are a darker blue than the last time I saw you." Daylphine started hovering above the ground, not even flapping her wings.

"That's something new," exclaimed Dalinda. "Orchid can do it too! Well, you and Orchid were glowing with dragon's light in the Pass, that has meant that you were reaching the next stage of your life. That said, though, it never included a rider before. Daylphine, any other abilities? Try breathing fire."

Dalinda backed up, and Daylphine concentrated on Firewind; flames came out of her mouth.

"Wow," Dalinda exclaimed excitedly. "Try another." Daylphine concentrated on her mom. Green acid came out of her mouth. She went through all the breath weapons she knew and breathed every one of them.

"You and Orchid have been given your third ability…. You can access everyone's breath!"

Orchid was walking to the last place she saw Drakk and Serephine. She ran into two other familiar faces first. It was her new friends, Maple and Dragonfly. Maple ran to her and gave her a big hug.

Dragonfly yelled at her, "Maple, where are your manners? She is the High Queen!"

"Not yet, she's not!" Maple hollered back at Dragonfly.

"Not till her coronation! Till then, she is my good friend whom I love so much and am incredibly happy to see alive."

Orchid squeezed Maple a little tighter than she intended to. "Hey, watch it Orchid, I'm a sprite, not a bear," she said. This made her happy, so much so that she swooped down and grabbed Dragonfly too, and they all hugged.

"How's Serephine?" asked Orchid.

"She is really bad now," stated Maple. Orchid looked concerned.

"I was hoping that she would be better by now."

"Oh, the shadow sickness is gone. She has something much worse now," answered Maple. "She was bitten by a bug."

"A bug?" asked Orchid.

"Yes, the love bug," Maple said with a straight face.

"Yes, and she infected Sir Drakk too."

"NO, I'm pretty sure Drakk started it," said Dragonfly.

Orchid laughed and let out a sigh of relief at the same time. "Orchid, how are you?" asked Maple. "You look different with blue hair. In fact, you look more like a big sprite!" Orchid laughed again. This is what she needed. She needed her sprite friends.

Gigi was heading back to Artistah. She and most of what was left of her army of eight hundred were going back to finish building the colony. The Hielflander riders would soon need to occupy the barracks and dragon stables. She knew that the Hielflanders were still there, building and cutting trees. The palace for Orchid and her court would have to wait; besides, she did not have any approved plans yet. She was hoping to talk the dwarves into coming, but they were completing the building of some contraption that Dayla came up with to transport the wounded to Triangulus, using wagons and Nen Yaksi. The lead dwarf, Rat, told her they had a much bigger project to talk over with Orchid. So, she had recruited Ashen Oak and Oaken Ash and four hundred seventy-five troops, all that was left of her army.

Aarik and Galadur had given orders to the survivors of their armies to get some sleep, and in the morning, to march to Northland. They themselves were heading to Triangulus. They were discussing the battle when one of Aarik's men approached them. It was one of his messengers, Donovan.

"Sir Aarik, there has been a change with the Queen. She has flown to Triangulus. Apparently, she and Captain Dayla had a disagreement, and she got mad and left," the messenger stated.

"What was the argument about?" asked Aarik.

"Sir Queen Orchid got mad because Dayla bowed to her, my king."

"Ah, I see. Okay, thank you for your report, Donovan." Galadur looked away.

"What is that all about?" he asked as he turned away. Aarik answered, "I think now that all this is coming to an end, she is feeling the stress of everything," Aarik stated. Galadur confided in Aarik, "You need to push her to find those she trusts and to put together a staff for her to dictate tasks to, so it doesn't burden her. Although she has royal blood, she has not been groomed all her life to know how to do these things."

"She will have the help of Queen Alora, and of course, me," answered Aarik.

"Good, very good," said Galadur.

Rat and one of his men rode on the first Nen Yaksi transport, as they now called it, to Triangulus. They were now helping with the unloading and helping get the wounded into the keep. After three long hours, they went looking for Orchid. They found her in the big field called Dragons Landing. She was talking to two small elves and another Hielflander with beautiful long black hair and blue eyes. She was holding hands with a Drakconian Captain. As they approached, Orchid spoke to him.

"Rat, nice job with that transport!"

"My Queen, it was Captain Dayla's idea. We have something important to discuss with you, My Queen."

"Well, let's all go in the keep. It is getting chilly outside." Orchid led the way; she had told Serephine and Drakk to join them, as well as Dragonfly and Maple. She also used telepathy with Daylphine and Dalinda. Alora was already in the keep. The first chamber was large enough to accompany everyone and not disturb everyone who was wounded or the healers. They were on the second and third levels of the keep. There was a big roaring fire here, and Orchid enlisted two or three servants to bring food and drink to the party. They all sat in chairs in a semi-circle, with Orchid at the front. After introducing everyone to Rat, Orchid gave him the floor. Rat began,

"Everyone, this is Windstone; he was captured and made a slave only a few years ago. He is from the Blue Mountains. I have asked him to explain to you what he explained to me."

Windstone stood up and looked at Orchid. "With your permission, Your Highness," he asked. "Granted," Orchid replied.

"Your Highness, may I give you a history lesson of my people?"

"Of course, proceed," answered Orchid.

"The Dwarven kingdom is divided into four factions. Each has its own ruler, but I shall not bore you with Dwarven politics. The basics are that a council chooses the leaders. The council is made up of ruling houses. These leaders are called Deshers. You see, Dwarven kingdoms are a caste-system society.

"A caste system is a class structure that is determined by birth. In other words, if your father is a miner, then all of his children are born into the miner caste and will have opportunities to be miners or do other jobs within the mining industry. Another caste is the merchant caste, the warrior caste, and the crafting caste. People usually only marry someone from the same caste. Some do not have a caste. These unfortunate souls do the dirty work. Most starve or are indentured servants for their entire lives.

"That being said, it brings me to how these dwarves came to be in your land."

"Simply because most were sold, they were tricked into going to the Iron Mountains. They were told that they would be apprenticed to different castes. When they arrived, they were given a warm welcome and then a banquet in their honor. The food given to them was drugged. When they woke up, they were on a ship heading to the arid lands. You see, slavers had made a deal with the Deshers in the Iron Hills. They were paid in gold for every dwarf they sold them. When the undesirable, un-caste ran out in the Iron hills, they put the word out to the other kingdoms."

Orchid was stunned. "Why tell me this?" she asked. Rat took the floor.

"My Beautiful Queen," he began. "We can never return to our various Dwarven tribes. We will be castless. I have a proposal for you, though, my Queen. We have close to fourteen hundred Dwarves, homeless and casteless, and we don't even know the customs and culture of our own people, 90 percent of the people here have only tasted the slavers and masters' whips.

They do not want to go somewhere where only the hand of the whip changes to our own people. So, while we were digging the tunnel for the dark one, we came across veins of precious metals and precious gems. This is our proposal. We will rebuild this fort into a defensible stone castle; we will build walls at the flats on the Travallah Pass to control the coming and going of people. We would feel much better if our Queen was protected by stone. We will build shelters for a contingent of dragon riders here as well as in the colony. We will share with you 80 percent of the gold and other gems and metals we retrieve from the tunnel to fill your coffers for four years. After that, we will ask to keep that 80 percent and pay a tribute of 20 percent. We also ask that the tunnel be given over to us as our new home. We will be known as the Travallah Mountain Dwarves. We will build a beautiful city within the tunnel, with a fort at each end to protect our beloved Queen, our savior, from the evils we endured."

Orchid had tears of joy running down her face. She quickly wiped it away before anyone saw it. She stood up and said, "ABSOLUTELY NOT!" Rat looked up at her with sadness in his eyes.

"RAT, Windstone, 70 percent will be more than enough to fill our coffers. I am excited to have you as neighbors and protectors. I have become fond of you."

The look on Rat's face was priceless. Windstone spoke up, "My Queen, I will be the first ambassador for the time being. You see, I am not a casteless Dwarf. I am from the Deshers class. I was sold by a rival for the throne, and I was captured while on a hunt. The slaver was told to take me to the arid lands, but his greed made his mind up for him. He was paid a lot of money to take me away. So instead of purchasing a boat and spending the money on expenses, he kept it all and sold me to the dark ones. I am not going to seek revenge or to put you in any danger. I have a chance to correct all the wrongs in Dwarven society. We have a chance to marvel the world with our talents and serve a queen who was willing to put her life on the line for us. Trust me when I say NO Dwarven King would have done what you did for us. We, the Travallah Dwarves, will proudly be the fourth race under your banner, my queen."

"I am proud to accept that alliance!" stated Orchid.

Chapter 31 The High Queen is crowned

It was now a week since the battle. Captain Tristan was now at the keep, as was Dayla. The two had sought out each other's company in the evenings to eat the evening meal together. Over the week, Dayla and Orchid had extraordinarily little time to spend together. Orchid was spending most of her time with Dragonfly, Alora, and Dalinda. The first few days, she spent some time with her cousin, King Galadur. Then he returned to his homeland with his troops, leaving some behind to further heal, like Tristan. As for Tristan, though, he was to establish an embassy here and serve as the first ambassador. This made Dayla incredibly happy. She enjoyed his humor and his company.

"My lady Dayla?" Dayla turned to see a royal messenger.

"Yes," she answered.

"My lady, the High Queen has requested your presence," stated the messenger. "She waits for you in her chamber."

With his message delivered, he turned and left. Dayla headed directly to Orchid. As she entered the chamber, she noticed all who were present. Dalinda was the only dragon; Alora, Dragonfly, Maple, and Aarik, whom she knew were leaving today for Landia. A few days ago, she and Orchid had talked about the saluting thing and had come up with a protocol. In official business dealings, she was to formally bow. However, in unofficial meetings, a right hand clinched over her heart and bowed head was all that was necessary.

Dayla walked twenty paces in front of Orchid and went to one knee. "Rise, Lady Dayla," commanded Orchid. Dayla stood up.

"Lady Dayla, after talking over with my advisors, I will hereby offer you an official position in my court. There are two suitable positions, and I will have you choose. Each position comes with an apartment here in the castle; this will need to be your new home if you choose to accept. The first position is Captain of my Royal Guard. In this position, you will handpick twenty Hielflander riders. Ten will travel, and ten will be on reserve. The second position is General of all my armies. This position will be required to travel between here, Artistah colony, and Northland, as well as Travallah Pass once the outpost and wall are built." Dayla thought for a moment. As much as the prestige of being the general of the armies appealed to her, she believed that her job was protecting the High Queen.

"I choose your protector as Captain of the Royal Guard."

"Very well, Lady Dayla, we will make it all official at my Coronation." Seconds later, Serephine came into the chamber. "Serephine," called Orchid, "I would like to offer you a position as General of my armies. This offer comes with an apartment here in the royal castle and lots of responsibility."

"I accept," said Serephine without hesitation. "Very well, starting right now, you will also earn your title of Lady."

"Serephine, take a knee, please," Orchid instructed. Serephine put her right knee to the ground and bowed her head. Orchid pulled her sword and knighted her.

"Serephine, I, High Queen of the United Lands, bestow upon you the title of Lady of the High Court and Commanding General of the Armies of the High Queen. Lady Serephine, you may rise." Serephine stood up and looked at Orchid. **Thank you. I will make you proud,** Serephine said in telepathy to Orchid. **You already have,** Orchid replied. Serephine smiled and then joined the crowd, where she saw and hugged Drakk. Lindale and Harmony came next.

"Harmony, I would like to offer you an official position in my court. Would you be the captain of my guard? Dayla will manage the royal guard. I would like you to manage the castle and outpost guards; also, I would like you to set up guard outposts in all major cities. And patrol routes for riding patrols. Your guards are to serve the people in keeping peace and protection. You will have an apartment at the colony in Artistah, as well as a private stall for Melody."

"I would love that, my queen," stated Harmony.

"Very well. Take a knee, please." Orchid then knighted Harmony as Captain of the Guard and the title of Lady.

"When you are ready, you can start your duties and start making preparations to move to the colony. I will have an official paper with my seal drawn up to show your official title. General Serephine will issue you the number of troops you need; just request them."

"Lindale, the position I have for you will be General of the Hielflander riders. My mother will, of course, be over the Dragons and Drakconian riders. You can choose where you want to make your residence. I would suggest both Drakconia and the colony at Artistah.

"With that all done, I will conclude this meeting."

Orchid now had people she trusted around her. She could feel the pleasure coming from Daylphine. Over the next few months, things were hectic. It was now the fourth day of the fourth month, Viresse, as it is named in Elvish. Spring was finally in full bloom in Hielflander. The Coronation of the High Queen Orchid was set for the sixth. The large field that at one time was called Dragons Landing was now full of wagons and vendors of every kind.

There were street performers, acrobats, fire eaters, and food of every kind. It was a carnival atmosphere. There were royal tents with banners mounted on tall poles outside the tents, fluttering in the slight breeze. People crowded the streets, and all were having fun. Harmony had regular patrols of guards to make sure there was no trouble. Northland guards were also very present in dress armor and brushed and bathed horses, with green vines or other flowers weaved into their manes and tails. Orchid was on her new balcony overlooking the scene.

Aarik was standing with her, holding her hand. Aarik had been riding back and forth between Landia and Triangulus. They had just eaten a delicious breakfast and were now thinking about going on a walk. Orchid was wearing her beautiful blue, royal leather armor with reinforced places like elbows, wrists, and hearts made from polished steel. All of it was covered in dragon scale; her pretty blue hair was about her shoulders. Her sword was at her side, as well as her old dagger. Aarik was wearing a shiny breastplate and leather riding leggings, and his sword was also at his side. His red hair was totally not cooperative today and looked like it was a wild mess of curls. They headed for the staircase leading from Orchid's balcony to the next level down, which was the throne room. Orchid's chambers had been redone by Windstone and his men. As you came in from the balcony and went left down the hall, there was a door that led to her chamber. There were two royal guards always stationed there.

At the bottom of the staircase, there were two royal guards, as well. Orchid's chamber had a massive bed and chests to hold things, a table and comfortable chairs and two exceptionally large fireplaces. There was a kitchen off to the right of her room, and the Hielflander woman who was assigned there was an amazing cook. Her name was Madeline. Each day she baked loaves of bread and pastries, sweet rolls, and other treats. When Orchid told her, she was not used to eating that much, she responded, "The guards would eat what you don't." So, Orchid didn't argue the point. It made Madeline an immensely popular girl. Overall, Orchid was having the time of her life.

Every day, she and Daylphine took an hour or two's flight to talk about things. Sometimes, Aarik came with them if he was not busy. Dayla also flew with them, on her own dragon, of course. As the royal couple stepped out of the castle, the smell of cooked food from the vendors assaulted their nostrils. Everyone was having an enjoyable time. The guards that were following them had been replaced by Dayla and Harmony, and they all started taking in the sights.

"Have you seen these, my Queen?" Orchid heard a familiar voice; it was Windstone. He gave her a short bow and handed her three coins. The first was copper; on the front, it had a dragon's head, and on the back was a crown. The second was identical but made of silver. The last was solid gold. The front had three crowns, and the back took Orchid's breath away. It was a likeness of her. Orchid looked at Windstone,

"That is beautiful workmanship!" she stated. "There will be your first payment tomorrow; all the gold, silver, and copper have been made into coins. One hundred coppers equal one silver, and one hundred silvers equal one gold. You are coming to my coronation, are you not?" asked Orchid.

"My queen, I would not miss that for all the gold in the cave. I have also sent a message to the other Dwarves settlements as to our intention of serving you and settling the new Dwarven clan. Do not be surprised if you see dwarves from the other clans," Winstone said.

"They are welcome," answered Orchid. "As long as they don't start trouble with our allies, including the Travallah Mountain dwarves."

The day was here. Orchid had been awakened early. She had a hot bath, and then she was tended to by the royal staff. Her hair and nails were done to perfection. She had dressed in a long light blue flowing gown. Of course, her hair was dark blue. Her ankle-high boots were dark red, as was a sash around her waist. Fastened around her shoulders was a long cape; it had red fringe around the edges, and the main part of the cape was green, jade green, to be exact. Drakconia was represented. She looked stunning!

She walked out onto the balcony, where she looked over thousands of people, hoping to get a glimpse of her. When they saw her, they cheered! She waved politely at them, and the cheers went even louder. Dayla came onto the balcony. She was wearing an jade green dress armor of a Royal Captain, similar to the armor that Drakk wore, only more feminine and pretty. She had on knee-high green leather boots, and her reddish blond hair looked even more red with a green background. On her shoulders was a beautiful red cape fringed in gold.

"Good morning, my queen," she said to Orchid.

"Good morning, my captain," Orchid responded with a girlish giggle. They both looked at each other up and down.

Dayla smiled and said, "Who would have thought when we headed out to hunt wolves, that months later we would be standing here, looking like this." Orchid laughed.

"I knew it all along," she said. They both laughed hard.

"Do I have anything to be worried about out there?" she asked, nodding her head toward the crowd. "Security wise?"

"No, I do not believe so. Word on the street is more about how much you are loved and excited to see what follows. Hielflanders really wanted this," stated Dayla.

"Well, I am not sure it's what I would have chosen, but…I am very honored," Orchid finished.

Dayla looke d at her and said, "I am honored that you chose me to protect you,"

"You are as close as a sister; of course, I would have chosen you. Together, we will travel and make new allies," stated Orchid.

"It will be fun," Dayla replied. Alora came upstairs to check on her. "Hey, girls! You guys got butterflies in the tummy like I do?" she asked.

"Sure do," they replied in unison.

"But why do you have flutters?" asked Orchid.

"I guess I am just really excited for you," Queen Alora answered.

"Before I forget," said Orchid, "Alora, thank you for accepting me and making me feel welcomed. You made me feel like part of your family. Well, I was kinda feeling sorry for myself before all this happened. Dayla and Serephine were the only "family" I had left. So again, thank you."

"My dear child, may I say it has been a pure pleasure. I have grown to love you in this short while, almost as my own child. You call Dalinda mother; if you want, I would like that too!"

"Really?" asked Orchid excitedly. "I would really love that, Mother!" They all laughed.

"Excuse me," came a voice from the hall leading to Orchid's chamber, "the ceremony is about to begin. They are requesting your presence."

"Well, we better go take our places," Alora said to Dayla. With that, they headed out the chamber door. Orchid's heart started beating really fast; she had to use her hunting technique to calm it back down. She walked to the top of the large stone staircase and took a deep breath; she then slowly started descending the stairs. She thought about hovering down the stairs and even to her place. It made her smile to think about it because it proved to herself that she was still a young, playful Hielflander girl—in her mind, anyway. As she came into view, she heard the music start. She recognized it right away as Lindale's lute. When she reached the bottom, she looked at the throne room. There was standing room only; a path right down the center was the only open space for her to walk to the stage where her new throne was and where the ceremony was to take place. There were three steps leading up to the stage. King Galadur was standing there waiting to perform the honors of her crowning. All the invited guests were bowing down on one knee. She saw most of the council members, the elves from the Tree Realm. She saw Tara Horsemen and her father, Gigi, Ashen Oak, and Oaken Ash.

On the right-hand side of the throne room, the roof was missing. It was open to the sky. Windstone was rebuilding that side but decided to leave it open for more room. He extended the balcony and reinforced it. Now it held Daylphine, Icewind, Firewind, and of course, Dalinda. As she started walking through the aisle, she saw more familiar faces. Windstone, Rat, and their wives were near the front. She saw some of the royal guards that were dressed in jade green ceremonial armor. They were standing at attention, but she could tell they were ready to pounce into action if necessary. Orchid had reached the bottom of the steps, and the music stopped.

A quiet hush fell over the room. She waited for Galadur to summon her. King Galadur looked out over the crowd.

"My ladies, gentlemen, and royal guests, may I present to you the Princess Orchid." The crowd cheered. Orchid walked up to the king and bowed her head. Aarik was there, sitting in the front row. He looked so handsome. He was wearing his father's crown. He had a private ceremony in Landia some weeks ago. Galadur had presented him with his crown also. Orchid and Daylphine were there as well.

"People of Hielflander, this is Orchid of Artistah and my cousin. She is the last of this bloodline, and I am enormously proud of her for finding her way back to being a royal. We, the High Elves of Caras Galadhon, recognize Orchid of Artistah as ruler over these lands." Aarik stood up and walked to the front.

"I am Aarik, king of Northland; we also recognize Orchid as the ruler of these lands, and in the coming months, she has accepted my offer of marriage and will rule as queen over Northland." The crowd cheered. Alora stood forward now.

"I am Alora, Queen of Drakconia; we, the people and dragons, also recognize Orchid as High Queen over these lands and pledge our support for her."

It was now Windstone's turn. "I am Ambassador Windstone. I am the leader of a new Dwarven clan living in the Travallah Mountains. We also recognize High Queen Orchid. We proudly call her our queen."

Orchid was blushing now. She did not like all this attention. Orchid now dropped to one knee. Galadur took out his sword.

"May the gods and goddesses of Tarsus watch over this young queen, and may your lands always be safe. I crown you, Orchid High Queen of the United Lands." Cheers from the dragons, and people were deafening. Even those who were not up here in the castle were cheering outside. The chant started, "Long live the Queen!" Orchid rose and then took center stage. She looked over the crowd and waited for the chanting to settle down. Eventually, it did.

"Royal guests, visitors, and my beloved people of Hielflander, today, I humbly accept the honor of being the first single ruler of Hielflander in an exceptionally long, long time. As much as I love our way of life, it was almost disastrous. By not having an army to protect us, by not keeping alliances fresh, and by caring only for our own people, we almost lost our country. I promise to reign as High Queen, to rule in what I hope is in the best interest of the united clans and countries. As for life in Hielflander, there will be changes. Some of you have already seen the new currency; this concept will be new to most of you but know this, we are all neighbors. If you are still comfortable bartering and trading for those things you need, then by golly, keep doing it. Just remember to keep taking care of each other. Your council members will still carry your needs and concerns to me, thereby keeping me informed. Guards will be directing small matters in the cities and also reporting back to me. Let us celebrate our victory!" The cheers were deafening.

Two months to the day, King Aarik and Orchid were married; it was a beautiful early summer day. Everything was perfect.

THE END

Made in the USA
Middletown, DE
16 February 2025

71015271R00134